Women
don't let him go

Translated from German
Love Novel
Frauen lassen ihn nicht los

Novel

Vera Wagenvoort

Women
don't let him go

Novel

Vera Wagenvoort

Imprint

Bibliographic information from the German National Library: The German National Library has catalogued this publication in the German National Bibliography; detailed bibliographic data is available on the internet at http://dnb.d-nb.de.

Edition 1 - © 2024 Vera Wagenvoort Cover design: Alex Beck, www.alexbeck.com
Unter Vewendung von Material von:
»Sabavector« und »Forgem« @ AdobeStock
Editing in German: Emma Sommerfeld
Translate: Vera Litti & translator

Imprint: www.vera-litti.de

ISBN: 978-3-00-076305-2

For

Michi, Chris und Neo

In need of a vacation, or what?

The air was wonderfully light. Birds were chirping in the trees along the roadside.

It was a wonderful, sunny morning on a Thursday in early summer when the five men stepped out of the café. The first one had stopped and waited until the last one had approached before addressing him.

»Mr. Freimut, please remember to email me the presentation documents!« The man with the sunglasses in his hand showed enthusiasm for Thomas Freimut's explanations.

Thomas' blond hair towered over the others by half a head. With his slender figure and sporty-elegant clothing, he stood out from the businessmen in the typical blue suits.

This business appointment was the only one that had been free in his calendar between meetings in Hamburg, Munich, Düsseldorf, and elsewhere.

»The documents will be sent to you in the next few days,« Thomas exuded energy. Smiling, he continued, »I find your idea of incorporating a sketch into the presentation excellent. I will pass that on to my assistant right away.«

The person addressed nodded approvingly. »I find your proposal for implementing the corporate culture, in turn, fantastic. You have just inspired me. Thank you very much!«

He extended his hand to Thomas as they parted ways, his handshake firm. »I look forward to a good collaboration. Thank you for finding the time to attend this meeting, even at seven in the morning.«

»No problem, I'm looking forward to it as well. And thank you, gentlemen, until our next meeting.«

It looks like you've repeated the previous sentence. If you have any more text or if there's anything specific, you'd like assistance with, feel free to let me know!

Thomas looked around for his Uber, his gaze searching. In one hand, he wheeled his silver deluxe trolley, and in the other, he casually draped his leather jacket over his shoulder. He couldn't believe that in a few hours, he would be sitting on the beach. Glancing at his Pepsi, impatience began to creep in. He had saved up for the watch for years. »Now, I really need to get to the airport. Where is that Uber?«

»There, at the intersection, Mr. Freimut,« the man with the sunglasses reassured Thomas one more time, patting him on the shoulder and pointing towards a waiting car. »I wish you a few relaxing days in the sun!«

»Thank you very much! I could use some relaxation,« Thomas said. He glanced around one last time. Had he forgotten anything? Then, waving his hand in farewell, he walked briskly over to the Uber with long strides.

During the ride to the airport, he emailed the documents to his assistant Monica to keep her up to date during his absence. He was determined not to let the business suffer just because he was on vacation. It reassured him when everything was in order.

After pressing ,send,' Thomas let his head sink back against the headrest and closed his eyes. With the traffic, they would need at least an extra half hour to get to the airport. Fortunately, he had allowed for enough time buffer. He tried to relax despite everything, thinking about a chilled gin and tonic he would treat himself to later.

Last month, he celebrated his 45th birthday – or rather, didn't celebrate, as on that day, he gathered his employees for training. He wanted to ensure that they would continue to maintain the high standard that made them appeal to even the largest international clients.

His three siblings had left messages on his voicemail - the two older brothers jokingly, while his older sister, as always, expressed her concern with affection. She feared that his job as a manager in a large marketing agency would leave him with little time for his personal life, especially considering he had already seen one marriage fall apart.

Thomas had an athletic build, a spring in his step, and was very sporty. He succeeded in everything he undertook, except for his marriage, of course. Most women couldn't resist his charming allure. »Work leaves me no time for a serious relationship,« he used to say. His occasional, yet constantly changing, female companions in his bedroom, he claimed, were solely driven by physical needs, nothing more. Or so he asserted.

His financial situation had allowed him to purchase a bungalow near Düsseldorf, a residence that seemed to beg not to be inhabited by just one man. This view was shared by numerous young and not-so-young women. However, when it came to his private life, Thomas remained discreet with his colleagues at work.

The plan to take a break had only developed a few weeks ago. Thomas had realized he was annoyed with his work. Initially, he couldn't pinpoint the source of this feeling. He had barely time to catch his breath, and everything had to be done all at once. He was the first in the office in the morning and the last one in the evening. Sometimes, he even brought folders home. However, in the end, it all became too much for him.

The decisive factor for his decision to take a few days off was then a single situation.

For a major corporation, Thomas had to conduct a marketing presentation. However, he lacked crucial documents to prepare for the talk, and the company kept him waiting. Impatiently, he reached for the phone.

»Yes, this is Wintermann AG, Mrs. Meier. How can I assist you?« An unusually melodic, young voice said. At that moment, it couldn't have sounded enchanting enough to have a soothing effect on him.

»Oh, no!« Thomas exclaimed into the phone. »Wintermann AG. Unbelievable! I thought you guys no longer existed.«

Mrs. Meier had recognized him right away by his voice and greeted him warmly. »Yes, Mr. Freimut, how may I assist you?«

With a tense smile, he replied, »You can guess three times what I want.« He impatiently tapped his pen on the desk as he spoke.

»Oh, a conversation with the boss, I presume,« the voice on the other end of the line responded in a drawn-out manner, trying to ease the tension she sensed from him.

»Bravo! Fantastic! That you guessed that right away!« He jumped up from his chair, pacing back and forth in the office. »Someone should nominate you for the Nobel Prize.«

»And you, it seems, for Man of the Year in terms of politeness,« she countered, but her voice still maintained its melodiously cheerful tone.

»Excuse me,« mumbled Thomas, taking a deep breath as he sat back down. After a brief pause, he realized how impatiently he had acted, even jeopardizing the business relationship. »It's just not my day today. I urgently need the documents for the presentation.«

»I've noted that,« Mrs. Meier replied, noticeably relieved.

Thomas' assistant quickly entered the room, quietly placed a folder on his desk, and promptly disappeared again.

»And?« He pressed the receiver to his ear with one hand while flipping through the folder with the other.

»Yes, just a moment, please. I'll connect you.«

»Thank you!« Annoyed, he rolled his eyes. Meanwhile, classical music played in the background. What does the woman behind that voice look like, Thomas wondered, he only knew her from the phone. Probably like ten thousand others. And how old could she be?

The business relationship with the company in Berlin had existed for years. At least once a year, he held a marketing seminar there, but the collaboration was not usually as sluggish as it was this time.

Without being focused on the task, Thomas flipped through the drafts his assistant had prepared.

Minutes later, the cheerful and friendly female voice reached his ear again.

»Mr. Freimut, I'm sorry, but it seems the boss is currently in a meeting. Can he call you back?«

»Yes, yes, he should do that. Goodbye! And have a nice day!« He hung up dissatisfied. Nothing seemed to be going smoothly.

He leaned back in his desk chair, feet on the desk, and crossed his arms behind his head. He wore a light brown suit paired with a light blue shirt featuring cufflinks, adding a distinctive touch to his outfit.

Since he wasn't on the phone anymore, his assistant came in, standing expectantly in the open office door. She leaned on the door frame with one hand and asked, »So? Have you had a look at the documents? I rushed to prepare them for you.«

»Oh, the documents,« Thomas touched his forehead and took his feet off the desk. He aimlessly sorted through the presentation folder. »Do you mean these?« He lifted the stack.

»Yes, exactly those.« She smiled at him. She liked her boss. Working with him and the team was pleasant. He was always courteous and polite, a charmer and a gentleman of the old school. That's why he was appreciated by his colleagues. Only recently, his behaviour had occasionally left something to be desired.

Perhaps it was due to stress. Probably it was due to stress.

»Oh, sorry, I haven't looked through them yet.« His phone rang, but he ignored the sound and stared thoughtfully at Monica.

»First, everything is super important, urgent, please today, preferably right now, and then...« she muttered more to herself, shook her head, turned on her heel, and clenched her hands into fists. »I spend the whole night working on it because it was soooo urgent… Typical! Lately, he's been really acting strange.«

On her way out, she nearly collided with Thomas' friend Ralf – his lunch appointment.

He sidestepped her and entered Thomas' office shaking his head, holding a bag in his hand. »What's up with her?« He gestured with a nod towards the hallway. »Oh well, today seems to be not our day. Good to see you. I can see you brought something for us?! Come, let's sit over here.« Thomas pointed with an inviting gesture to his round conference table.

»Sure. You can choose. Döner or Lahmacun?«

Ralf placed the bag on the table, and they sat down. While Ralf unpacked, Thomas said, »Oh, thanks. Lahmacun for me.«

Ralf looked over with concern as he handed him his food. »And then I've got your drink here, it gives you wings.« With a fist, he jabbed him on the right upper arm.

Sighing, Thomas nodded. »Yeah, wings wouldn't be bad, considering the workload around here. I don't know how I'm going to get it all done!«

Ralf paused, gazing deeply into his blue eyes, took Thomas by the arm, and said with a firm voice, »I don't mean to alarm you, but - you seem pretty stressed out. The last time I saw you like this was after your divorce. Be careful not to have a heart attack!«

Thomas laughed. »Me, have a heart attack? It's just a lot to do right now. You know how it is, lots of work and not enough staff.«

»What do you do on your days off? Do you relax? You're overworked. Take a trip to the seaside or the mountains,« Ralf paused briefly, then continued immediately. Concern was evident in his voice. »Spend a lot of time walking in the fresh air, that will do you good. And let work be just work for once. Maybe you should take a vacation!«

»Oh, vacation? That's just not possible right now!« He shook his head vigorously. As he took the last bite, he changed the subject. »Of course, I do relax after work. One could retire to bed with their chosen partner - the most enjoyable pastime on earth.«

With a broad grin, he looked at Ralf. »Vacation? Honestly, I can't afford that right now. I've got better things to do.«

Shaking his head, Ralf remarked, »If you think you're in-dispensable... Do you really believe you're immune to a heart attack? You still remember our school friend who passed away last year, don't you?«

Thomas nearly choked on the memory. The shock from last year still reverberated within him. A classmate, his age.

Ralf didn't stop urging him earnestly. »You probably have enough overtime piled up. And your boss would rather have a healthy employee than see you in the hospital or, heaven forbid, at the cemetery. Please, think about it! „ He said, raising his arms in mock despair. „It's your life! But if I may say as a friend: You look really bad.«

»Really?« Thomas looked at him, surprised.

Ralf had been his best friend since school, always honest and reliable. Back then, he never snitched on him when he skipped class, and their mutual loyalty had only grown stronger since then.

Thomas couldn't help but notice how content and balanced Ralf seemed since he had a family. His little daughter was his sunshine.

»Moreover, you're not even fully present here at work. Your assistant, in my opinion, looks especially lovely today, works tirelessly, and you don't even notice,« remarked Thomas.

Deep down, Thomas had been dreaming of a break for a long time. Ralf was right. What good was all this if he were to have a heart attack or even a stroke tomorrow? Being in his mid-forties was a dangerous age, even though he felt more like he was in his late thirties.

Thomas had thought long and hard about it. After a brief back and forth with his boss, he managed to secure a week off. The accumulated 200 overtime hours he had amassed played a significant role in the discussion. After all, since his colleague had left, he had been doing the work of two people.

Once Thomas had become accustomed to the idea, he was eager for a few days of respite. In the sun, preferably all-inclusive, so he wouldn‘t have to organize anything himself. Therefore, he tasked his assistant with booking a last-minute week-long vacation for him, anywhere.

Monica was pleased that she could do something good for her boss and set out to find the best hotel with a pool and all the amenities. Ready for an island getaway, she booked a trip to Lanzarote.

Finally, he settled into his seat on the plane. He had a window seat in the business class, with a middle-aged couple beside him. He observed the cloud formations, his thoughts lingering on work. »Monica will handle everything during my absence. What would I do without her?« he wondered.

Since the woman next to him kept glancing over, he felt compelled to strike up a conversation with his seat neighbours. He smiled at them. »Isn't it wonderful, flying above the clouds like this! Are you also going on vacation?«

The woman had been waiting for an opportunity to share. »No, it's a family visit. We're visiting our daughter; she's married to a Spaniard in the Canary Islands. You know, I'm going to be a grandmother for the second time. I'm so excited. The little one is three years old now, and soon he'll have a little sister. The due date is in two weeks, and we're staying for six weeks to help our Sandra out a bit, you know?« She glanced over at her husband, who nodded and grinned.

»That's wonderful! I'm sure your daughter is thrilled to have so much support,« remarked Thomas warmly.

»Yes, our son-in-law is helpful, oh, the whole family is. You know, Spaniards are very family-oriented; everyone helps each other,« the woman added with a smile.

Thomas nodded politely, then took a newspaper offered to him by the stewardess and began to read—or at least pretended to. Slowly, his pulse calmed down. Time flew by, and before he knew it, they were landing.

Polite, Thomas bid farewell to the soon-to-be grandparents as they disembarked. »I wish you a pleasant stay and all the best to your daughter,« he said kindly.

»Thank you. We wish you relaxing days,« they replied warmly.

Each person retrieved their carry-on luggage, and slowly they made their way down the aisle one by one.

Thomas hoped strongly that he would find relaxation. However, he felt somewhat reserved about it since he was unfamiliar with the resort and the island. Monica had been enthusiastic about the hotel, and she would have loved to come along. He was curious to see if it would meet his expectations.

As Thomas waited for a taxi to take him to the hotel, he looked out of the open window eagerly, observing the radiant blue sky, the palm-lined avenue leading along the sea, and he felt the warmth of the air enveloping him.

Houses painted in shades of orange-yellow and white, adorned with blue or green shutters, lined the street. It was beautiful with the small balconies where colourful laundry hung out to dry. Geraniums twined around the grilles, and colourful flowers lined the streets. It was typically Mediterranean, a sight that was instantly soothing. People sat in street cafes, adding to the vibrant atmosphere.

Thomas leaned back into the cushions and felt the stress of the past few days slowly melting away. Would he be able to let his soul unwind here?

He had earned his vacation. How quickly things could change! Just that morning, he had hastily hosted a business breakfast in Düsseldorf – and a few hours later, he was in the Canary Islands. Summer, sun, beach. The atmosphere, the weather, the landscape – picturesque.

An hour's drive from the airport was his club hotel. Monica

had enthusiastically told him it was one of the top-rated ones, situated in a beautifully expansive park with stunning, colourful flowers and palm trees. He was eager to see it for himself.

After seeing the brochure, his anticipation grew. It was a wellness hotel with entertainment, seminar rooms, sports facilities, swimming pool, sauna, and everything else. The hotel's private beach offered loungers with blue umbrellas. The beach amenities were impressive. In addition to beach volleyball, bocce, canoeing, and surfing lessons, guests could go jet skiing, play tennis, or simply lounge in the sun. Everything was there to ensure a comfortable and enjoyable stay. As a guest, he could use it all.

An entertainer drove him to his bungalow in a club car. The individual bungalows, which made up the hotel, were scattered across the expansive grounds, ensuring that guests never felt crowded.

Upon arriving at his bungalow, he was amazed by its size and coziness. The furnishings included a queen-sized bed, a desk with a chair, a wardrobe, a two-seater couch, a chest of drawers, and a rocking chair. The television was mounted on the wall facing the bathroom, and a ceiling fan spun above. Everything was to his taste, decorated in light tones with turquoise curtains, bedding, and pillows adding a pop of colour. The bathroom was functional with a shower and a window. Outside, each bungalow had a small veranda with a round table and two comfortable chairs. Thomas was thoroughly impressed with his new retreat. Monica had chosen something charming. His initial scepticism about a club hotel being suitable for him was at least dispelled by the first impression.

He unpacked his suitcase and neatly placed his belongings in the wardrobe.

Afterward, he strolled to the pool bar in shorts and a short-sleeved shirt with his backpack to treat himself to a refreshing beer and a small snack. The warm sea air had left him thirsty. Barely had he sat down and placed his order when his phone rang. A WhatsApp message from the office. »You haven't made an important decision regarding Brunner and Brunner yet? How should I proceed? Monica.«

Thomas felt torn. It wasn't always easy to delegate responsibility, but independent employees were worth their weight in gold.

Dear Monica, please make the decision for me. I'm on vacation and don't want to be disturbed anymore! You can handle it! Have a nice day, Thomas."

Lost in thought, he gazed ahead. She usually knows everything, so she can handle it. Monica! – If I didn't have her! She is an excellent asset. Never misses a deadline. She is always there when I call her or need her, and her performance is impressive.

The waiter placed the food and his beer in front of him, putting an end to his contemplations. He took a sip and as he ate his sandwich, he looked around.

Near the bar, there was a small pool with a slide, where children played with an inflatable crocodile. In the other pool, some guests, along with the entertainer, were having fun doing aqua aerobics to hot Spanish tunes. The adults goofed around just like the kids.

Behind the pool bar, a group of teenagers attempted to play darts in the most outrageous manner possible. They knelt on a mat and tried to hit the dartboard from various positions, all while being very playful. Some were holding their stomachs from laughing so hard, making it even more challenging to throw the darts.

Further away, other guests sat there and enjoyed doing nothing, soaking up the sun and the view of the sea. Thomas greatly enjoyed sitting there quietly, sipping his cold beer, and relishing the fact that nobody was interested in him, and nobody wanted anything from him.

Later, he stood on the terrace of the hotel, gazing out over the blue sea, stretching his arms out, feeling the wind play with his hair and brush against his face.

»Ah, finally, vacation, fantastic!« he said to himself, trying to convince himself.

He had read somewhere that if you said something often enough, you would believe it eventually. He put on his sunglasses.

„The sun was shining in the cloudless, blue sky. ‚What a glorious day! Incredible!‘„

He wasn't a sun worshipper, but nonetheless, he loved the warming sun, the beach, the endless expanse of the sea. Finally, away from work. Time to think and relax. To find clarity about his life. What more could he want? He stood there, closed his eyes for a few seconds, let the sound of the sea wash over him, felt the gentle, refreshing wind brushing against his skin, and took a few deep breaths.

He walked down the stairs to the beach by the sea. How long had it been since he had taken such a relaxing vacation?! He wondered. It didn't come to mind. His kind of vacation? - Was pure adventure - but not all-inclusive with entertainment. A new experience.

Monica had said it would be like a health resort. You didn't need to worry about anything, and there were entertainers who motivated you to participate in the sports programs offered. Entertainment from morning till night.

Down on the beach, only a few of the blue and white patterned parasols and dark blue loungers were occupied. The hotel didn't seem to be fully booked. He placed his backpack on one of the loungers and sat down to observe his surroundings better and to enjoy the vastness.

Out on the water, a few windsurfers were out with their orange sails. It was a captivating sight as they rode the waves. They surfed skillfully, exuding joy, and excelling at riding the waves without falling into the water.

They reminded Thomas of his youth and how he used to surf with his friends at St. Peter Ording on the North Sea.

Long-forgotten memories that instantly came flooding back. He felt the urge to give it a try himself and get on the board.

Further to the right, away from the hotel beach, Thomas noticed a woman with an easel that didn't quite fit into the scene of bathers and water sports enthusiasts. He became curious, grabbed his things, and slowly walked along the water towards her. When he got close enough, he saw her capturing the fascinating beach landscape with the sea, the surfers, and a white sailboat passing by on the horizon on her canvas.

Thomas stood two meters behind her and watched the young artist from the right side as she dipped her brush into the colours with great passion, capturing the crashing waves with sweeping strokes.

Thomas took his small SLR camera out of his backpack. As a hobby photographer, he always had it with him. »May I take a few photos of you? It's beautiful how you're standing there...« he asked politely.

She turned to him, and her blue eyes scrutinized him. »Yes, why not, I don't mind,« she said, her tone revealing her amusement at the question.

»Perhaps I should start charging if I'm this photogenic. I didn't know it myself until now, but who knows?« she joked.

Thomas took the shot. A snapshot. She moved very gracefully, occasionally brushing a blonde strand of hair away from her face. The rest of her hair was pinned up with a brush.

»It's fun watching you work. By the way, I'm Thomas Freimut,« he said.

She quickly painted the final strokes before turning to him with the brush in her hand.

»Pleasure to meet you. I'm Lydia Fröhlich, but everyone here just calls me Lydia. I work here at the hotel, and we use informal language with the guests,« Lydia grinned at him, placing the brush on the easel's shelf.

Thomas lowered the camera and looked at her picture as he

took a few steps towards her. »Oh, great, I think that's much better anyway. You work here? As what? Let me guess, as a painter?«

»Do you paint as well, or do you prefer photography?« Lydia asked, eyeing him up and down.

Thomas stood right next to her. »I also paint occasionally, but unfortunately, I don't have enough time to indulge in my hobby. Photography is also one of my hobbies; it's quicker,« he replied.

She nodded in agreement. »Yes, I know the time problem well. I turned my hobby into a profession. I'm an entertainer here at the club hotel, and among other things, I offer painting classes to the tourists.«

Thomas nodded approvingly. »That's really nice, Lydia. I think your last name suits you very well. You have such a cheerful and fresh demeanor. I don't know if I'm allowed to say this, but somehow you have something very fascinating about you.«

Lydia looked at him with wide eyes, eagerly awaiting his response. »Yes, and what?« she teased him.

»Well, I'm not quite sure myself at the moment. But I'm sure I'll figure it out,« Thomas mused, teasingly.

»Since when have you been here? I haven't seen you around before,« Lydia asked.

»You couldn't have seen me before. I arrived today, and I must say, it's beautiful here. The sun, the warmth – everything is just enchanting! The contrast of the colourful shutters against the white bungalows, with the blue sea!«

With a broad, sweeping gesture, he indicated the waves, then laughed. »One instantly feels much more cheerful here. At home, there's more rain than sun, and it immediately affects your mood.«

Lydia looked at her painting, checking if it was finished, as she continued speaking.

„I believe you. It's a dream to be able to work here under palm trees, where others vacation. As the saying goes, ‚One should not dream of life, but live one's dreams,',, she said, taking the brush in hand, placing it between her lips, and pausing briefly.

»That's easier said than done. I envy you for that. Who has such an opportunity?« Thomas replied.

As Lydia continued painting, Thomas observed a father and his son trying to fly a kite. At first, they struggled, but then, with the next gust of wind, it soared into the sky. The little boy was delighted to see it dancing in the wind. Not only the father and son, but also Thomas, watched the colourful kite with fascination, enchanted by its gentle movements against the vast sky.

Thomas' thoughts drifted back to his childhood.

»*Isn't flying a kite similar to my childhood dreams? I dreamt of being free, of observing everything from a bird's-eye view. That's why my childhood dream was to become a pilot,*« he chuckled at the thought.

»*Come to think of it, as a frequent flyer, I'm not that far off from it. It's something you don't even realize. It's become routine,*« Thomas reflected.

He watched as the boy struggled to hold onto the string while his father supported him.

My first flight was incredibly exciting. I had a window seat and watched the clouds. Some looked like mythical creatures, and as they moved, I invented characters and stories... strange, why is that coming back to me?"

»*Life is strange indeed. I've achieved so much, yet I've completely forgotten the ease and the ability to dream,*« Thomas reflected.

Lydia's voice brought him back to the present.

»Actually, every man and woman have the opportunity to do what they please and pursue their dreams. But few seize the chance or have the courage to leave their stagnant and secure jobs to do what they truly desire. And even if they have the courage or just contemplate it, then the next obstacle arises,« Lydia remarked.

She paused briefly. »People—friends or relatives, that's the cruel part—usually dear people who scoff and say that it's not possible to just live out your dreams. That you must wake up,« Lydia added.

She turned to Thomas, looking at him challengingly.

»But why exactly can't it be done? True friends fully understand and support you in your endeavor, but unfortunately, there aren't many of those,« she said.

Nodding, he put the camera back in his backpack. He sat on a lava rock right next to the easel, resting his arms on his knees. He gazed at Lydia, who stood there opposite him.

Their gazes kept meeting. She smiled and hummed a tune.

»Yeah, I completely agree with what you're saying,« Thomas cleared his throat. »You can not only bring fabulous images to the canvas, but you've grasped the meaning of life. Amazing—and you practically radiate with energy,« he added.

With her charismatic aura, she practically drew the guests in, she was aware of that.

Lydia laughed. »Oh, that's obvious! When you can do what your heart desires, energy can flow freely. It's just how it is. Then you have fun, you're happy, and it reflects in the person and is contagious,« she explained.

She turned back to her easel, added the final touch of paint, and nodded contentedly. Lost in thought, she gazed at her painting, the brush still in her hand.

Thomas watched her. *How old could she be? Definitely younger than me—late twenties, perhaps?*

He said aloud, »Where do you get the courage? I find it impressive that as a young person, you just do what you enjoy.«

»Hey, young man!«, Lydia replied indignantly. »You're not that old yourself. Let's keep things in perspective! Taking responsibility for one's life has nothing to do with age.« She gestured wildly with the brush in her hand, sprinkling small paint dots on the sand and her feet.

»Ok.« Thomas pondered. »Let me ask differently. Why do you think so many people don't just do what they do best? Have they just been lucky?«

»I don't think it's just luck,« Lydia replied. »There are many factors at play. Fear of failure, societal expectations, financial constraints, lack of self-belief, and even comfort with the familiar can hold people back from pursuing their true passions and talents. It's often a complex interplay of circumstances and mindset.«

Lydia smiled thoughtfully and replied, »There are many reasons for that. Some people fear change or hesitate to try something new. Others feel constrained by external circumstances, societal expectations, or financial constraints. Sometimes there's simply a lack of confidence in one's own abilities or the courage to step out of the familiar path. Luck certainly plays a role, but ultimately it's about whether one is willing to leave their comfort zone and pursue their passions.«

Lydia put down the brush and turned to Thomas. Her expression was serious. »No, Thomas, it's not just luck. You seem to be one of the optimistic people, and that's the small difference. I believe that everyone is responsible for their own happiness.«

Thomas raised his eyebrows. »What do you mean? Surely, I'm one of the optimistic people. True. But what does that have to do with it?«

Lydia shook her head slightly. »There's a connection, Thomas. Optimistic people tend to see challenges as opportunities. They believe they can actively shape their lives and are willing to take risks to pursue their dreams. That's an important factor in doing what one does best and being happy doing it.«

»It's just the perspective on how one sees life and what each person makes of it. You know it: Either the glass is half full or half empty.«

Slowly, she packed up her painting supplies and put them into her large woven basket bag with leather straps.

Thomas leaned forward.

»Of course, the optimist and the pessimist. I know that well. At work, I also talk to my colleagues about different perspectives. Additionally, as you reach middle age, you have more responsibilities and society's expectations grow. Lately, I've been so busy with everything, and I get annoyed by those negative thinkers. It's terrible! They complain about everything and think they know better. It really brings me down.«

Lydia nodded. »The negative thinkers! Hmm, I know them too well. It could be so nice. Sometimes you're in such a good mood, and then the manager has to come and get upset about some stupid little thing that's actually so trivial that you think he can't stand it when others are in a good mood. It's like: If I'm not doing well, then you shouldn't be happy either.«

Thomas nodded briefly. He was lost in his thoughts and continued talking. »Yet everyone only has one life to master. But sometimes I think some people believe they'll get a second chance,« he said, energetically brushing his long hair out of his face. »Life can be so beautiful, you just have to know how to live and enjoy it. Life isn't about what you get, but what you make of it. I have so many ideas, inspirations, and I want to experience so much that I regret not being able to clone myself. I'm needed everywhere and sometimes I don't know where to go.«

He looked so helpless when he said that, that Lydia laughed.

»Well, it's not that bad yet. But what I wanted to say is: It's often a matter of perspective whether I'm happy or unhappy. But most people forget that. I can only be responsible for my own happiness. Once a guest said to me: ,Yes, young lady, you are to be envied, you can always work in the sun, it's like a permanent vacation.' But it's just as much work as any other job - just in a nicer place that I chose for myself. So, where and what one enjoys doing most is in the hands of each individual. If working in sales at the store no longer brings me joy and satisfaction, then I must do something else that brings me more joy. Somehow, it all works out, you just must have the courage to do what you love.«

»And that, dear Lydia,« Thomas emphasized with his hands to underline his words, »is the problem with most people. They can't change who they are. And they lack the courage.«

Since the paint needed to dry anyway, she sat down on a rock next to Thomas right away.

»Yeah, yeah. I used to say the same thing, that this doesn't work for this reason, and that doesn't work for that reason, and I admired others who worked abroad. Then I did a semester abroad in Ireland, which brought me many new insights, and my father encouraged me to take this job. So here I am,« she smiled.

Thomas nodded approvingly. »Did you have any difficulties with the language? And what did you do with your apartment during that time? Those are the typical questions one asks in such situations, right?«

Lydia laughed. »Oh yes, those typical questions! The language was a bit challenging at first, but I got used to it over time and learned a lot. As for my apartment, I sublet it, and that worked out quite well. It was definitely an adventure, but it was worth it.«

»The questions are certainly valid. There are many arguments we often tell ourselves about why something can't be done. I told myself: Lydia, you can do it, and once you've achieved it, you can look back on it successfully. Regarding the apartment, there were indeed some problems, but ultimately, everything can be solved. At the time, I was living in a shared flat and simply sublet my fully furnished room. It all worked out wonderfully.«

»And did you pass your exams despite the language difficulties?«

»Of course, I managed it. No pain, no gain! I was confident. But it was still super important for me to have a friend who encouraged me a lot and, above all, believed in me. He was the only one I had regular email contact with over the months, and he reaffirmed my plans. At least that gave me positive and, above all, happy thoughts when things weren't going so well.

Especially then, it's important to have someone who says, ‚I'm here and believe in your abilities,‘ when others give up on you or think pessimistically. In my eyes, he was somewhat special. He was like a coach.«

Thomas nodded and took his cigarettes out of his backpack. He had realized early on that it was best not to rely on anyone. Freedom, independence, and his own gut feeling were most important to him. He offered the pack to Lydia, but she politely declined. Then he took out a cigarette and placed it between his lips.

He had already received several marketing awards and achieved professional success through his hard work, initiative, and perseverance. He was in the right place at the right time and had the right business partners. He searched for his lighter in his pocket, found it in his shirt pocket, and lit his cigarette.

He had always wanted to quit smoking but had never managed to do so. The first thing you needed for that was motivation and perseverance. He currently had neither.

Lydia was relieved that the cigarette smoke drifted away to the other side.

»Indeed, but still, self-motivation is the most important thing in my eyes. You must not become dependent on anyone. You just have to believe in yourself: that you are a unique person.«

»That's probably true, and also that one loves oneself. Nevertheless, I tell you that every person, including you, dear Thomas, somewhere has someone who motivates them, in whatever form. Be it that there is someone who looks up to you, is excited about you, or gives you positive feedback, or that you have a friend who loves you absolutely and gives you this love, which in turn inspires you. So somehow there is some person.«

Lydia became increasingly animated. »So, I can't imagine that you've accomplished everything solely from your own motivation. Of course, every action triggers a ripple effect, and at some point, you can no longer distinguish intrinsic motivation - that is, self-motivation - from extrinsic motivation - that is, external motivation. Because when you're happy and radiate happiness, it comes back to you as feedback, even if it's just a smile. And it's precisely this smile,« her voice rose, »from someone else that motivates you, reaffirms your actions, plain and simple! You're happy when someone pays attention to you, aren't you?«

Thomas was impressed. *Wow, what a strong woman! Well, she's right.*

I have to agree with you, Lydia. I receive recognition from my colleagues, employees, and fellow human beings. I get uplifting emails from many kind people that truly bring me joy, or friends come to me for advice, but - nevertheless, I say, one shouldn't let oneself be too influenced by external factors and should believe in oneself. „

»Sure, if nobody else believes in you, then do it yourself. At least you'll have one fan already,« she said with a slightly cynical tone, but she quickly composed herself.

»Of course, self-love comes first. However, I must say, receiving recognition further strengthens your belief that you're doing the right thing, and you put even more power into it when you receive acknowledgment. I can only speak for myself, but I have to say, it thrilled me when I received a positive, encouraging email from that person, making me feel like I wasn't alone in this world. There's someone who believes in you, likes you, and is proud of you when you overcome whatever difficulties you face. They share your joy but also your sorrow. I could have managed without them, surely, but it's so much nicer when there's someone you genuinely like, who likes you back and celebrates your success with you. You can't tell me you don't celebrate your successes with anyone, Thomas, can you?«

»Phew,« he pushed his hair back before continuing. »I do celebrate my successes with dear people, but if no one's around, then I reward myself. Though it's certainly nicer when you can celebrate your success with someone who has been there with you from the start. I can't argue with you on that, Lydia.«

Lydia's smile was triumphant. »Exactly! Everyone needs recognition. But it's the happy thoughts that make you happy, and that happiness is contagious and comes back to you. And that, in turn, makes you happy again, that's it. A cycle. Happiness is not related to a relationship with another person. Happiness can have many facets. It's inside you. I agree that you have to believe in yourself first, and of course, your self-motivation is key.«

»Ah, look at that, so you do have self-motivation after all,« Thomas grinned. »I enjoy it when it rains. Why? If I don't enjoy it, it would still rain. Nothing changes except my attitude.«

„Exactly! When I was feeling down because my job wasn't enjoyable anymore, I saw it as an opportunity. Perhaps it was finally my chance to pursue my studies, which I had always wanted to do. I told myself, ‚Lydia, you should see this situation as an opportunity. Who knows what good may come out of it.‘„

Confidently, Lydia added, »I told myself: I am too good for this position and deserve something better. So, my resignation offered me a wonderful fresh start in a new city. The pessimist would have said: You don't give up a secure position! Who knows what will happen. I pursued my studies, as I mentioned, went abroad, met many nice people. Certainly, there was also pain when my long-term relationship ended, but still: Who knows what good came out of that.« Lydia smiled and made an open-handed gesture.

Thomas shook his head. »And the end of the relationship didn't hit you hard?«

»Ah well, I would say, the end of a relationship is like a turning point in a relationship. Of course, it's not pleasant, and I was certainly down and sad. The unexpected loss of a long-term relationship is a painful experience, but you must make the best of it. Either change the situation or change your attitude! I changed my attitude and told myself, the time with him was nice, it was enriching for me and my life. It was an inner voice that said, surely something new will come, this can't be everything.«

Thomas nodded. »I tell myself that over and over again: This can't be everything. Someday, I'll experience true love and happiness. Not just in material terms, I'm doing quite well there. I mean beyond that, personal happiness. You know what I mean.«

He had barely spoken the words when he stopped abruptly, startled. Did he just say that?

Lydia didn't seem to notice anything unusual about his statements. »I have a great poem about happiness, not sure who it's by, a friend emailed it to me once when I was going through a rough patch. I printed it out and always carry that email in my bag. When I'm feeling down, I take it out and read it.«

She leaned forward, pulled her bag closer, rummaged around in it, and pulled out a slightly crumpled piece of paper.

„Good fortune isn't all that rare,
many things can make us care,
it's how we view life's every turn,
so let joy within you burn.
Happiness is each new day,
it's all we love along the way.
It knows no season, cold or hot,
Happiness is music, even if it's fraught.
Happiness is found in a hearty laugh,
with this wish, I bid you a peaceful night's draught!"

Thomas had listened attentively. »That's very nice. But, as you said, only a few people find their personal happiness. What does happiness mean to you?«

As soon as he posed the question, his thoughts circled around the meaning of happiness. *To be here now, philosophizing about life with a stranger, a charming woman with a refreshing, insightful, and yet cheeky demeanor. She had a way of saying what needed to be said without sounding preachy. No, quite the opposite; her delivery added a charm to it...*

Lydia picked up where she left off.

„Once, a princess asked a wizard if a person's happiness resided atop a shining star. In response, he said: ‚No, true happiness is only found within one's heart.'„

»Indeed, you're quite the poet,« Thomas remarked appreciatively. »It's true, there are always people who find something to complain about everywhere, and others who still seek the sunny side of life despite everything. I say, we belong to the latter. The sun shines for us. *We always look on the bright side of life.*« Encouraged, he hummed the melody.

»What do you do for a living, Thomas?«

»Actually, I work as a marketing consultant,« Thomas replied. »I've been in the field for quite some time now, and it's been a mix of challenges and achievements.« In a few words, he explained, adding, »I really enjoy it. My job allows me to travel across Germany. Our consultancy group operates internationally, for example, in Switzerland, Austria, England, and occasionally in America – New York, San Francisco, and so on.«

Lydia nodded approvingly. »Wow, not bad. Man, you must get around a lot. Hats off to you, you're one lucky guy.«

Thomas lit a cigarette. He didn't take a drag, feeling restless. He needed something in his hand.

»Ok, you travel a lot from hotel to hotel, and you don't always get to see much of the beautiful city. When the sun is shining outside, you're sitting in a darkened room with your participants. You've got it better here,« he said with a slightly lopsided grin. »You can enjoy the sun.«

»True,« Lydia replied. »Sometimes the sun is so hot that I'd be glad to be in a darkened room. Somehow, we're rarely satisfied with what we have, even though it's the same for others. As the saying goes, *'The grass is not greener on the other side.'* But apart from that, besides the hotel grounds, I don't get to see much. I need my day off to relax, and then I prefer to paint and, of course, enjoy the sun. There's not much free time when you work in the tourism industry, so getting out to see something else on the island is a treat.«

She rose from her seat and turned back to her landscape painting. With her finger, she felt the canvas to see if it was dry. Standing by the easel with a serious expression, a small dog came running towards her, barking loudly. She flinched at first, but he was immediately called back by his owner.

Relieved, she placed her hand on her heart. »Wow, that scared me,« she exclaimed. They both laughed about the situation.

Gently, she took her painting and leaned it majestically against her bag. »I'm done with my work,« she announced, then proceeded to pack up her easel.

Thomas stood up to admire her artwork.

»That's really beautiful. I try my hand at acrylic and water-colour, but I'm not as good as you.«

Lydia laughed. »Oh, come on, I'm sure you paint quite well, just differently, as every artist has their uniqueness, every person their own perspective on the world.«

»Quitting time for today,« she said, slinging her bag over her shoulder, clutching the easel under one arm, and her artwork under the other. »I can give you lessons. Every Saturday and Tuesday morning between 10 and 12 at the Palm House of the Club Hotel.« Lydia was about to head towards the hotel.

He stepped aside to clear her path. »If that was an invitation, I'd be happy to take you up on it. Tomorrow, I'd like to explore the island, and if you're willing, I'd love to invite you to dinner tonight. I saw a beach café down there,« he gestured towards the beach.

»Ah, at Pedro's,« she acknowledged.

»Yes, exactly, at 7 p.m.? But only if you want to,« he replied.

»Tonight, I already have plans. But how about tomorrow? Let's say 6 p.m., I won't say no to that,« she replied.

She was thinking: *Tonight is my free evening. Men should be kept on their toes anyway. I have better things to do than wait for Prince Charming and go out to dinner with him right away. Or who knows what else they might want. Well, he's not unlikable. It was only now that she properly scrutinized him from head to toe as he stood before her with his broad shoulders. Tall and charismatic. He definitely had sex appeal.* Thomas's excitement was evident from his face. »I'm thrilled, so we'll definitely see each other tomorrow evening at 6 o'clock, but perhaps even earlier.« He winked at her. »Ciao, until then!«

Lydia, who was finally ready to leave with all her things, looked over at him with a smile.

„Alright, Thomas, here we don't say ‚Ciao,' that's Italian. Here we say ‚hasta luego!' and I'll say to you ‚hasta mañana!',„

Pure relaxation

Lydia was cheerful and enjoyed life in the sunny south. She had a great time painting with the guests. Of course, it was sometimes exhausting, but she usually recovered quickly. Even after several months, she still approached her job with enthusiasm. It rarely got boring for her, as there were constantly new guests and variety. Moreover, she was an artist, organizer, entertainer, and team leader. Sometimes she had little time to indulge in her dreams. On her day off, like yesterday, she usually did something enjoyable. The good sea air, the sun, the beach, and the palm trees - they quickly made her forget about the stress.

Thomas was certainly one of the welcome hotel guests. Besides him, there were the nitpickers, the annoying ones, the know-it-all who weren't so beloved, and the pushy ones, mostly single men. Fortunately, there were few of those.

She looked forward to dinner with Thomas. For the occasion, she wore her new summer dress, which she had bought with her colleague Tina in town the day before. It was made of a soft, flowing fabric in royal blue, which complemented her long blonde hair and accentuated her blue eyes, which shimmered greenish depending on her mood.

The invitation was a welcome change from the hotel dinner and the evening program. Tonight was game night, which Tina loved and enjoyed moderating. On a night like this, it was hardly noticeable if one of the entertainers was absent. So she was lucky. Additionally, she equally cared for the well-being of the guests. For the time being, it was Thomas.

She looked at herself in the mirror. *Yes, you look enchanting, Lydia.. Now, the lipstick, my favourite scent, and off you go!*

She threw on a sweater, left her bungalow, and walked down to Pedro's beach café.

Thomas waited for her. He stood casually, leaning against a wooden beam of the veranda, his leather jacket slung over his shoulder, smoking leisurely and watching Lydia as she approached with her light, airy stride. Before she reached him, he quickly stubbed out his cigarette in a small ashtray in his hand and tucked it into his jacket pocket.

»There you are,« his smile showed his delight. »You look lovely, really beautiful dress, suits you perfectly.« He hugged her gently and kissed both her cheeks.

»Thank you, Thomas, you've dressed up nicely too, so sporty yet elegant,« she said with a wink, smiling at him.

They walked onto the empty terrace and found a nice spot with a view of the sea.

In a traditional manner, he pulled out a chair for her. Surprised, she turned to him, »Oh, thank you, very thoughtful.« He then took a seat opposite her.

Pedro approached them immediately. »Ah, querida, Lydia. Me alegra verte. Oh, buenas tardes, señor.«

»Hola, Pedro. Yes, I'm glad to see you again. Could you please bring us the menu?«

»Ah, la carta, por favor!« Pedro grabbed two menus from a side table and handed them to the two of them.

»Muchas gracias, Pedro.«

As an appetizer and for refreshment, they ordered cocktails.

Thomas immersed himself in his menu. »I'm not sure what to eat – can you recommend something?« He looked at her somewhat perplexed.

»Maybe la sopa – a soup, or la ensalada – a salad. The salads here are always very refreshing and generous, but the vegetable pies are also excellent. Hmm, I think I'll have a traditional vegetable stew with a small salad, and they always serve homemade papas fritas with it,« Lydia suggested.

»That sounds good. I think I'll order that, a good choice!«

He closed the menu and placed it next to his table setting. They smiled at each other.

Pedro brought the cocktails. »For the lady, a Pina Colada, and for the gentleman, a Flying Kangaroo,« he said, then took their orders.

»How did you actually come to this island?« Thomas wanted to know after Pedro had hurried away.

»After my studies, I had a boring desk job. Stress with my boyfriend. It was, a friends-with-benefits situation, if you know what I mean, but I wanted more.«

She sucked on her straw.

»The position as an entertainer was advertised, so I applied on a whim. Sort of ripe for the island. I was lucky to get into this club. I like it.«

»I see, a little luck is necessary for everyone, isn't it, Lydia?« She nodded. »And where did you learn Spanish?«

»Before, we often vacationed with the family in Spain. Additionally, I took a few Spanish courses during my studies. And now, here, it's amazing how much you can learn when you immerse yourself in the country and interact with the locals,« explained Lydia with a smile. »I love the music and the easiness of the Spanish.«

The sun was slowly sinking into the sea. Only a few vacationers came for dinner so early. Murmurs drifted over from another table. In the background, the sound of guitars could be heard. Lydia enjoyed the atmosphere and felt a bit like she was on vacation herself. Then, their meal was served. It looked delicious.

»Enjoy your meal! Buen provecho!« Lydia wished.

»Gracias, igualmente!«

»Yes, I can speak a bit of Spanish,« Thomas replied with a smile.

»Well, just a few words, nothing to write home about. I

went to Spain often with my parents,« he grinned back.

»Well, then we already have something in common,« Lydia remarked happily.

Thomas took a forkful of his vegetable stew with legumes. »Mmmh, excellent! And to enjoy the view of the beach from this terrace!« Chewing contentedly, he gazed thoughtfully into the distance. »It makes you forget time and space when your gaze is fixed on the horizon. How infinitely vast the sea is ... - and that sky!«

Lydia nodded and ate her fries with her fingers. »Enchanting! Such magnificent colours, I couldn't paint them better in the sky, such beautiful combinations of colours! You must watch the sunsets every evening, Thomas. Each one is more beautiful than the last. Sometimes it's red, sometimes it's yellowish or even pink, but always stunning,« she enthused.

»Completely losing oneself in the sight nature offers. The sound of the sea is like a melody in the ears and brings complete peace. I could sit here for hours just watching the people and nature,« Lydia expressed.

She speared the last piece of salad with her fork and popped it into her mouth, all the while gazing deeply into his eyes.

He grinned. »From what I can see, you're a romantic. I understand that well, I feel the same way. Just letting the soul unwind and switching off from all the everyday stress.«

Silently, they sat facing each other. As Lydia savoured the fruits of her cocktail and grinned at him, Thomas's thoughts drifted away.

Is she flirting with me? She has such beautifully curved full lips. An attractive young woman. What if we're meant for each other? Oh, why am I thinking like this again...

»The food was excellent,« Thomas waved to Pedro and took care of the bill. Lydia thanked him several times for the invitation.

»May I give you a gift?« he asked as they were leaving.

Lydia wasn't sure if he was joking. »Another gift? But Thomas, I can't accept that,« she said.

»Yes, you can. Come on, Lydia, I'll give you a walk on the beach, will you accompany me?«

»With pleasure, con mucho gusto, muchas gracias, vamos a la playa!«

Thomas took her hand. »A qué esperas? What are you waiting for? Let's go to the beach!«

As if it were a cue, they ran down to the water, arms outstretched, the wind in their hair, and the salty air on their skin.

They took off their shoes, left their belongings on the beach, and delighted in the footprints they left in the warm, moist sand. The next wave carried them away again, and they jumped around wildly to leave new ones behind.

Abruptly, Thomas stopped. »Come on, hop on my back. Brrr,« she jumped up, and he galloped with her to the water and back again.

Like carefree children, they had fun. »Come on, my little horsey,« and she tapped his backside with her hand. Lydia laughed heartily.

»Why are you laughing like that?« Thomas asked, amused.

»I was just thinking about what a funny pair we are, goofing around like this, really funny!«

Her laughter infected Thomas. Unable to hold her, he fell to the ground with her, laughing. Quickly, he got up and helped her to her feet.

Then she ran off, calling back over her shoulder, »Catch me if you can!«

Laughing, he caught up to her and grabbed her from behind, holding her arms. »Gotcha,« he said.

»What is it, Lydia?« he asked, curious.

»Oh, it's nothing special,« she said, smiling mischievously in return.

She glanced at him cheekily from the side, tucked her hair behind her ears, and said, »Oh, nothing!« before laughing.

They picked up their shoes, jumper, and jacket.

They continued walking barefoot.

It felt like they had known each other for an eternity as they walked side by side along the beach. It was no coincidence that they had met each other.

»Yes, I can't remember the last time I was so carefree. When you're working, you have to be serious and grown-up.«

»He smiled contentedly.«

»It's not accepted to be allowed to be a child sometimes. Yet, it's liberating to do something crazy. But with you, it was especially easy for me. You're so captivating.«

Lydia beamed at him. »It's time to do things we wouldn't normally dare to do.«

At this time, the beach was empty. The hotel guests were at dinner. Only a few locals were taking their evening stroll. One destination was the lighthouse, which sent its light out to sea.

»That's true. It's crazy how as you get older and look back, you realize you've become more serious and responsible. I'm not as spontaneous and carefree as I used to be. I remember coming out of the club with my friends and thinking about where we should go for breakfast. One of my friends suggested going to Paris. We immediately got in the car and just drove off. Looking back, it's hard to imagine how we used to be.«

He tied his shoes together to carry them along with his jacket over his shoulders.

Lydia laughed. »I also remember such actions. Just great!«

With the sweater over her shoulders and her sandals in hand, she spun around in a pirouette.

»To be so carefree is simply wonderful and it awakens the creativity within a person. Unfortunately, it's underutilized. When you're an adult, you're expected to behave like one. Why is the child within us suppressed? Aren't children the ones from whom we can learn to go through life carefree and worry-free?«

Thomas looked directly into her eyes, then sighed. »If only it were always that simple! Life is better lived, but one cannot be entirely without worries or problems. You can only change your inner attitude towards life, as you so aptly said during our first encounter.«

»Think positive« is the keyword! Isn't that right, Thomas?

He paused for a moment. »In my presentations, I often use the example of ‚The Little Prince,' do you know it?«

»What? ‚The Little Prince' by Antoine de Saint-Exupéry? Of course, I know it. What's so exciting about the story?«

»Yes, it's a children's book, but equally for adults.«

»Aha! And?« She didn't know what he was getting at.

»I like to use fairy tales and stories to make difficult topics as understandable as possible. So, about the topic of problems, there's a beautiful passage. It's about how the little prince talks about how problems and worries aren't actually that difficult.«

Lydia listened with interest.

»Well, the complicated problems are often much less intricate than one thinks, and they have the strange property of resolving themselves as if by magic when the solution comes just at the moment when one least expects it,« Lydia said.

»And something like that is in ‚The Little Prince'? Wow, I always thought such lofty wisdom was only found in psychology books,« Lydia exclaimed.

»No, as I mentioned before, for my participants, I make it as simple as possible so that everyone understands it, without all the psychological terms,« Thomas clarified.

Thomas offered her his arm, but she didn't link hers with his. At first disappointed, he took note of it. He wasn't used to being rejected. They walked along the sandy beach in step with each other.

»Anyway, there's some truth to that. Sometimes problems solve themselves if you just wait or leave them be. It doesn't always work, but somewhere I read: There are no problems. Problems are just challenges.«

Thomas nodded, smiling.

»Challenges - instead of problems? Yes, I understand. That sounds good,« he repeated. »There are no problems, only challenges or new opportunities. You use a different word, and it has a different effect.«

A fisherman was preparing his fishing boat to go out at night. Lydia greeted him as she walked by. When he saw her, he waved back.

»Yep, with a suitcase full of thoughts and problems, no - challenges, as you say - I came here. Basically, ready for the island. I just want to sort out my thoughts a bit and find some peace. To be alone and switch off from everything!«

She glanced at him from the side. »I understand, that's how it is for many vacationers who come here. What stress do you have at home, if I may ask?«

The hotel guests who passed by were greeted with a smile and a wave of her hand.

»Difficult to put into words,« he pondered.

Thomas admired the landscape, which looked bizarre in the setting sun and rising moon.

»But I can try. I ran away. I need freedom and, above all, time to think. No, that's not true,« he paused. »To be honest, my friend Ralf convinced me. Without his advice, I wouldn't be here at all. Right now, I'm working for two. He thought I needed to relax and unwind. He's right. I have a lot on my plate. Both personally and professionally. I need to think about that, and that's why I'm here.«

Lydia listened attentively.

»You know, it feels like you're an old friend of mine,« he said, looking at her. »We hardly know each other, yet we feel so familiar. Normally, I don't engage in such intense and open conversations with someone I don't know yet. I mean, it doesn't happen often. It's usually more superficial, you know?« He realized he was struggling to find the right words. »But with you, it's different. I feel comfortable.«

Lost in thought, they continued walking. It was a wonderful, balmy summer evening. The sound of the waves was soothing.

A thousand things were going through his mind. Where should he start? Should he entrust this woman with his life story? On the other hand, why not? She was an impartial person—sympathetic and trustworthy. A woman who had her feet firmly on the ground, who knew her way around, confident, intelligent, and open-minded. It was easy for him to talk to her. He didn't know why, it just was.

The easiness was gone. Thomas's face had become serious, and the tension had disappeared from his posture.

»Do you know, Lydia, as one slowly age, they begin to reflect on their life. Then they look around at their circle of friends and realize that most of them are married, have children, planted a tree, and built a house. That's perfectly fine. However, it stirred something within me. One day, the thought occurred to me: No, Thomas – this isn't how you imagined your life! I want to leave something for posterity. Something significant – you know. So far, I've just lived my life in relationships, but now I'm beginning to doubt the correctness of my life. Sure, I've had a successful career.«

A smile flickered across his face. He pulled his shoulders back, proud of them. Lydia gave him her full attention.

»However, I have decided to clean up my life. Something must happen. That's why I'm here, because I want to clear my head.«

Thomas saw a lava rock suitable for sitting and headed in that direction to take a break. Lydia followed him. Both settled down on it. He ran his hand through his hair, surprised at himself for how openly he could talk with Lydia.

»After my divorce, I've only had casual relationships. Somehow, I never found the right one to whom I could give my heart. I don't know...« He shrugged.

Lydia nodded. »I completely understand! I went through something similar after my last breakup. I loved him, but I felt like he just liked me. Liking and loving are different. After that, I had to realign myself, and that takes time.«

Lydia frowned. »How long were you married then? Or rather, how long and why did you separate?«

»We were very young. Early 20s. She was my first great

love. I moved to another city because of my studies, so we only saw each other on weekends. She left me for someone else who was local and had more time for her,« he shrugged. »I wanted a relationship and eventually a family. Besides studying, I was already working because I wanted to build my career. I succeeded in that. But my marriage suffered as a result.«

»Okay... and why hasn't the right one come along yet?« Lydia looked at him.

»Well, I'm kind of caught between a rock and a hard place - somehow I've also had bad luck with women.«

He pressed his lips together. Next to Lydia, he felt comfortable yet also surprised by his own openness. It felt good to talk about his situation. She lent him her ear and asked interesting questions.

»The girlfriend after my marriage just left me in the lurch one night and shortly after married someone else. You can't convince me she really loved me if she moved on so quickly,« he said.

»Did you live together?« he asked.

»No. We had separate apartments. Besides, it wasn't possible. She was studying in Leipzig, and I was working in Düsseldorf. So, it was a classic weekend relationship, but one day she was just unreachable. It's silly to break up like that and leave the other person in the dark, especially after all I did for her!«

Lydia looked at him questioningly.

»I supported her as much as I could during her studies, and when she graduated, she packed her things and left. Just like that!«

»Hmm, strange indeed,« Lydia sounded pensive. »Sometimes people can be odd. A friend of mine ordered a moving van while her husband was away at a training session. She was done with the relationship. When he came home, half the apartment was empty, and she was gone. She handled everything else through her lawyer.«

»Exactly,« Thomas was glad that Lydia seemed to understand him.

»But in the long run, we wouldn't have been a good match. We were too different. She was very messy,« he added. »That wouldn't have worked out well.«

»And what is she doing now? Have you heard from her again?«

»Yes, a few years ago I ran into her by chance while shopping in Leipzig. She's married now. And as far as I know, she has two children.«

Thomas looked at her and made a gesture indicating it was time to leave. They stood up and continued walking.

»And you?« Lydia nudged a seashell with the tip of her foot. »Are you in a relationship again?«

Thomas frowned. »Yes and no! I'm constantly on the go and have a lot on my plate, so I can't really relax properly. I don't know … Which woman likes someone who's always on the move? That's not something most people can handle in the long run.«

A jogger ran down the stairs. Above the cliffs, there was a sports facility. Children's laughter from playing football reached them from below. The floodlights illuminated half of the beach.

In the floodlights, Lydia couldn't help but notice that he seemed annoyed and troubled.

»I'm not sure if that's the case,« she replied cautiously. »I think if you love each other and have common life goals, you can find common ground. There are many professions where one travels a lot, and the wife stays home with the children. In such cases, good communication is especially important. You can communicate via email, phone, or through Skype or Zoom. It doesn't matter where you are, even if you're abroad. Unlike before, that's not a problem anymore these days.«

Thomas seemed unconvinced. »I think it's difficult,« he said.

Lydia didn't give up so easily. »Maintaining a relationship is always challenging, in that regard, I completely agree with you. I wonder how women managed in past centuries. Times change, but certain things never do. That longing for a perfect, loving partner, right? They should be there when you need them, not constantly on the go,« she remarked.

Silently, they walked along the beach. The palm trees swayed gently in the wind. The sea became restless, waves slowly approaching. As tumultuous as the sea, so were Thomas's thoughts.

It took a while before he spoke again, and when he did, his voice sounded unusually soft.

»Imagine, after two years, my girlfriend Ute left me last week. Everything had started so beautifully and promisingly!«

Thomas sank into his thoughts.

Then he slowly recounted how he had met Ute.

»It all started on a beautiful day in May. I was on my way to one of my lectures, as usual, this time on the ICE train to Frankfurt. That's when I saw her. She was sitting across from me in my first-class compartment. Her long, blond curly hair cascaded over her shoulders; she wore a delicate green pantsuit that accentuated her figure very well. Her skin glowed as the sun shone on her face.«

Lydia laughed. »Do you remember all of that?«

»Oh yes! She looked stunning. I tried to read my documents, but I was more interested in this woman. When something fell from her hand, she bent down and gave me a glimpse of her full breasts, which were revealed by the blouse with the deeply cut neckline, as she looked up at me and our eyes met...«

He saw everything vividly in his mind again.

»Are you looking for something?« I asked.

»Yes, my pen, it fell down,« she said, looking to the ground but not finding it.

»I reached between my feet. ›Here you go.‹ It was a fancy pen, and I handed it to her.«

She thanked me with a smile. »I'm lost without my writing utensils.«

I felt that gratitude in her smile, as she showed me her beautiful white teeth. Her big, expressive blue eyes sparkled, her long, luscious eyelashes and her gracefully arched eyebrows, everything fit together perfectly. Her charisma was captivating.

As usual, I joked around. »Yes, one's pen, another's laptop, but we must keep working, right? Where is your journey taking you if I may ask?«

With a broad smile, she looked at me. »I'm going to Frankfurt,« she said softly.

»Are you there on business?«

She set aside her writing tools. »Yes, I'm a journalist.«

„I became curious. ‚It's rare to meet such a nice journalist. Let me guess, you're not exactly writing an interesting report about Frankfurt, are you?'„

„She leaned back in her seat, adjusting her hair. ‚No, I'm attending a lecture there because I'm writing a report on ‚The Employee of the Future and Ego Marketing.'„

»I perked up. ‚Oh really? Don't tell me we're headed to the same event.«

»No, I can't believe it either – you too? The future of work and how to market oneself best? That's truly hilarious,« she laughed in surprise.

It was no coincidence that the journalist was sitting directly opposite me. She was literally my type.

»I should introduce myself. My name is Thomas Freimut. I'm the marketing director who will be speaking about ‚Ego Marketing' there. It's sure to be nice and exciting.«

»Yes, indeed! Very exciting! My name is Ute Mondschmidt. I came all the way from Hamburg just to hear you here in Frankfurt, and I meet you already on the train! That's something!«

She shook her head, her long blonde hair swaying in rhythm.

„I became braver. ‚That's wonderful, isn't it? It's a pleasant journey, and the sun is shining as well. Since we're both professionally attending the same lecture, we can use the informal ‚you‘. I'm Thomas.‘„

»Okay, I have no problem with that. I'm Ute.«

»So began,« said Thomas, looking at Lydia embarrassed. »Somehow, the train journey flew by. We had a nice conversation and exchanged thoughts about our topic in depth. I was confident that Ute would write a good article. And that's how I met her, on the train, on the way from Düsseldorf to Frankfurt.«

»And did you two meet up at the conference afterward?« Lydia wanted to know.

»Completely innocent, it just happened. My presentation went smoothly, and Ute wrote a very good article. She took great portrait shots of me. At the hotel bar, it got later and later, and we had long and deep conversations. There was a spark between us. Then one thing led to another, and yes – eventually, after a few glasses of wine and sparkling champagne – we danced our way to my room. I'm not quite sure how it all happened. We kissed, undressed each other, and ended up in bed. She felt incredibly good, and she looked amazing. How can I put it, Ute is an attractive young woman, she could kiss passionately, and I forgot everything around me. It was an intoxicating and erotic night. For me, Ute was the queen of the night.«

Thomas noticed Lydia's surprise, and his eyes sparkled even more.

»On the following day, we happened to have the same route back home. We got along right away and were on the same wavelength.«

„He looked at Lydia. ‚Do you understand? She lives and loves life just like I do.‘„

Lydia frowned. »But if she lives in Hamburg and you're in Düsseldorf, when did you two see each other? Was it like a classic weekend relationship?«

They strolled along the water. The lighthouse was getting

closer. Thomas continued with his explanations.

»Oh, her publisher had a branch in Cologne, so despite all the circumstances, we saw each other regularly. Düsseldorf and Cologne are just a stone's throw away. Ute commuted between Hamburg and Cologne anyway. Almost every week - she always had her weekly meeting there on Wednesdays and stayed until Thursday. That was very convenient for me, to have a relationship on Wednesdays.«

»Exactly, it was often on Wednesdays, but occasionally we would spend a whole weekend together, right?«

»Oh, every now and then. Every two months, I would spend a weekend with her in Hamburg. It's quite a distance. I didn't have much business there. It was more convenient for me if she came down, then she didn't need a hotel room.«

»Okay. For love, no distance is too far.«

»Nah, but...« Thomas left it at that. »Hamburg is a beautiful port city with lakes. So, in the summer, it's pleasant. It's nice to have breakfast on Sunday morning at the fish market, watch the hustle and bustle, with all the vendors selling various things. We enjoyed browsing there. I always find it fascinating to observe people and tourists. Not only is the city worth seeing, but there are also many charming little cafes with live music, and during the day, you can enjoy a nice shopping spree. In good weather, a harbour tour is worthwhile. Once, Ute really surprised me.«

Lydia asked, »What did she do that was special?«

»As a journalist, she has special connections, so she got press passes to the premiere of a musical and invited me. That was quite impressive, being among all the celebrities on the red carpet!«

»Of course, with a charming young woman, every visit and everything you do is enjoyable, no matter what. But attending a premiere is certainly hard to beat. But isn't a weekend relationship, or rather a Wednesday-Thursday relationship, stressful?«

»Why?« Thomas looked at her with a puzzled expression.

»That simplifies things. So, I thought it was great. It allowed me to manage my time effectively. If I couldn't make it on a Wednesday, we'd meet another time or on the weekend, or the following week. Like me, Ute, being a journalist, travels a lot, and occasionally we'd meet in some other city where I was holding another marketing event, and otherwise ...«

Thomas gestured vaguely with his hand. He looked out over the sea to the horizon, barely visible in the darkness, and Lydia noticed that he seemed quite calm, considering that Ute had left him.

»What else?« Lydia frowned and stopped in front of him.

Thomas watched a white sailing ship, visible in the moonlight. The dark sky was reflected in the sea. They watched the play of the waves hitting the shore for a while. Then Thomas turned to Lydia.

»There was also my long-term relationship with Carmen.«

Lydia jumped to the side in surprise.

»How? You were still with another woman? At the same time?!«

»Yes.« His response startled Lydia. She looked at Thomas with wide eyes.

»How, yes?!« She looked over at him. »I'm having trouble following you right now.«

Before stepping onto the promenade, she put on her sandals. In a calm manner, he untied his shoes, knelt, and put them on, grinning mischievously. »Yes!«

He stood up. Lydia looked at him incredulously before they continued the last 50 meters to the lighthouse.

»I've been with Carmen for four years. I think,« he calculated briefly, »no, it's been six years now.«

Lydia shook her head. »And she knows nothing about Ute?«

Thomas seemed surprised. »No, why would she?«

»Yes, exactly,« Lydia replied, nodding. »It's all about managing time effectively.«

Lydia had stopped and looked Thomas directly in the eyes. »Because Ute can only meet on Wednesdays, you have time for

Carmen on the other days. You can't be serious!«

Thomas shoved his hands into his pockets and looked down at his shoes. How should he tell Lydia that there was more to it…?

Thoughtfully, he continued walking. She followed him, trying to understand his words.

They had arrived at the lighthouse. At the base stood a bench where a couple in love sat. They circled around the lighthouse and then slowly retraced their steps back the same way.

»Listen, Lydia, you mustn't hold it against me. Carmen is a love! But then, one day, I met Ute, as I told you, on the train. Ute is so different from Carmen, just in appearance alone. With her long, blonde, curly hair, Ute looks like an angel. But« he shrugged, »Ute is a completely different type. She's livelier, like a colourful butterfly. When she moves while dancing, she has a feminine allure, she's more erotic, fuller of life, and curious. That's part of her job. We could exchange thoughts wonderfully and talk about absolutely everything.«

Lydia frowned. »Didn't you say she broke up with you? Then you should be happy, one less… or did she find out about Carmen somehow?«

»I don't think so, how could she? I always hid everything about Carmen when Ute visited. I never met Carmen on Wednesdays anyway, and if the phone rang, I just didn't answer, simple as that.«

He shrugged, raising his hands. »No, she's a different type!«

»How cunning of you. And now you're hurt because she broke up with you?« Lydia's voice sounded sharp-tongued.

As Thomas didn't respond, she continued. »But you weren't honest beyond that, were you? Did you come clean with her, or was it just friends with benefits?«

He felt caught. He watched the moon, which illuminated their path. So, they walked back along the beach path.

»No, Ute and I had a relationship. When we were together, I was only there for her, all my attention was solely on her,« he said.

»Always just on Wednesday evenings, right?« Lydia looked at him sharply from the side, but Thomas didn't rise to the provocation.

»She was very much in love with me, and I loved her. But,« he nodded, as if confirming it to himself, »I can say that. She is an open-minded and enthusiastic person. What I liked most was her spontaneity, doing whatever pleased her. And above all,« now he looked Lydia directly in the eyes, »spontaneous sex.«

»Oh, typical man. You didn't have that with Carmen?«

»At times, yes,« Thomas looked out to the sea. »After six years, spontaneity fades a bit. Besides, it was nice with both. I can't say whom I love more.« Thomas seemed pensive suddenly.

»I think I love all my women equally, that's precisely my problem,« Thomas admitted.

He looked at Lydia, as if hoping for a sympathetic word from her. »Each in their own way,« he said.

Lydia became alert. ‚All my women‘? What did he mean by that again? She posed the question back.

Lydia asked, »How did you meet Carmen? That interests me now. You've been together for six years? What kind of person is Carmen? What did Carmen have that Ute didn't?«

In the meantime, the moon was high in the sky, and the stars twinkled. Lydia pulled her sweater over her, as the thin dress felt too cool in the evening air.

Thomas felt warm. His jacket hung casually over his shoulder.

As they passed by the sports field again, the game had ended. A group of teenagers came running down the stairs to the beach, shouting.

Thomas responded to her question. »I've been with Carmen for about six years. There were ups and downs, as often happens in relationships. There was a period where we didn't see each other regularly. We didn't want to fully break up. It was more of an on-off relationship. We had little time for each other, even though Carmen lives nearby. Eventually, we parted ways amicably. But whenever we had time again, we did everything together. Then, when the next vacation came around, which we spent together in Africa, we were a couple again. We never really let go of each other. That's been about two years now.«

Thomas paused for a moment and cleared his throat.

Lydia frowned. »How did you come up with the idea of going on vacation together in Africa if you were actually on the brink of breaking up?«

Thomas took his jacket over his arm, put his hands in his pockets, and strolled alongside Lydia.

»I had always wanted to go to Africa, and Carmen is open to adventure trips. Not every woman is someone you can take along, but with Carmen, I wasn't afraid she would annoy me. In this case, we shared the same interests and views, and since I didn't want to travel alone, I asked her, and it wasn't a problem.«

„He told it as if it were a matter of course. ‚We hadn't really fought when we split up. We were still friends. It was more like each of us went our separate ways, and we enjoyed continuing to have a good friendship. But that vacation brought us back together. Suddenly, there was that closeness and desire for her again, which I hadn't felt for a long time.‘„

Lydia had become pensive. »Sometimes it's strange. I've seen a lot here at the hotel. There are couples who don't like to travel together because they get on each other's nerves and end up fighting the most. The most common divorces happen after vacations. It's a different situation than at home. There, you can more easily avoid each other. I often see cases where a man goes on vacation with his mistress, leaving his wife and children at home. But voluntarily going on a trip with an ex-girlfriend because you get along so well, that's rather rare. The question is: if you get along so well, why did you break up in the first place? And how did you meet Carmen?«

Thomas took his jacket in hand. They continued walking in step.

»How did I meet Carmen? Hmm - I was invited to a birthday party of a friend at the time, yes. I think it was in Duisburg. Or was it Oberhausen?«

He ran his hand through his hair.

Lydia rolled her eyes and jumped ahead of him. »But you must know where your friend lives!«

»The thing is, he's moved so many times, and it's been a few years already. Anyway, it was somewhere in the Ruhr area. The party was already in full swing when I arrived. I found it kind of boring, to be honest. Parties like that aren't really my thing, especially when it's mostly couples. There was plenty of food and drinks, so I headed straight to the buffet – I'm always hungry. Carmen was there, helping herself to cheese bites...«

He chuckled at the memory. »She seemed to be alone because she was standing there, looking a bit bored, watching the lively scene.«

»I walked over to her and struck up a conversation.«

»I said to her, ‚Leave some for me,‘ and grinned at her.«

»They're really delicious,« she said as she popped one cheese cube after another into her mouth, giving me a challenging look. She took a cheese cube in her hand and instructed me.

»Very delicious cheese. As I was told, the ingredients for organic cheese naturally come from ecological farming. I must say, the taste is simply unbeatable. Give it a try,« she said before I could say anything, popping a cheese cube into my mouth.

I obediently chewed. »Mmm, delicious, really good. What's the ...«

»I don't know what the cheese is called, but it definitely tastes better than the regular one, doesn't it?« She looked at me expectantly with her big brown eyes.

»I was laughing. „No, actually I didn't want to know what the cheese is called, but what your name is.«

We laughed heartily at the comedic situation.

»Oh, so what's your name? My name is Carmen, Carmen

Botticelli,« she said, brushing her long brown hair back with her hand.

She looked like an angel. Friendly, and when she laughed, dimples appeared in her cheeks.

»Nice to meet you, Carmen Botticelli. Are you Italian? Well, silly question, one can tell from the name. But you speak perfect German without an accent, or...« I thought of another possibility, »are you perhaps married to an Italian?«

»My hopes sank, hopefully not married, because she didn't look like an Italian at all.«

»No, I'm single, not married, no bambini, and I'm in the third generation in Germany. Occasionally, Nonno Marco calls from Italy. I only know a few words in Italian; I understand him well, but I don't speak it. My parents aren't both Italians. My father rarely speaks Italian. Naturally, we end up speaking German. Another cheese bites?« She held one out to me, smiling invitingly.

»All right, also single, that's good to know. Talkative little thing, she should better eat something herself from time to time,« I thought back then. She didn't let me get a word in edgewise. Or maybe it just seemed that way because I was so captivated by her red lips.

Carmen wore a black blouse with a deep neckline and a floral velvet skirt, to my surprise, she paired it with sturdy lace-up shoes. But that's what made her so different. Unabashed and sexy.

»Yeah, sure.« I took the piece of cheese from her fingers. »By the way, you have beautiful brown eyes.«

Her eyes sparkled as she looked at me.

»What do you do?« I asked.

»I'm a copywriter at an advertising agency. You must be super creative for that, but it's not always easy to come up with something productive. Sometimes you must get inspired at a party,« she replied.

»Yes, I can understand that. It's an interesting profession you have!«

»Right, but it's often very tough. Sometimes it's very successful, then the prosecco flows, but on the other hand, tears often flow too. You know, Thomas, do you know what the most expensive piece of furniture in our office is?«

I shrugged. »No, I have no idea!«

»I can tell you, the most expensive piece of furniture in an advertising agency is the trash can. It swallows more ideas than get printed or broadcasted, really!«

»I hadn't known that, but I can imagine. It makes sense.«

»And it's true. By the way, all our wastebaskets are colourful, so it's not all grey in grey. And what do you do for a living?«

»I'm an employee at a large company, giving presentations and teaching the bosses and supervisors about the latest marketing projects. I'm often on the road and rarely at home. Even my cat couldn't stand it with me anymore and ran away.«

Carmen looked at me sympathetically.

»Now I have plenty of cat food, but no cat anymore. Too bad.«

I paused and waited for her reaction. When she looked at me with wide eyes, I added, »Well, the cat isn't dead, she belonged to my neighbour, who moved away and took the cat with them. And what am I going to do with the food now?« I looked at her. »You don't happen to have a cat, do you?«

Carmen laughed so hard she had to hold her stomach. »And now you have to eat the cat food? Then please don't invite me for Dinner.«

»No, don't worry, I'll find a way to get rid of the cat food. But you've given me an idea. I'd love to invite you for dinner, then I'll cook something delicious for you. I'm actually a pretty good cook.«

She tilted her head, resembling a kitten, and her voice sounded like a purr. »What would you conjure up for me?« She looked at me seductively, with a flutter of her eyelashes.

»What would I conjure up for you? I don't know yet, let yourself be surprised,« I replied.

»Oh, I bet you can't really conjure up anything. Do you even have a real magic wand?« she flirted with me.

Grinning, I responded to her flirtation. »Of course, I have one. But I can only show you my magic wand at home, you'll have to come visit me for that.«

»You've piqued my curiosity,« she chuckled. »I'd definitely like to see this magic wand sometime.«

We flirted and had a great time. Carmen was really in the mood.

In the background, music was playing, and Carmen moved to the beat. She hummed along as she slowly guided me onto the dance floor, which was sparsely occupied. Taking my hand, she led the way as we danced. She followed my lead well.

Carmen was in an adventurous mood, I could tell. Her pupils had dilated, she moved with enthusiasm, and she teased with glimpses, as the top buttons of her blouse were undone. She seemed a bit tipsy. »Where do you live, actually?« she asked.

»I'm from Düsseldorf,« I replied.

She looked into my eyes.

»Wow, really? What a coincidence! We could have formed a carpool.«

What I would have loved to do. I found her charming. Maybe we could meet up sometime? I could feel the tension between us. »We could make up for it sometime.«

»Are you still sober and able to drive?« She looked at me challengingly.

I had drunk a non-alcoholic beer, so that wasn't an issue. I had been offered to stay at the hosts' place, but I prefer to sleep in my own bed at home, so I just don't drink alcohol.

»I'm definitely driving home; do you want a ride?« My hopes rose, my heart leaped, this was the opportunity.

»I think you can read minds. I only had three glasses of wine, but it hit me hard, so I can't drive anymore. And I don't want to sleep here, I'd rather be at home.«

»Hopefully you could bring me back here tomorrow morning so I can pick up my car.«

That was exactly what I wanted to hear. Tomorrow morning, and the night with me!

»No problem, we can do that,« I said, brushing her arm. Her skin was soft. She responded to my touch with a smile. I would have liked to feel more of her skin at that moment, but maybe later.

At that moment, I heard the first notes of one of my favourite songs by Santana, a cozy tune. The dance floor quickly filled up, and the lights dimmed. Slow dancing always worked, we used to say. Carmen nestled against me, and I held her tightly in my arms. Her perfume smelled good, and I gave her a kiss on the cheek. Just like that, but she seemed to like it. She was my type. Carmen wasn't opposed to it. It didn't take long before we wanted more, and we danced closer. I would have liked to know how she kisses, but I didn't dare in my friend's apartment.

Thomas was lost in thought, traveling back in time, and there was a broad grin on his face. »That was nice!«

Lydia brought him back to the present. »What kind of person is your Carmen?«

They passed by the sun loungers of the neighbouring hotels and decided to make themselves comfortable on the chairs. They sat facing each other, and Thomas, being a gentleman, placed his jacket on the sun lounger for Lydia to sit on before he continued speaking.

»Oh, did I forget to mention that? Carmen is rather tomboyish, not feminine. Ute was the complete opposite. With Carmen, it's just her Italian temperament. Not in a sexual way, no, just her overall aura. She has a beautiful smile. When she looks at me with her big, mysterious, brown eyes, I become weak. You can't help it. Plus, she can cook incredibly well. Honestly, she can turn water into a flavourful soup. She has shoulder-length dark brown hair and is overall a sporty type. She enjoys horseback riding and owns a horse together with her sister. Carmen is very companionable, so you could say that I hit the jackpot with her, and we can share any secret together.«

Lydia looked at him questioningly. »I don't understand: If you love Carmen, why did you start something with Ute? Why haven't you two gotten married after so many years? I mean, after six years, it's about time, isn't it? Otherwise, it might never happen.«

»I don't know,« Thomas shrugged. »It just never happened. Who gets married these days? If things aren't going smoothly after a few years of dating, you want to see how you fare on the market as an attractive man. Marriage isn't on the table – something better might come along.«

»Typical man! Attractive?! Don't get too ahead of your-self,« Lydia laughed. »I always thought that if you love each other and are sure about it, then you get married. But I think it's a societal issue right now – people just don't want to com-mit. ‚Therefore, examine who binds himself eternally, whether something better can be found,‘ as Goethe said. Then one is forever searching. Isn't that a shame?«

She scrutinized him. »Honestly, Thomas, could it be that you're going through a midlife crisis? I feel like men in their early to mid-forties, especially if they're not married yet, are constantly searching. But what are they searching for? To hold onto and keep searching? The search never ends because ulti-mately, they don't find it – there's no such thing as the perfect person. Aren't you around the same age?«

»What do you think? How young do I look?«

Lydia sensed that he was fishing for compliments. »I don't know, early forties?!«

»Thanks, your kind,« he said, feeling a bit hurt but trying not to show it. »I'm 45, but I feel like I'm 30.«

»So, it is the midlife crisis after all,« Lydia laughed, then shook her head. »Of course! Typical man! That's why you're still flirting with someone else. But when a relationship is stuck, you can work on it. I think it's up to both people to make something of it. Or don't you love each other anymore? As soon as a problem arises, you leave your better half behind and keep looking? Typical! It's not just the throwaway society that makes everything faster, but also the lack of willingness to work on something. A relationship is work!«

Thomas let his gaze wander over the sea. The beach was illuminated only by the hotel complex. He pondered: What is a relationship anyway? Work sounds like work... Do I want that?

He said aloud, »That's true, every kind of relationship is work. Essentially comparable to business. There, you make acquisitions again, only in your partnership you ignore that. It's exhausting to work on the relationship. I feel that Carmen is in love with me.«

He pondered. »But I can't say it any differently. She anticipates my every wish and is understanding about everything. On the other hand, she has a strong sense of security.«

»What do you mean by that? What does love to have to do with a sense of security? And don't you Love her?«

»Well, she wants to be sure that I'll always be there for her, that we should move in together, etc. You know,« he looked at Lydia and attempted a smile.

»Just as soon as you give a woman an inch, she wants the whole mile. Do I love her? Well, in a way, yes. But the passion, like it was in the beginning, isn't there anymore.«

»That's understandable with a woman, of - how old is Carmen? At some point, she wants to know where she stands. And you should know if you love her!«

»Did I not mention it before? Carmen is 33 or 34 years old. No, I don't know if it's my great love. Many things just fit well together when she's not causing stress.«

»Thomas!« Lydia shook her head. »You don't even know the exact age of your girlfriend! A woman of 34 years would like to know where she stands after six years of relationship. That's completely normal. Do you perceive that as stress?« She exclaimed, slamming her hands on her knees.

»She's annoying with that. It's always like this: When are we moving in together? Should we do this on the weekend, should we do that? What are your thoughts on starting a family? What do you think about children? I can't stand it anymore,« Thomas's voice sounded impatient.

Lydia sighed and discreetly studied him. He looked good. She almost hoped for something more. Hadn't he flirted with her? But like this... No, thanks! Not another man with this problem! She always seemed to encounter such types. Although, this time was different. She wanted to understand Thomas's behaviour. Why he reacted this way. She wanted to explore the species of man, especially the one who didn't want to commit or marry. What problem lay behind the problem?

Lydia's tone was one of understanding and sarcasm mixed. She seemed to be analysing Thomas's situation, pointing out his fear of commitment and his lack of genuine love for Carmen.

She highlighted the complications that marriage or moving in together would bring, implying that Thomas's aversion to these commitments stemmed from his desire for freedom and independence.

Thomas nodded thoughtfully. »It's possible. Carmen puts pressure on me and wants to see me more often.«

»Believe me: A good relationship is a good mix of love, romance, action, drama, and sex - and if you find this in a woman, then I believe you're ready to marry her.«

»Maybe you're right. It certainly sounds good.« Thomas let his gaze wander.

Lydia was curious. »By the way, when do you usually see each other? Carmen also lives in Düsseldorf.«

»Carmen fortunately lives on the other side of the city. I've advised her against spontaneous visits since I'm often on the road anyway,« Thomas replied.

»You are quite clever; you've thought of everything.«

Thomas became embarrassed. »Well, sort of. Otherwise, we always met whenever I could. I'd call her spontaneously, but it was mostly on Thursday evenings, occasionally on Saturdays and Sundays, or then again on Mondays.«

»Your Carmen doesn't have it easy with you. You live nearby and still don't see each other often. It's obvious she doesn't know where she stands with you. You're not thinking about marriage, and not about kids. Don't you want any?«

»Oh Lydia, I haven't really thought about it. I do love kids, yes. But right now, I'm just enjoying my life, and I'm not convinced that they're welcome now – maybe someday. Well, when I find the right woman... – I'm not sure about that right now.«

»Wow, great response. If you relay this to Carmen, then I can understand why she might want to get moving. A woman's biological clock does tick a bit faster than a man's. It annoys me; the man lives, loves, travels, and enjoys life, builds a career, and eventually, around the age of forty, he'll take a much younger woman and start a family. As a woman, you're always at a disadvantage. Then you build your career, and before you know it, you're 35. Carmen is now at an age where she slowly but surely wants to have children, whether with you or without you. So, she can start looking for someone else in time, before spending the best years with someone like you. And it doesn't get any easier as a woman gets older.«

»Oh, I don't believe that she wouldn't have a chance with others. I understand that for you women, the clock is ticking, but she doesn't need to nag me about it. There's still time.«

Lydia shook her head vigorously. »Thomas, a woman needs to know where she stands with her partner. Either you love her, or you don't. If you truly loved her, it would surely be your greatest desire to be with her, to spend as much time as possible with her, and not just one day a week. Then, the conversation about children and starting a family wouldn't scare you off; you would openly express your views on it, but it wouldn't annoy you. No woman wants to waste her best years. If you're not ready to give her a definitive answer, she will eventually find someone else, just like Ute did. Exactly right.«

Thomas took a deep breath in and out.

»My goodness, you're really letting it all out. I'm disappointed that Ute left me. I want a woman. And love? What is true love anyway? Love fades.«

Lydia sighed. »Thomas, it's not going to work like this! A woman doesn't wait forever for a man to make up his mind about his plans. No woman wants to constantly wonder: does he love me, or does he not want children right now because Mr. Right is in the mindset of his career. If you find other things more important than taking care of your relationship - fine, then you might end up spending your twilight years alone. Are you sad that Ute left you?«

»Ute never talked about children. I think she didn't want any, she just enjoyed life.«

Lydia laughed. »Sorry for being brutally honest, but do you think a woman doesn't notice what you're up to? It's all about feelings. Maybe she also felt that you weren't 100 percent committed to her. But to get a grip on the problem, we need to look at both sides. Do you seriously believe she shouldn't worry? She can only come when it pleases the Lord and if there's space in his schedule. Otherwise, he's just passing the time with other nice women. Or am I mistaken? Do you also offer time management courses? I mean, Carmen on Thursdays, Ute on Wednesdays, and do you have any more slots available?« She looked at him penetratingly, as if she could read his thoughts.

»I actually love all my women, and vice versa, I hope. Because you quickly notice whether you like each other and feel somehow attracted to the other person. Is that love then? I don't know! Somehow, I have a problem committing myself. And with the children...«

Lydia moved her feet in circular motions in the sand, looking contemplatively at her circles. Thomas had settled comfortably on his lounger, smoking a cigarette, and gazing at the starry sky.

»If a woman really wants children, she might not necessarily tell you directly, but she hopes that you are the one with whom she can start a family. However, if a woman realizes that there's no future with you, she'll keep you around until someone better comes along, or until she gets pregnant by you. It's as simple as that. Men aren't any different. Ute and your ex-wife did the right thing. Also, if you love a woman and want to spend all your time with her, then you shouldn't have a problem saying that you love her or want to have children with her. You'd be willing to do anything for her.«

»Well, maybe you're right. Perhaps I haven't found the great love you're talking about. Anyway, I've seen Carmen the most frequently, so she really doesn't need to worry or complain.«

»I think you have a problem! Either with women or you have a general relationship problem.«

»I love too many women at the same time. That's my problem.«

As soon as he said that he smiled awkwardly.

Thomas felt respected by Lydia. She had a calm, pleasant voice, and he felt comfortable. He had the impression that she wanted to understand him. Since he had already started, Thomas was ready to tell her the whole truth.

»So, every other weekend I meet up with Margit.«

Lydia made a horrified face. »You're not serious, are you? You must be kidding! Not another relationship!«

»No, I'm really serious. There's also Margit,« he said hesitantly.

Even though part of her was shocked, Lydia couldn't help but grin. She found it highly interesting to get to know someone like Thomas and wanted to learn more about him, Margit, and the other women. A modern-day Casanova! She had never met anyone like him before.

»And where and when do you meet Margit?« she asked eagerly.

»Margit is from Frankfurt,« Thomas stuttered. He paused, his thoughts swirling.

»Now or never, spill the beans! It's interesting to talk so freely with a woman about my relationships, who listens openly and

explains to me why and how women react like that.«

Honestly, I don't have time to think about it. Or I would have time, but I don't want to admit it. Maybe I have a fear of commitment or am even unable to commit? On the other hand, I'm fascinated by women, their different bodies, and being desired by women, being in the spotlight. And ultimately, they have been just as positively impressed by me. What am I supposed to do? On the contrary, I really enjoy it when women idolize me. I'm doing well, I could have at least five women on each arm. Sure, I'm not the best-looking guy, but I'm aware that I have charisma and my charm works on women. They fall at my feet. I can't and don't want to resist it. I feel incredibly flattered that women of all ages and professions find me attractive. It's my ease in dealing with people, my casualness, my captivating stories, and charming performances that especially appeal to women. Of course, men are impressed by me and especially by my knowledge, so I'm often invited to events. Overall, I can't complain I'm doing exceptionally well, I'm successful both professionally and personally. But the situation is still unsatisfactory. It doesn't make me happy. I'm still looking for the perfect relationship or for the one true love that, it seems, I haven't found yet.

After a short pause, he continued calmly.

»I think you're right, Lydia. I do have a fear of commitment. Maybe you can help me sort out my life. You're already doing that.«

Lydia was pensive: *How does a man in his mid-forties manage to juggle three relationships at once? With Ute, Carmen, and now Margit! Well, Ute broke up with him. She was fed up with being a Wednesday girlfriend. I would have done the same thing in Ute's place, at least if nothing progresses after a while. Occasionally spending a weekend together, or meeting in a city. Well, I wouldn't be up for chasing after a guy like that. No, if someone wanted something from me, the man should make the effort and not the other way around. Although, looking at him now, I wouldn't have pushed him off the bed; there's something about him.*

I can relate to Ute, Carmen, and Margit; he's quite a fascinating man. Why can't men like him commit? They're not the happiest in their relationships, which is a shame! Everyone aims to be in a happy, harmonious relationship, to be loved and to love in return. They search for something and never find it because they don't start searching with their hearts. It's a pity! Especially when he always portrays himself as single, yet he's just playing with his feelings. Except today, with me, he's sharing his stories about women. Oddly enough, it's with me! There's something that connects us. I know I can always rely on my intuition. In my eyes, he's afraid of women, of committing, of taking on a responsibility. But why? I want to find out, but not today!

Lydia stood up, returned his jacket, and glanced over at him.

»Thomas, please forgive me, but it's late and I'm really tired. I need to be fresh for my guests tomorrow morning, even though I would have loved to hear more about your interesting love story with Margit.«

Thomas looked downcast. »Will we see each other again tomorrow? Then I can tell you more.«

»Sure! You can accompany me back to my bungalow if you'd like,« Lydia offered.

„While Thomas got up and put on his jacket, he continued speaking. ‚But of course, I'll do that. I can't leave you here alone. By the way, thank you for the walk on the beach, it was really refreshing. I hope I didn't bore you?'„

„ ‚Bored?' Lydia laughed. ‚I haven't been entertained like this in a long time, really! I'm looking forward to tomorrow, to see what happens next.'„

»They climbed the steps up to the hotel complex. There were no guests to be seen, the bar had long been closed. The compound lay quiet and sleepy before them. Even the night porter had fallen asleep in front of the television. Thomas accompanied Lydia to the Bungalow.«

»So, here we are!« She stood before him, tired. He, on the other hand, took her hand, pulled her close, and gave her a kiss on each cheek in farewell.

»Good night, dear Lydia. Sleep well and dream sweetly. I look forward to seeing you again tomorrow. And thank you for your company.«

Her eyes flickered, and a smile crossed her face. She was somewhat shy. »Good night, Thomas! Get home safely.«

Thomas lit a cigarette and made his way, humming. He hopped from one foot to the other like a child as he thought about the evening.

It was a successful evening. Tomorrow, I'll see her again, maybe I'll surprise her... I could visit her at the painting class, yes, that's what I'll do. She'll be surprised, let's see what else happens. She's different from the other women. Likeable, and has an attractive manner. Oh, now I'm raving about Lydia. No, she's just nice ...

A Love-Story in Section

The next morning, Thomas woke up early, put on jeans and a T-shirt, and headed to breakfast. On the long hotel terrace, he enjoyed a cigarette with a good cup of green tea. He loved to have a hearty breakfast. The buffet offered a rich culinary selection, unlike at home. It wasn't worth it for him to fill the fridge just for himself, especially since he was often on the go. Besides, it was more fun to eat in company.

From his secluded spot, away from the other guests, Thomas could observe everything. A few tables away sat a woman, in her mid-thirties or early forties. He scrutinized her from head to toe. He found her attractive with her long, flowing hair, lost in thought as she sipped her tea.

What is she doing here alone? I have nothing better to do, why don't we roll in the sand, then kiss her sweet mouth and... I want to sort out my life and not hop into bed with the first woman I meet! It would be nice to give in to my feelings... Oh yes! Every man's dream! No, Thomas, that's not good. She is seductive, but it's pointless...

He was snapped out of his daydreams when his phone beeped, and he looked at the screen. Ah, a WhatsApp message from Monica!

Thomas, I've saved your project again! Please get in touch, it's urgent!

He pushed out his lower lip. Why should I get in touch? Urgent?! Monica has already taken care of everything for me.

I don't need to waste my time on that, I'm on vacation, and besides...

He lifted his head and glanced over to the table, but the attractive stranger had left in the meantime. He turned around, unable to spot her anymore.

Thomas arrived punctually for the start of the course at the palm house of the club hotel. A large open space with many small tables and a few easels. The large window front faced the courtyard, which was planted with cacti and palms. At first glance, the room seemed warm and stuffy, but a fresh breeze blew in through the open sliding doors.

Most of the participants were women, but some men also joined. Lydia distributed a watercolour pad or canvas to each person. A large container with various brushes and all kinds of colours were available for the participants on a table near the entrance next to the sink.

»How nice to see you all here again today!« Her eyes lit up for a moment when she saw Thomas.

»Hey there, Thomas! Nice to see you,« she said, approaching him. »I'm glad you decided to join us after my invitation.«

»All mines!« The joy was written all over his face.

»You can sit wherever you like, there are no assigned seats. The nicest spot is here in the front by the window,« she gestured there with an open hand.

»You have plenty of light there, standing right next to a shade-giving palm, and you have a view over the entire room,« she explained.

»Thank you for the tip. I've never painted in the shade of a palm tree before,« Thomas replied.

With the canvas in hand, he approached his table, examining his spot closely. Quietly, he said to himself, »It's the perfect space to let my creativity flow.«

At the neighbouring table, there was a loud rustling of paper. Overall, there was a relaxed mood and a pleasant atmosphere. Soft relaxation music played in the background. Among the hotel guests, there was a sense of familiarity, and they exchanged tips on various painting techniques. It was a real buzz of conversation and laughter.

Lydia tried to make herself heard and said with a loud, strong voice to the group: »A warm welcome!«

Everyone was busy with themselves. One person got water, another searched for the right brush, or prepared their colour palette.

»While you unleash your imagination, I'll tell you something about the theory of colours. If you have any questions, feel free to ask at any time!«

Slowly, calm settled in, and everyone went to their place. Mostly, people painted whatever they liked: landscapes, still life's, flowers, or the view from the window.

Her voice was softer than at the beginning. More melodic and almost a bit mysterious. She stood in the middle of the studio, having claimed her space, as she began her presentation.

»Colours are harmonious, mysterious, and sometimes exciting. The shapes and colours in rooms or on a painting influence both the large and the small aspects and are crucial for the dynamics of the overall image,« she said, moving slowly, almost floating, around the room, observing the painters over their shoulders.

»The language of colours can have a supportive influence on people. Accordingly, colours can control the aura and effect of spaces and revitalize the energies within a room. Not all colours are equally suitable for all rooms or office spaces, so I will only focus on a few particularly important colours and briefly describe the characteristics associated with them,« she explained.

Lydia made a brief pause and looked around the room, but everyone was diligently occupied, and no one needed her assistance. So, she continued:

»Let's start with the friendliest colour, which is YELLOW. Yellow denotes the sunny side of the colour spectrum. This colour creates a neutral sympathy, and spaces adorned in yellow tones should be sought out when seeking encounters with the world of communication. Hence, the Palm House of the club hotel is painted in a fresh shade of yellow. Yellow, as the colour of the sun, is cheerful, bright, friendly, and symbolizes a keen mind and the ability to analyse. It signifies maturity, agility, concentration, exchange, and communicativeness. When used as an accent or dominant colour, it supports knowledge, intellect, imagination, ideas, and human creativity. The emotional significance is warmth, laughter, joy, openness, ambition, adventurousness, and a desire for freedom, but also fear and cowardice. For example, colour psychologists attribute a healing effect to the colour yellow, such as promoting concentration, courage, knowledge, and intellect, as well as the ability to organize thoughts, clarify mental connections, and strengthen mental creativity.« At the last sentence, she glanced over at Thomas.

Thomas painted a picture in shades of blue. He couldn't think of a suitable subject. Hesitantly, he painted the sea with a blue sky.

While listening to her presentation, Thomas had thoughts running through his head: *Oh, what she doesn't say, yellow promotes concentration and helps to organize my thoughts? Well, if that works! It's nice that painting has a liberating effect. I can't believe I haven't done this in so long, well, I never really have time for myself. Every weekend on the go, then here, then there, then Ute, Carmen, and so on... Where is the time for me?*

Lost in thought, he painted his shades of blue, and suddenly the horizon disappeared into the blue of the sea.

Even Ute criticized that I hardly had time for her, it's annoying, and then she's nagging at you, totally terrible! ... On the other hand, Ute was right. If I spent less time with Carmen or Margit, then I would have more time for her, but none for myself, or the woman would demand more from me, I'm afraid of that. It's better to have several relationships, then I don't need to commit to one, and besides, you enjoy the time together. I can't commit. The feeling of having my freedom, being single, I need that, and if they don't like that I have so little time for them, then they have to leave, end of story! The main thing is, I still find time for myself.

He noticed that he had missed something important during Lydia's presentation; the others had become silent.

»... ORANGE gives the impression that something could suddenly happen or will happen; it is the colour of change. Orange is stimulating and signals full activity and open cheerfulness. The spiritual meaning of the colour orange is individuality, deep insight, devotion, and the need for belonging. The mental significance is wisdom, endurance, indecision, optimism, energy, ...«

Lydia paused as side remarks were made and the guests laughed heartily.

»Where was I? Right, joy of life, courage, strength, ambition, openness, self-confidence, sociability, tenderness,« a murmur went through the room, »and warmth,« she added with a smile.

»The colour orange promotes the development of self-esteem, it also enhances responsiveness, the joy of learning, and brings more vitality.«

Thomas looked up from his painting: Is that why she's wearing an orange dress today? The colour of change. It suits her, for sure. It complements her natural complexion. She's doing great, keeping her people engaged and imparting knowledge. The way she stands there, so confidently, and talks with ease and poise. Almost like I always do. I find orange beautiful. Am I already in the mindset of a transformation? Who knows?!

Lydia stood by the window, gazing at the sky, and enjoying the breeze. Then she resumed her presentation.

»Now let's talk about another colour, blue. BLUE has a psychological effect of being cold, like the blue sky or the endless and eternal sea,« she said, extending her arms outward to the sides.

„Blue makes the distance to the wall appear greater than it actually is. As Kandinsky said about blue: ‚The darker it becomes, the more it calls humanity into the infinite, awakens in it the longing for space and expansiveness, and ultimately into the supernatural.‘„

She looked at Thomas's painting from a distance. Slowly, she walked through the rows again. Occasionally, she gave tips or answered questions.

»Blue, as the colour of distance, is the colour of loyalty, friendship, and trust. As the coldest colour, it is the symbolic colour for pride, peace, calmness, security, inspiration, patience, devotion, and communication. The mental significance of the colour represents intuition, diplomacy, leadership, uniformity, authority, willpower, and wisdom. Blue tones help promote expression and concentration. Rooms painted in strong blue or pastel tones do not seem intrusive but create an atmosphere of grace.«

Lydia stopped by a guest who asked her a question. Smiling, she answered him softly.

With a loud voice, she continued. »Hence, this colour is extremely pleasant in lounges and waiting areas. In the hotel, the lobby is kept in a blue colour. It allows tourists to relax first. The choice of colours and colour combinations therefore influences every painting of the artist, but also the rooms. - Yes, dear guests, I will not be able to describe all the colours in detail, it was just meant to give a small insight into colour theory. I thank you very much for your attention.«

Applause broke out.

Thomas's favourite colour was blue, just like his painting. Perhaps that's why he preferred going to the sea rather than the mountains. He hoped that the vastness of the ocean would clear his thoughts. Often, he sat on a rock or in the sand, listened to the sound of the sea, and gazed into the blue. Sometimes, the boundary between water and sky was barely visible, while on other days, the water shimmered more turquoise and stood out against the light blue sky. Every day brought a different experience, just like the weather and the view at this club hotel.

Lydia sat down at the front table, one leg resting on the ground while the other dangled in the air. Her gaze wandered around the room.

»Yes, it's already time for today. You're welcome to take your paintings with you and continue next time.«

The vacationers packed up their colours, cleaned their brushes, and said their goodbyes.

Most of them had worked up an appetite and headed over to the restaurant for a meal, taking their paintings with them.

Lydia went over to Thomas and admired his artwork. »It has turned out really beautiful. The way the different shades of blue blend together. Just like in my lecture. Fantastic, so you also master art theory?«

»Yes, I attended courses and gained experience for a few years,« Thomas replied.

»That's obvious. You tried to convince me that you can't paint,« Lydia shook her head.

»Amazing how colours affect us. I must have instinctively chosen the right colour. Blue – the longing for space and time. Peace and relaxation. What I experienced here again is mindfulness towards oneself. Focusing on one's inner self. Concentration. It's best to be completely in the flow and not even notice the others.«

In the meantime, she closed the sliding doors and looked at him expectantly. »Aha! Maybe I can still learn something from you.«

She was visibly impressed that it had triggered something in him. Since he was the last one in the room, they left together before she locked the door. He stood right behind her.

»May I accompany you to dinner?« Thomas enjoyed Lydia's company and their conversation. A scent wafted from the restaurant toward them.

Lydia had nothing better to do at the moment. Her main task was to take care of hotel guests, entertain them during meals, organize sports activities, and host an evening show.

The program ran on a biweekly schedule. Every week, there was a significant turnover on arrival and departure days. Then, each member of the team was assigned a few guests to look after. The guys tended to focus on the ladies, while the girls took care of the gentlemen. They were encouraged to pay special attention to the solo travellers, ensuring they had someone to talk to if they desired.

It seemed that Thomas particularly needed her attention.

»Oh yes, my stomach is rumbling loudly. Giving a class and entertaining like that is exhausting and makes one hungry. Come on, let's go!«

Together, they walked side by side along the path to the hotel restaurant.

»How did you like it, Thomas?«

»Somewhat it has brought me a little further. I mean, I haven't looked at the world of colours in such detail before, so you really inspired me again.«

During lunch at the buffet, his thoughts wandered.

He would have preferred a private painting class with Lydia, where he could express his ideas alone with her. He dreamed of what it would have been like in his studio at home.

I would have covered the floor with large sheets of paper. First, we would undress, then creatively paint each other's bodies in all sorts of colours. This body painting engages all the senses and offers the opportunity to get to know each other in all facets. The art lies in bringing images onto paper. And what could be more exciting than joyous, passionate erotica, … even to the point of ecstasy. Thank goodness no one can read minds. That would be embarrassing. Oh, there I go again with my daydreams!

With their plates filled, they walked outside under the shaded seating area. It was cooler there. They took a seat at one of the rear tables, a bit away from the other guests.

Lydia ordered a carafe of water from the waiter. With so much talking, she was thirsty.

Lydia looked at him attentively. »I'm glad it was beneficial for you.«

Immediately, the waiter placed the water with two glasses on the table. Thomas poured them each a glass. He was thirsty after the class as well.

It wasn't a coincidence; he believed more in destiny, that he had crossed paths with Lydia. But he didn't want to talk about that now. Thomas took a deep breath before responding. »What kind of paintings do you usually create?«

»Oh, it depends. I prefer to paint landscapes and modern pieces in acrylic. As a child, I used to love painting sunsets and sunrises; nowadays, I prefer to photograph them,« she said, popping a lettuce leaf into her mouth. »And you? What do you like to paint the most?«

»At the moment, I haven't had much time for painting. Last year, I participated in a figure drawing class. I love landscape paintings, and I enjoy taking photographs as well. I often paint the scenes at home,« he replied.

»Indeed, it is a shame. Hopefully, I'll find some time to get back to it soon,« he replied with a hint of longing in his voice.

»But painting here is also quite enjoyable. I admire the way you conduct the classes,« he said with a smile. His plate was now empty. »So, what's next on your agenda?«

»Not much, really. Some program arrangements and office work. Then I have the afternoon off until tonight. Yes, and tonight we have a Latin American dance party,« she said as she stood up.

»Oh, that sounds great. After eating, you should rest or take a thousand steps. How about we continue our beach walk?«

»Yes, I'll be done in half an hour. I don't mind at all. I just need to do some office work, and our office is right behind the reception. Are you coming there?«

Thomas nodded. Quickly, she walked towards the reception.

Thirty minutes later, she checked the lobby to see if Thomas was already there. He was sitting in a chair, waiting for her.

Quickly, she disappeared behind the »Staff only« door and emerged again with a backpack and sunglasses.

Together, they walked down to the beach. Like the days before, it was a beautiful day for vacation. Thomas enjoyed being out with Lydia. She was so carefree and relaxed. Her hair and the colourful scarf she wore around her neck fluttered in the wind. To shield herself from the sun and tame her hair a bit, she put on a cap. She was an extraordinary woman, and he wasn't sure why he felt that way. Perhaps it was because she approached life with such ease. She seemed balanced and happy, which left a lasting impression on him.

»I must say, getting to know you has been enriching for me.«

Lydia laughed. »Oh, come on!«

They walked along the path by the water towards the lighthouse once again. They strolled slowly side by side. The blue lounge chairs were all occupied. Children screamed in the water whenever a wave came.

»No, really, you listened to me the whole-time last night, and for that, I want to thank you again. I hope you slept well after our hours-long conversation and had some pleasant dreams.«

»Yeah, everything's good,« replied Lydia.

She hadn't been able to sleep. She thought about her last relationship, it had just fizzled out. One day, he showed up with another woman by his side. Out of frustration, she had packed her bags and flown to the Canary Islands. Men were so hard to understand! Just then, Thomas came along and told her about his relationships with women. Lydia didn't want to talk about her past love, so it worked out well that she was curious about their conversation.

They took off their shoes. Lydia tucked hers into her backpack while Thomas carried his in his hand. They felt the warm sandy beach beneath their feet, pleasantly soft.

»So, yesterday we left off with your friend Margit. You

could just continue from there. Tell me, how did you meet her?«

»So, I met Margit at a seminar in Munich, one of those weekend seminars. I was giving a lecture on marketing and how to develop new ideas using creative techniques. After I finished my presentation, she approached me...«

»Mr. Freimut, do you have a moment?«

„I turned around and looked into two expectant brown eyes. ‚Sure, I have a moment,‘„

»Great! My name is Margit Waldmann. I found your presentation simply fantastic, almost refreshing, how you can convey such concentrated knowledge in a relaxed, cheerful, and free manner.«

»As always in such situations, I grinned. It was fantastic to receive this feedback, but it‘s particularly charming when it comes from an attractive woman. And she was. ‚Oh, I do that with my eyes closed,‘ I said.«

»No, really, Mr. Freimut, I‘m impressed. I work at a big bank in Frankfurt and occasionally hold employee seminars there. Sometimes I find it difficult to make a dry topic engaging and interesting, like you did.«

»Margit didn‘t leave my side. She stood right in front of me, a head shorter than I. With her blue suit, red leather bag matching her shoes, her scarf, and lipstick, she looked stunning. Everything was perfectly coordinated.«

With a smile, I said, »Then we‘re colleagues in a way.«

Margit smiled at me and continued with her pleasant voice, which caught my attention immediately. »Personally, I find this weekend seminar very beneficial, especially from the perspective of personality development, idea generation, and creativity. Unfortunately, it‘s often challenging in our company to properly engage the employees, so I think the idea of using creativity techniques for that purpose is brilliant. I haven‘t thought of that before. Currently, we often just have endless debates that are often fruitless and unproductive.«

I nodded in understanding. »I understand that well; it can be very draining in the long run. There are ways to break free from the constraints of traditional confrontation in debates and ultimately bring the employee meetings and conferences to a productive conclusion.«

I was in my element as usual and continued talking. »There's an exciting method. It's like a game. The Indians say, before you judge someone, you must walk a moon in the other's moccasin. Only then can you judge the other's individual situation. So, it's about the shoe game, where employees can actively contribute their creativity in a project work.«

»That sounds interesting,« Margit said, hanging on my words. I didn't find it unpleasant. »Tell me more about it!«

»Nothing would please me more. I took her by the arm and led her to a cozy corner of the hotel, where we could talk undisturbed over a delicious cup of coffee.«

»There are six different types of shoes. Each shoe has its own meaning. Depending on which model is addressed, you consider the upcoming project from this particular shoe perspective. You then metaphorically put on this shoe and view the whole thing from that angle.«

»How am I supposed to understand that?« Margit sat back in her chair, holding her coffee cup.

»There are the models of blue sports shoe, light street shoe, yellow summer shoe, green hiking shoe, barefoot, and black lace-up shoe.«

Margit looked at me with great interest as I continued to speak.

»The blue sports shoe, in this case, represents the critical examination of our own thinking. We ask ourselves questions such as: What do we need to do next? What have we achieved so far? Where do we need to go to reach our goal and in what time frame? Just like in sports, hence why it's closest to the sports shoe.«

I looked into a puzzled face. From my presentations, I know

that it's best to simplify complex topics so that everyone can understand them. It's best to explain things vividly, so that the listener can better remember and visualize them. So, I continued with my explanation.

»You have to imagine it like this: you're putting on different models of shoes, and the sports shoe is worn at the beginning of a discussion to determine what you're going to debate and what the conference is actually supposed to achieve. The prerequisite is that everyone is explained this creativity technique beforehand, so that they know exactly how it works.«

Margit nodded slowly.

»Therefore, the blue sports shoe represents the organizer, who among other things determines the sequence of the other shoes. He moves from one standpoint to the next.« He looked directly into her eyes.

»The summer shoe represents sunshine and optimism, hence the colour yellow. A summer shoe is light and open, it allows everything and is open to everything. It helps to see the advantages of a situation.«

Margit was hanging on his every word and nodded in agreement.

»The green hiking shoe makes us think of nature and plants, which in turn remind us of growth, energy, and life. Therefore, the hiking shoe is associated with creativity. That means, when suggestions, ideas, or inspirations need to be developed or changed, the hiking shoe is put on. New paths are taken,« he said, making an open hand gesture. He had good control over his arms and hands.

»Going completely barefoot, as you might expect, represents emotions, sensations, feelings, and intuitions. When you walk barefoot, you feel everything precisely under the sole of your foot: warmth, cold, and the texture of the ground, whether it's pleasant or rather unpleasant. You understand why you like certain things or have a dislike for them. When walking barefoot, you have the opportunity to let your feelings run free,« he explained.

»The black lace-up shoe, on the other hand, represents caution, the notorious pessimist who ties everything up. This lace-up shoe is meant to prevent us from doing things that could harm us; it should alert us to risks and dangers, so to speak, pull the laces. So, whenever a problem arises, it can be solved quite nicely and quickly by incorporating this shoe game,« he concluded.

Margit was impressed. »That's really a fabulous idea, Mr. Freimut. I'll incorporate this into my next board meeting. Excellent! I'm excited.«

»I can recommend a book on creativity techniques to you. You'll surely find various ideas in there about what you can do.«

Somewhat tipsy, my old colleague Jan greeted me as he saw us from a distance and walked over to us. Without asking, he plopped down on the empty chair. Before I could introduce him to Margit, he said, »Hi, I'm Jan.«

Margit looked puzzled by his behaviour; she was not accustomed to being addressed by her first name so directly. I could tell that she felt a bit offended, and I understood: etiquette was important to her.

»I'm Thomas,« I said, extending my hand. »Shall we use first names among colleagues? Allow me to introduce my old colleague Jan.«

For Margit, the situation seemed to become a bit more comfortable; she had no objections. »Pleasure to meet you, Margit. I'm surprised, I'm not usually on a first-name basis so quickly,« she chuckled awkwardly.

»Typically, you mention the first name but continue to address each other formally. But, oh well,« she turned to me. »Thank you for this private expert lecture. Would you, no, would you be willing to give such a presentation in our company?«

»I'm glad we're on a first-name basis so quickly; it reduces the distance. „Sure, why not? We can schedule a date for that,« I replied.

Lydia interrupted his thoughts. »Thomas, you're somewhere and you meet a nice woman like Margit, but you don't immediately get together, right? How do you do it?«

In the meantime, they had arrived at the lava rocks and settled down there.

»It was just a professional encounter. This seminar lasted the entire weekend, so we became friends right on Friday and went out to dinner together, exchanging ideas. Margit gives seminars on business etiquette in both professional and personal life. We talked for hours.«

Lydia found it exciting to learn more about Margit. »What is she like?«

At the lava rocks, Thomas observed the geckos, which briefly basked in the sun and then disappeared into a small cave.

»She's close to my age, around forty, with a sporty figure, dark, short, curly hair, and beautiful doe-brown eyes. Just a pretty woman. Margit is someone who's grounded, who knows exactly what suits her best. She's a reserved person who not only teaches manners but lives by them.«

Lydia pursed her lips. »So old-school and etiquette-driven, quite terrible, don't you think?«

»Sometimes yes, sometimes no. It's appropriate at times, although I do break etiquette rules occasionally. Being reminded of it can be bothersome, especially when I'm on vacation and just want to relax.«

Lydia was surprised. Vacationing together? How could he do that if he's in a relationship?

»You went on vacation with Margit? Have you been together for long? And when do you see each other?«

»I think,« he paused for a moment, pondering, »I'm not quite sure, but I guess we've been together for about two years now. It's a typical weekend relationship; we see each other once or twice a month. At the beginning, I used to travel to Frankfurt, and later, she came to visit me. Margit values orderliness a lot, so my apartment was always tidy when she came. It has its upsides. Still, it can be exhausting,« he grinned at Lydia.

»I didn‘t feel the need to do that for others. But with her, I would have felt too embarrassed. Otherwise, it was more pleasant to go to her or to fly there. Plus, you could move around more freely in Frankfurt, as there wasn‘t any Carmen around,« he smiled.

»Of course!« Lydia slapped her forehead in an exaggerated gesture. »How could I forget that? None of your friends at home could find out that you were in another relationship.« She looked at Thomas thoughtfully. »Did no one ever notice?«

»No. It depends on whom I introduced my women to. Most of the time, I met with friends alone, or they were business associates, so it was never quite clear whether I was involved with the woman by my side or not. It‘s nobody‘s business. Purely private!«

Lydia nodded in agreement. »I see, I can still learn something from you. You not only master time management, but also have the finesse to be alone with your women. But if you‘re constantly on the go like you are, others can surely understand that you‘d like to be alone with your girlfriend.«

Thomas was surprised by her perceptiveness and ability to connect ideas. He had decided not to be surprised by Lydia anymore and told her so.

»Wow, you understand me quickly. I‘m amazed by your empathy. Should I continue?«

»Oh yes, please,« she said, standing up and continuing forward. He followed suit. The beach was empty at that spot, with only a few walkers making their way to the lighthouse.

»Okay. Where did I leave off? Oh yes, the first meeting with Margit was then a preparation for my seminar, purely business. I held it at her company in Frankfurt. There were follow-up meetings for that, and so after a few meetings, we really got together. Yeah.«

He smiled at the memory and brushed back his hair. »Margit has a feminine, reserved manner that I really appreciate.

On the other hand, she's, well, you'd say: outwardly conservative! It just takes time, but once she warms up, she's quite lively. We then went together somewhere in East Germany and led a seminar together for her bank.«

He chuckled. »That was quite delicate, even my dear Ute was there.«

»In all honesty,« Thomas replied, »it was a bit awkward at first, but then we managed to keep it professional during the seminar. Margit and I discussed beforehand how we would handle the situation, and thankfully, it all worked out fine.«

»Very casually, I introduced the two of them and then told Ute that I still had some things to discuss with Margit regarding the evening program. Actually, Ute wasn't supposed to be there at all; another journalist from her publishing house was supposed to come. That wouldn't have been a problem, but the journalist fell ill, and Ute stepped in for her at the last minute. She had no idea about my seminar; she was visibly surprised. And I acted as I always do, as if I had never expected anyone else. Thank goodness she had to fly back on the same evening because she had stepped in at such short notice and her time budget was pretty tight.«

Lydia laughed, then shook her head. »Man, Thomas, you lucked out! Imagine if she had stayed and was in the same hotel! What would you have done then?«

Thomas shrugged. »I don't know. But honestly, I was nervous. I didn't even dare to go to the bathroom and leave them alone. But since it was purely a business meeting, you keep things low-key in public anyway. So, it was just a peck on the cheek. We had another cup of coffee together, and then our paths diverged again.«

»Unbelievable, the luck you had! And they didn't realize they were sharing a man?«

Lydia was horrified, »I just can't believe it. Two women meet and don't know they're sleeping with the same man.«

Thomas viewed it pragmatically, »It was a completely official meeting, and they addressed each other formally. Secretly,

I even had to laugh. I think I handled it elegantly.«

»Elegantly resolved, you sly fox!« Lydia shook her head again. »Unbelievable! I would have been sweating bullets in that situation.«

»Well, that's me, you can believe that. My hands were really sweaty, and I was relieved when the precarious situation was over.«

As they arrived at the lighthouse, this time the bench was free, so they sat down and enjoyed the view.

It was on the tip of Lydia's tongue to say that he had caused this situation himself, but she refrained from doing so. She found it remarkable that Thomas was so open with her. She had often been surprised at how openly some guests spoke about their most intimate affairs. Thomas confided in her with his story completely. Perhaps it's easier to confide in a stranger about personal issues than a friend. You just talk, and then you fly back home and never see that person again. Sometimes a connection is formed.

»What do you think, Thomas - the sun is getting too hot. Shouldn't we sit down there in the dunes under the palm tree and just enjoy the sea?«

»That sounds like a great idea, Lydia. Let's do that,« Thomas replied with a smile.

They left the bench and climbed down the cliff to the beach near the lighthouse. It was shadier under the palm trees. Lydia spread out a large towel she had brought in her backpack. Then they sat down and shared a bottle of water.

»Oh, you think of everything, Lydia. You're a fantastic woman!«

Lydia laughed. »Oh, thank you. Women's intuition,« she winked at him.

»How poetic,« Thomas remarked, surprised himself at how impressed he was by her. She was younger than him, yet she had a way of seeing the world that he found incredibly appealing. She had already gathered many experiences in her life.

He rummaged in his pocket for his cigarettes, lit one with

a match, and smoked leisurely as he gazed out over the sea.

»Some people seem to have other vices besides love stories,« Lydia grinned at him from the side.

»Sometimes I could sit here for hours, just gazing into the distance. The sound of the sea, a few palms providing shade… How beautiful it is here!« She took the soft sand in her hand and let it trickle down thoughtfully.

Thomas watched her as she did so. When he was with Lydia, he could unwind. She was so cheerful, always in a good mood and infectious, but that alone wasn't it. It was undoubtedly no coincidence that they met. Surely their encounter had a deeper meaning, one that Thomas wasn't consciously aware of. Perhaps it was because they could talk so well with each other? Or was he even in love? He felt so light and carefree in her presence.

Lydia noticed he was observing her. »You look so thoughtful. What are you thinking about?«

»Nothing specific, just enjoying the moment, sitting here with you. It's beautiful!«

Lydia closed her eyes and stretched out on her towel. She was tired and relaxed in the shade of the tree. She had stripped off the straps of her dress on the sides, and her long legs glistened in the sun. A gentle breeze blew over her body, soft and refreshing.

Thomas wanted to get some colour as well, so he took off his shirt, exposing his upper body.

They weren't exactly sure how long they had been lying there, but the sun was still high when they started to make their way back.

»I hope you can take some time here to think about which of your women you love the most. You're a very interesting man, Thomas. I've met many men before, but never one who simultaneously has as many relationships as you do.«

Slowly, they strolled along the beach in silence. The waves lapped at their feet and legs. The seawater was pleasantly refreshing, and the sand beneath them was soft. There were hardly any stones or shells around.

In the late afternoon, many people were on the beach. Children played water polo, others snorkelled, and teenagers let themselves drift on a board with the waves. Further out, two surfers were trying their luck.

Shortly before reaching the hotel, Lydia was burning with a question on her lips. »Tell me, have you never met a woman through the internet?«

»Yes, you see, one leaves no stone unturned. My first experiences with internet acquaintances were when I placed an ad on some sort of dating website.«

»Does that cost anything?«

»No, that was free. You just enter your text, name, age, and whatever else you want to share about yourself, and that's it.«

»Did that work?«

»You won't believe it, but I saved some emails on my smartphone because I found them so nice.«

Lydia grinned, and he added, »Well, I wanted to think about my relationships again here, so I thought, take everything with you, maybe it'll make the decision easier.«

»I'm curious about that. But you surely won't show them to me or let me read them...« She looked at him expectantly.

»Oh, come on, no problem. I can show you, my smartphone. They're not that earth-shattering anyway. Now you already know so much about me, so it doesn't matter anymore.«

»Sure, go ahead! I just need to stop by the reception desk to see if there's anything important.«

»No problem, see you at the bar?« Thomas had already turned away.

»Okay, wait for me,« and Lydia disappeared quickly towards the reception.

Upon arriving at the hotel bar, Thomas ordered himself an

ice cream sundae. All the bar stools were taken, so he sat at a small round table under a large blue umbrella.

It didn't take long before Lydia returned. She waved to him from afar as she approached. After getting herself a drink, she joined him at the table.

»Here I am again. There wasn't anything, so I have time,« Lydia said as she joined him at the table.

She sat down next to Thomas. In the meantime, he had opened the corresponding file and handed her the smartphone. He indulged in his large refreshing ice cream sundae with lots of fruits and cream.

»Well, I'm curious,« Lydia said as she took it in her hand, but before she could look, Thomas continued.

„Yeah, one day I thought, ‚Man, what so many others are doing, you have to try it!' I wrote an ad, something like: ‚He's looking for her, long-term relationship: imaginative and tender, Thomas, 37 years old.'„

Lydia interrupted him. »But you're much older, aren't you? Or was that a long time ago?«

She drank her water in one gulp, she was very thirsty. Then she turned to the waiter, pointed to her empty glass, and ordered another one right away.

He grinned sheepishly. »Don't you think I could still pass for 37?« Then he took a spoonful of ice cream into his mouth.

Lydia smiled. »Okay, but that's cheating, you're in your mid-forties. You probably placed the ad just to check your market value, right?«

Thomas felt caught. *My goodness, Lydia is quite clever.*

The waiter brought Lydia a glass of water and asked if they wished for anything else. Thomas was completely satisfied with his large portion of ice cream.

»You know what, if you're really interested, I'll just show you all the emails,« Thomas said.

»Sure, go ahead!« Lydia leaned forward to read the display better.

»So, well, look here, as I said, I placed this ad:

Hi, I've stayed young at heart, love to travel to distant lands, am very creative, full of life, and would love to enchant you. I want to lean on you, pamper you, and go on dream trips with you. I love it when you can laugh and aren't prudish. I enjoy nature, want to enjoy it with you, and lie in the grass. That's when the best ideas come to me. Get in touch if you're looking for a confident person, Thomas!«

»And? Did you get any responses?«

Lydia felt a bit uneasy at his words because long ago, along with her friend, they had responded to an advertisement from a Thomas, but she had forgotten the content of the ad. Hopefully, it wasn't him. Otherwise, she would keep her secret to herself and hope she wouldn't blush out of embarrassment, fearing he might notice something.

»You know, the funniest part was that my friend Ute actually responded to my ad.«

Lydia laughed in relief. »No way! How did she come across it?«

»According to her, completely by chance,« Thomas shrugged. Before his ice cream melted, he quickly ate it.

Lydia played with her glass out of embarrassment. At the neighbouring table, a young couple sat, both looking at their phones. Was this the new way of communication? Everything online. No real conversation anymore.

When Thomas had eaten half of his ice cream, he continued, »Alright, as a journalist, you need to be good at researching, but she's really super perfect at finding things. Whenever I needed something, an address or contact details, seminar materials from another speaker - Ute knew everything. But in this case, I was really confused, I must admit. What Ute wrote to me was nice. Wait,« he tapped on his smartphone for a bit, »here I have it. Let me read you the email.«

He cleared his throat.

„Dear Thomas,
Your name is quite fascinating and makes me incredibly curious about you. I apologize for only reaching out now, but I've been very busy with work and travel. I am the best thing that has ever crossed your path, and the sweetest woman in this universe. I am very creative, imaginative, and love nature just like you. Like you, I am looking for a tender and imaginative long-term relationship. It's a shame, I always thought I had found it, but somehow, I am only disappointed by men. I hope you are different and can enchant me. Occasionally, I become wild and then do very naughty things. I think you'll like it.
You're dealing with a very confident, intelligent, pretty, attractive, fascinating, colourful, child-loving, nature-loving, adventurous, expressive personality here – namely ME – the sweetest and craziest woman there is!
Well, if you've fibbed about your age – never mind – as they say in Cologne – I'll take you as you are. Well, if you feel addressed, please get in touch with your most beloved Ute.
Can't wait to hear back from you. I hope you're serious – or have you ever received the craziest declaration of love of all time via the internet? Either way, I think you're fantastic! You're my prince and I'm the queen of the night – or have you forgotten that? I'm sure you didn't expect that!!! I'd almost propose to you myself, but that's the man's job, and if it happens, it should come from you.
With love and 100,000,000 kisses,
Your Sweetheart."

After he finished, he called the waiter and ordered a coffee.

Lydia had listened attentively and shook her head. »Wait, she recognized it was you right away?«

Would I react like that if I saw an ad from my boyfriend on the internet? How did she recognize him? It‘s strange. Maybe she found it funny and responded like that for fun. Why didn‘t she have any doubts that he had serious intentions with this ad? The trust and love must be incredibly strong to hope for a marriage proposal after something like that. There are indeed crazy women. Ute must have loved him very much. Otherwise...

Thomas shrugged. »Must have been. Probably from my photo.«

»And how did you react?« She looked at him with wide eyes.

»I didn‘t really react until she brought it up,« he said.

Lydia slammed her hand flat on the table. »Typical man, isn‘t it? Here we are, coming up with all sorts of things, and then we get no feedback. But you must have felt great and flattered, didn‘t you?!«

Thomas grinned from ear to ear. »I found it amusing. I can‘t help it if women keep giving me compliments all the time.«

»No, of course not! But it‘s strange that men just accept it as if it were self-evident. When in fact, it‘s wonderful to receive a compliment from a loved one. It motivates you for the whole day, puts you in a good mood, and makes you accomplish a lot. Have you ever thought that it might have been frustrating for Ute to first find your ad on the internet and then not get any feedback on her response?«

Thomas looked at her with a puzzled expression. »Yeah, but,« he stammered, pushing his empty ice cream bowl to the centre of the table, »I can‘t help it if she happened to come across my ad.«

»Come on, no, Thomas, you shouldn‘t have put one up at all if you really love Ute,« Lydia leaned forward, looking Thomas squarely in the eyes.

»You can tell me whatever you want, but I believe an intelligent woman like Ute quickly realizes whether you're being sincere or just feeding her a line. In your eyes, it wasn't a serious relationship, more like holding on while still searching!«

Thomas felt caught and annoyed. »But Carmen and Margit didn't notice anything. No, I would have seen that.«

»Typical, maybe, I won't deny that,« Lydia said, calming down and leaning back.

»But Carmen has been with you for over six years, she thinks she's the only one in your life and wouldn't even entertain such a thought. She's so sure of herself that she doesn't notice these subtle hints anymore. As for Margit, I don't think she would ever expect you to cheat on her behind her back. That woman has class, and she expects that from you too. Ute, on the other hand, is aware of her situation. She senses that she's somehow being deceived. When a woman truly loves a man, when she's deeply drawn to that person, vibrations or energies are released that the person picks up on subconsciously. I think Ute has that ability to connect with you without you even knowing it. That's why she realizes she's not the only woman in your life.«

»Ah, nonsense! That's too esoteric for me; I don't believe in that kind of thing. And I don't think about her at all when I'm with Carmen or Margit.«

Lydia could empathize well with Ute. After all, she had once been in a similar relationship herself.

»But because Ute cares for you so much, she just senses it. It's a feeling, it can't be described, you just have it. There aren't many people who still possess these innate qualities. Maybe she already sensed something during the meeting with Margit? Or do you think it left her completely indifferent?«

Thomas denied it, saying, »Oh, come on!«

He thought, »Even though I've received emails from Ute before, where she mentioned noticing me checking out other women, I don't like discussing negative things. I prefer to avoid them. How does Lydia know all this? Can she empathize so well with Ute's situation? Or do all women think alike?«

»Like always, you're right, Lydia. I remember receiving an email from Ute. It really hurt her and didn't leave her completely indifferent. In it, she mentioned wanting to talk to me about it. And she correctly identified the situation with Margit. And do you think Ute really loved me? - I saved Ute's email. Wait, I can read it to you.«

Thomas scrolled through his emails, searching for the one from Ute.

„Here it is:

> *Hello, my (not always) dear Thomas,*
> *As for the ad story, I still don't know what to make of it. Are you really looking for another woman?!*
> *Your secrecy is starting to get on my nerves.*
> *I must say, the whole story is indeed murky, but on the other hand, it's a bit amusing that I stumbled upon it of all people. There are no coincidences!*
>
> *I think - and there's no avoiding it - we should have a serious talk about our relationship. With your great talent for time management, I'm sure you'll have some time for me to calmly discuss one thing or another. I think it's very important to talk about the relationship from time to time, what the other person has on their mind, where life's journey is headed, or, as you wrote, your dream journey.*
> *You know that I take our relationship very seriously, and you should be aware that I'm sometimes very frustrated by all of this. I have real heartache and sleepless nights. And all because I don't know what all of this means, and you quickly come up with an answer when I accidentally catch on to it.*

Now this thing, because you supposedly are conducting a new market research on behavior in online dating. But you won't get an easy victory with me; I am strong enough to stand my ground. Your evasive maneuver only confirms that you really have a guilty conscience and fear confrontation.

Furthermore, even with your busy schedule, it's possible for you to meet other women. You're constantly on the go, and who knows if someone might catch your eye along the way ...

How was it back then at the event with Margit? You're also quite frequently in Frankfurt - strange, isn't it? Did you think I wouldn't notice how you looked at her? There was something in your gaze, in the way you acted, you were almost sweating bullets, afraid something would come out. Maybe you really do have something with her.

I don't know. It was purely a business matter. One thing I can tell you, though, if Margit found out, you wouldn't have anything to laugh about. There would be fireworks between you two, or the plates would fly. She wouldn't put up with something like that. And if I bring it up to you, you clam up...

I have no idea what bug bit me that I had to fall hopelessly in love with you of all people. No, I'm not looking for the man who comes home on time for dinner in the evening, you know that yourself. Just someone I love and who loves me, who appreciates me and spends time with me, just like last weekend, I really enjoyed that.

I have a lot to do, I'm often on the go, and I also have to plan, but I think if you communicate that to the other person, they can understand the whole thing better and won't be disappointed. I find it stupid myself to have to bring it up every time, but as long as YOU don't comment on it, it will just keep getting postponed, and ‚No Comment' is simply not a solution to our problem.

This will be my last email on this topic for now. I hope we can find a solution together because I've been avoiding this for a while. The frustration is growing and becoming unbearable, which I naturally don't want.

Therefore, my request is to set a date (preferably a weekend) where we can talk about this matter calmly. I care a lot about you and our relationship. Unless you no longer have feelings for me, but then please tell me, and don't keep me waiting any longer. At least then I know where I stand. Otherwise, it's not enjoyable for either of us. It's a pity what a lack of communication can destroy!

Your (sometimes annoying) and always loving Ute."

Lydia took a sip from her glass. Then she slowly set it down.

»Yes, I think she really loved you very much. She didn't want to lose you, yet she had already lost you a long time ago because your heart never belonged to her. That email was her last cry for help. It's a pity!! It's a pity that you men often only realize how much you loved someone when the relationship is over.« Lydia's voice sounded sad.

Thomas looked concerned. »But then I don't understand why Ute didn't fight for me. If she really loved me, why did she just leave? Did she find someone else?«

»I really don't need to tell you that, do I?« She looked at Thomas with a sharp gaze. »So, if I'm going to help you ...«

Thomas cleared his throat. He looked bewildered...

»Okay. I must tell you. So, here it goes. She found out that you're looking for someone else, a long-term relationship, a woman to go through life with. She writes you long emails, and you don't say anything about it. She feels deeply hurt and unloved by you. Now tell me: Why should she fight for your love if there's no love from your side? Also, why didn't you fight for love?«

»For the first time, Thomas appeared helpless... 'You might be right, but I still care about her a lot,' he said softly, biting his lower lip.«

Lydia leaned forward. »But liking someone isn't the same as loving them! When a woman like Ute realizes, 'The man doesn't love me,' she looks for someone else. I told you; Ute is looking for a man for a long-term relationship, not a short fling. What do you men seek? You post an ad, and you already have everything you need.«

Thomas pondered. »From this perspective, I hadn't really considered the whole thing seriously, and I felt sorry for Ute. I didn't want to hurt her. I thought she was enjoying life, but I never fully realized how much she loved me. Or maybe I didn't want to admit it. Because then I would have had to commit.«

He nodded in agreement and turned to Lydia.

»Finally, I can understand the women. I didn't make it easy for them. Least of all for myself, I love them all and can't decide. I haven't found the woman or the love that embodies everything. Of course, I hoped that none of them would find out about the others. Ute caught on to me and eventually left. Rightly so. They already loved me, but maybe I'm incapable of commitment. I was afraid of giving up my freedom and everything if I were in a relationship.«

The waiter came and brought them both water. He winked at Lydia and made a suggestive head movement towards Thomas. When she didn't react, he promptly left again.

Thomas looked out at the sea and observed the beachgoers slowly packing up their belongings as he continued speaking.

»After my first big love, who broke my heart, I didn't want to be a fool again. I showered her with affection. She was always calling me, but that didn't bother me. I fulfilled every wish she expressed. And then…? Then she left me for someone else! Within four weeks, I had to move out of our shared apartment because she was the main tenant. That's how it was! That's how women are!« He raised his eyebrows.

»Since then, I swore to myself not to let a woman influence me anymore. I never wanted to be so foolish as to fall in love with a woman again. My heart was broken. Since then, I've kept my feelings under control. As soon as I started to develop feelings for a woman, I simply avoided her and looked for another one. Dates were not kept, calls on the answering machine were simply ignored. I went out and quickly met someone else, and the game started all over again.«

He looked at Lydia. »You've figured it out. In any case, I'm one step further now.« He sighed. »Can't I truly love a woman? And yet, I miss Ute.«

Lydia scratched her nose. She watched as her two colleagues finished their archery program and took a break.

Her colleague Tina arrived and began her activity with the children's animation.

Lydia had some time left.

»What else did you find out from your internet research? Surely it wasn't just your friend Ute who responded,« she turned back to Thomas.

»No. It was exciting. Every morning after waking up, I checked my mailbox right away. Some are provocative, and with others, I play the role of Doctor Sommer; I'm ready to provide advice and assistance on all questions. What are they? – Oh, here's one from a hot chick!« And he handed Lydia his phone so she could read it better.

I just came across your personal ad. It seems like you're looking for the same thing as me, an adventure without any obligations. I love being single, but what's lacking are the hot fantasies. And I can't get enough of them. I don't want them to remain just fantasies. I love to be stylishly seduced and to seduce in return. But at the same time, I'm up for some wild stuff. My favourite positions are 'whether it's 69, 66, or 88, I enjoy outdoor SEX.

And if you happen to be really into me, drop me another email right away. Attached is a little picture of me in case I'm not your type! Hope to hear from you to arrange a casual date, to get to know each other over a cup of coffee, to see if there's any chemistry.
Kisses, wherever you like them, Sabine!'

Lydia looked up from his smartphone.

He took it again to continue looking. »Not bad, huh? Some people are direct. But actually, I'm not looking for an Adventure.«

»Really not?« Lydia raised her eyebrows. »I thought that's exactly what you're looking for. I mean, one might get that impression, right?«

»Maybe so, but I'm looking for a long-term relationship, or at least hoping to find the right one. Well, this email falls into the category of ‚erotica,' you never know. Oh yes, here I have more interesting emails. Take a look.«

He handed her his smartphone again. She read quietly to herself and kept swiping the screen to prevent it from timing out.

„Hi Thomas,
I stumbled upon your advertisement and couldn't resist replying to it. Could it be that your zodiac sign is Aries, Aquarius, Gemini, or Pisces? If you were born in spring, we could soon celebrate our birthdays together and realize all our dreams and goals. By the way, I think your information matches pretty well with me and my expectations. I'm looking forward to your prompt reply, and I'll tell you more about myself in due course. ...
Bye, your Messenger of Good Luck!"*

»Sure, I remember. I found that one interesting, so I wrote some responses. Would you like to read them?«

„Of course, it's getting more and more intriguing! Lydia played with her hair and read eagerly, while Thomas kept swiping the display to prevent it from dimming.

Hi there, dear Messenger of Good Luck,
I greet you warmly. It would be nice if you could tell me a little about yourself. Yes, it's true, my zodiac sign is among those you listed. I'm curious and a bit excited.
Get back to me soon, and don't keep me waiting too long! I was – as you probably were – on vacation and was particularly delighted by your email. I think it's good and exciting. You have to tell me all about it.
Looking forward to your reply,
Your Thomas.

He ran his finger across the display, searching for the other E-Mail so she could continue reading.

Lydia leaned forward. She found it amusing and exciting how people get to know each other over the internet.

»Come on! What's the next one?«

Title: He Who Seeks, Shall Surely Find Soon...
Hello Thomas,
thank you for your kind words, which brought me much joy. My lucky number is 13, so I replied on the 13th, and lo and behold ... Actually, I don't know where to begin ...

Well, I've never placed an ad on the site myself. It was probably a twist of fate that the dear Lord or someone else tapped me on the shoulder and prompted me to open your ad. Well, the thing with the zodiac sign was great; I guessed right and got yours. Yes, dear Thomas, as they say, everything in life is a first. Some try a hundred times to find the right life partner through an ad, and it just doesn't work out. Who knows, maybe you're an exception in this regard and have already found more than one partner through your ad? Well, as far as looks are concerned, I consider them secondary when it comes to a person. Personally, I place much more value on their character. I've never been married and am, as they say, free of baggage.

60 kg would be distributed over a normal figure with a height of 170 cm. My blond hair is very long. My eye colour sometimes varies a bit. Sometimes my eyes are green, sometimes blue.

My hobbies are similar to yours, especially photography, traveling, hiking—whatever is fun, really. Additionally, I'm passionate about cooking and enjoy reading fairy tales. I love having children and animals around me, and of course, nature. I hope you also like children. Yes, I'm not prudish. Howe-

ver, I'm truly looking for a man for life.
How would I describe my character? Hm? I'm so-
metimes quiet and sometimes a bit wild, but general-
ly, I'm a balanced person and embody the qualities I
desire in a life partner.

That means open-minded, creative, open, abo-
ve all loyal, reliable, optimistic, sociable, tolerant,
warm-hearted, romantic, well-groomed, homely
(but not overly), sensual, helpful...

What I absolutely don't like are envy, secrecy, lies,
selfishness, arrogance, untidiness, and stubbornness.
Why am I writing you so much? Does it have to be
like this when you don't even know someone? Well,
maybe in the middle of this email, you've already
told yourself that this won't work out for a shared
journey in life.

Or maybe you're already quite euphoric and can't
wait until we see each other for the first time, hug,
and see where it goes from there? Speaking of »se-
eing each other for the first time,« like you, I'm very
sociable and enjoy meeting new people. Especially
when they're as nice as you probably are!? So, shall
we meet soon? What's stopping us? After all, one
should live each day as if it were the last.

So, dear Thomas, I hope you can now imagine a
little more about me, and I look forward to hearing
from you. In that spirit, I wish you a lovely evening
and a good night with pleasant dreams...
Many warm regards, Your Karina. Your Messenger
of Good Luck

P.S.: I'll just go ahead and write ‚Your Karina.' Well,

who knows? As for why I didn't mention my name in the first email, I simply forgot in the heat of the moment.

Lydia looked at Thomas, who grinned and brushed his hair away from his face.

»Am I really boring you with this? You can tell me honestly,« Thomas seemed uncertain for a moment.

Thomas nodded. »Then you can read the response here,« he said, handing her the phone.

Re: Seek and ye shall find!
Dear Karina,
I can hardly believe that our ambitions overlap to such an extent. Actually, I can't add anything to your »partner requirements« and feel absolutely addressed. I am looking for a life partner with whom I can have fun and experience everything. By the way, I like blue and green eyes.

A little bit about me: I really like children (especially the ones I produce myself), although I'm a complete novice in this matter, even though I'm already over thirty. I hope that's okay. At the moment, I feel like I'm thirteen. Maybe it has something to do with your lucky number. With my mostly positive mood, I look youthful. I like to dress casually, but unfortunately, my job doesn't allow it. I often must make a serious impression, which is sometimes difficult for me. But that's how I earn my bread. I'm a marketing consultant and speaker on various topics. I really enjoy it because I can bring a lot of spirit into it and only do what I like. So, I'm doing well.

What really brings me the most joy in life, though, is

pursuing my hobbies, for which I have far too little time. It's a pity! I'm almost always on the go every day, but mostly at home at night.
Nature is toootally important to me. That's why I go on crazy trips. Last spring, I spent two weeks traveling in Mexico. Very, very beautiful and very exhausting. I love exploring foreign cultures and landscapes. Yes, so that it's not just a dream, I make it happen. I hop on a plane and off I go! I love animals and enjoy having them around. I live in the vicinity of Düsseldorf in a house that should provide enough space for my family.

I plan to do more for myself in the future. I often feel lonely. I wish for a loving partner with whom I feel safe and at home, with whom I can go on many small and big trips, with whom I can cuddle without inhibition, because sex plays a big role for me in feeling completely happy.
Yes, about my appearance! I've just crossed the age of 40, but nobody will believe that. I look younger. It's all about attitude. I am 185 cm tall, slim, with blue eyes and shoulder-length blonde hair. Well, it's best to experience me ‚live‘. In principle, I'm a chaotic person, can't keep things organized, forget appointments, etc., but I have a dear assistant who always reminds me of everything.

I'm humorous, can tell exciting stories, love music, Theater, and art, painting, and so on. I'm a sensual type. You can tell me the truth, even if it hurts. Most of the time I'm dominant, spread good vibes, and generally know where things are headed. I'm romantic, naive, a bit childish, and enjoy reading fairy tales and stories.
As you can see, dear Karina, I'm probably one of the

craziest guys you'll ever meet. And the best part is, except for occasional stress, I'm doing well and I'm unattached. No woman has endured the turbulence for long so far. Until now, they've all wished I'd be nice and home by 6:00 p.m. But that's not the case. I'm often out and about, especially in the evenings. And when I'm at home, I'm either working on the next presentations or enjoying a delicious cappuccino at a café. And I smoke. Depending on stress, sometimes a bit more. However, I'd like to quit, maybe you can help me with that...

I would love to pamper a woman, but she's not here. Now you know a hell of a lot about me. I would be very happy to meet you soon. I'm sure you're busy on Sunday, wherever you are, because you plan ahead. I would have time. And if I didn't have time, I would make time. I'm very curious to see how we will like each other.
That reminds me, I don't even know which city you're from. If you think we should meet, why don't you make a suggestion! Starting from Tuesday evening, I'll be in Vienna for a few days to take care of a dear client. But after that, everything will be back to normal. If you can manage it, I'm eager to meet someone who seems like a soulmate to me, like you, Karina.

Dear Messenger of Good Luck, I had completely forgotten to wish you a good night with very sweet dreams!!! Your Thomas!

Lydia had become silent as Thomas showed her the email correspondence with Karina. She immediately noticed that the email address belonged to her best friend Karina. They had once made a pact to respond to personal ads together. And now, she was walking along the beach with Karina's dream man. What a coincidence! Back then, she found this Thomas very interesting. She empathized with her friend's feelings. But now, knowing Thomas and his issues with women, she wasn't sure if Karina would have been happy with him. Probably not! Karina had been very sad when he suddenly stopped contacting her. He seemed to have everything she desired: charisma, a love for travel, appealing to her, fond of children, and above all, she thought Thomas wasn't as dull and conventional as other men.

Thomas didn't notice Lydia's reaction at all. He was staring at his smartphone, searching for the next message, and then handed it back to her.

Title: We're on the Right Track.

Dear Thomas, I apologize for replying only now, but I was away all weekend. Hopefully, I still have the chance to reach you before YOU are gone again.

First of all, thank you very much for your kind words! That all sounds extraordinary. Somehow, there is an unconsciously growing promising sympathy between us, without us ever having spoken a word to each other or seen each other before. Don't you think?

I think every person is an individual and interesting in their own way to another person. However, when two people meet who have a lot in common, this feeling becomes even stronger. It's nice to hear what you share about yourself. Well, you have a job you enjoy, you live in a nice house. You can be proud of that – and the only thing missing for your happiness is the right woman, I understand.
Sometimes life takes strange paths. And perhaps it

had to be that way, that I rejected some marriage proposals because I felt inside that there is the right one for me in this universe! It's probably been similar for you too, you haven't met the one hundred percent right person yet. Although I don't want to claim at this point that I am the one. Anyway, I can understand you well. I am convinced that the right partner exists for me. But maybe I can whisper an answer into your ear in 50 years?!

Dear Thomas, don't you also feel that since last week everything is a bit different in your life? Honestly, I feel the same way. Although I can't tell you why that is. It probably even affects both of us?

I unfortunately have little time for my hobbies and often feel lonely. Sure, I go out with friends, but there's someone missing to lean on, someone who comes home and is happy to have someone there. I quite like traveling, preferably several short trips, either a sightseeing tour, city tour, or simply a relaxing vacation. I'm not a sun worshipper; on vacation, I'm very active, whether it's hiking, swimming, or lying on an alpine meadow and forgetting everything around me – that's really beautiful. Sex is important to me, but more on that when we meet ...

In terms of clothing, I have everything in my wardrobe. From lace to sporty for underneath, and from evening dresses to jeans for over. Yes, just like you, I need to have the appropriate outfit in my closet for every occasion. When we meet soon, what are you in the mood for? Of course, I want to please you with my look.
It's strange, isn't it? You only know a person from a

few lines, and already you're making plans together, starting to dream ...
And the beautiful thing is, there's nothing stopping us from realizing these ideas. Originally, I just wanted to briefly respond to your email. And lo and behold, quite a few lines have accumulated again.

Have a great time in Vienna and lots of love!
Yours, Karina.

Thomas made sure Lydia was still interested and glanced briefly at her. She sat motionless, staring at the display. It was clear that reading her friend's most intimate emails was uncomfortable for her. He didn't know she knew Karina, and she didn't tell him.

They both ordered milkshakes, and while they waited, Thomas showed her more emails.

Re: We're on the right track.

Hi Karina,
I'm delighted to have received such a lovely email from you. I'm curious to meet you soon. I enjoy your words, and I get the impression that you've known me for a long time already. And who knows, maybe we've already crossed paths. If you're brave enough and decide to give me your phone number, I'd be happy to give you a call.

If we meet, I will hope you wear your favourite casual clothes. I'll do the same. Then I'll treat you to a delicious meal. Perhaps there will be a sweet dessert too. Who knows. Please get back to me soon. I'm very eager to learn more about you. For example, why does your eye colour change? When is your

birthday? In which beautiful city do you live? What's currently occupying your mind the most? And why has so much changed for you lately? Don't keep me waiting too long and tell me before I'm away for a few days again. Wishing you a good night, a kiss wherever you like, and sweet dreams.
Your dear Thomas.

She looked up as the drinks arrived. He picked up his glass and took a sip. She left hers untouched for the moment.

»Yeah, pretty amusing, those emails, right? Got them all nicely sorted, didn't I?«

Lydia nodded and glanced again at the display of his smartphone.

Re: Gutelaune-Mail...

Re: Good mood E-Mail …

Dear Thomas, thank you very much for your reply. I hope you had a good night and dreamed something nice.

I don't know where to start and which of your questions to answer first. I'm getting impatient to meet you. You make me curious because you give the impression that we know each other. And who knows, maybe you'll feel the same way, that you'll be in a situation and think, 'Hey, she seems very familiar.' Weird, isn't it?

Your suggestions for meeting with me sound good; I like 'the idea of going out to eat, I'm always hungry. Since I have a sweet tooth, I'm excited about a sweet dessert.
Ah, sorry for the confusion. I was referring to the

sense that we seem to understand each other without even meeting in person, like we're communicating telepathically. As for your eye colour changing, it's just an observation I made from your description. It's interesting how they appear darker by candlelight compared to sunlight.

Ah, interesting! It sounds like you have some exciting changes coming up, especially with your birthday and potential relocation. Moving closer to Düsseldorf could be quite an adventure!

It sounds like you have a diverse and engaging career as a freelancer. Describing it in detail would indeed require quite a bit of time!
It's nice to hear about yourself. Well, who knows, maybe we'll work together someday?
Sorry, I couldn't find the poem. Could you please provide the text of the poem so I can translate it for you?

> *Arrived on an island.*
> *Celebrating reunions with the wind and the vastness of the horizon.*
> *Nowhere else does the sky merge so much with the sea.*
> *Nowhere else does happiness taste so salty.*
> *Leave the past behind and look forward to today!*
> *Here you can be completely yourself.*

Many warm greetings, wrapped in radiant sunbeams, are sent to you, even if it's raining now.
Your Karina."

Lydia's thoughts raced: My God, Karina had written so much. And with her poem, it really hit the mark… arriving on an island, yes, that was me back then… and I had written her that poem… Crazy world!

Lydia continued reading.

Re: Good morning E-Mail
Dear Thomas, I hope you had a good stay in Vienna. It's a pity that I haven't received a response to my email yet. But maybe you didn't have the time or the opportunity to reply.

I look forward to hearing from you and hopefully we'll see each other soon. With that, I wish you a wonderful »Good morning« and a great start to the new day.
Yours, Karina.

Thomas looked at her. »Why are you so quiet? Is everything okay?«

Lydia nodded. »Yeah, it's strange what someone writes, isn't it? There aren't many more emails from Karina, then I'm done.« He placed his smartphone on the table.

Re: He who seeks will surely find soon.

Hi dear Karina,
I haven't forgotten about you. But it's true that I'm very busy at the moment.

Probably I'll have the chance to report more extensively in a few days. Right now, I'm working on a presentation for a dear client again. Yeah, sometimes it gets a bit crowded.
In any case, it's nice that you haven't completely given up on me and have patience. I'm looking for-

ward - selfish as I sometimes am - to your message.
Your Thomas.

She caught a brief glance at Thomas, then continued reading.

Re: Re: Whoever seeks, will surely find soon.

Hello Thomas!
Thank you for reaching out, I'm a bit stressed now
and could use some mental boost, how about you?
I can come to Düsseldorf this weekend. Please let
me know!

Warm regards and kisses, Karina.

Lydia couldn't remain silent as she continued reading. »Well, that's just typical of men. The woman makes an effort to keep the contact alive, and what does the man write?«

»That it's nice to hear from her and that he's still waiting for her message,« Lydia said, shaking her head in disbelief and annoyance.

Thomas remained silent about it.

He opened the last E-Mail for her:

Title: Too bad, waiting for your response!

Dear Thomas, it's been two weeks since you last
contacted me. It's a pity, I had hoped we were on
the same wavelength and could have built a future
together, but I was mistaken.

I haven't given up hope yet, please get in touch with
me, and we can talk about everything. Maybe you've
been too busy with your job until now. However, my
initial excitement has been dampened.
Please, reach out!

Pensively, she set aside his smartphone.

His gaze fixed on her face, so he asked with concern, »Are you okay? I must be boring you with my stories about women, right?«

Lydia didn't show any sign of discomfort. She finished her milkshake.

»No, no, sorry, I was just lost in thought. You're not boring me at all. I find it highly interesting. I swear! I just don't understand why you ended the contact if it sounded so promising?! Or why didn't you give her your number so she could call you?«

»Oh,« Thomas shrugged, »I don't know. What are just a few emails? I never met her, and even if I did, I wouldn't immediately think about something serious.«

Lydia thought to herself, »Typical man.« As a woman, every word is taken seriously and feelings develop, while for the man, it's just a game. Poor Karina... She suffered so much when he stopped contacting her. Lydia was angry at how he played with her friend's emotions.

She looked at the clock and, for the first time, felt relieved that she had to end the conversation with Thomas. The situation with her friend was weighing heavily on her.

»Oh my, it's almost four o'clock already! I nearly forgot. I must go to the next activity. I swapped with my teammate. Hey, Thomas, do you feel like joining? Water aerobics.«

»Where are you doing that?«

»Down by the sea.«

»Alright. I'll come down there. I just need to grab my towel.«

She didn't want to offend Thomas and hoped that during the water gymnastics, she could clear her mind.

Lydia found it challenging to switch gears suddenly and

jump into a lively and carefree mood. So far, she had managed it well.

On her way to the beach, she asked all the guests at the pool if they wanted to join. Some guests got up from their sun loungers and followed her. At the pool bar, it was difficult to convince anyone to do water aerobics. They preferred holding onto their beers.

Lydia cheerfully skipped down the steps to the beach, putting on an »I'm in a great mood« I. No one here cared about how she really felt inside. The guests wanted a lively entertainer. In this abrupt switch, she was professional.

Lydia always enjoyed doing water aerobics in the sea. The other entertainers preferred the pool because they had music there. Lydia didn't mind. She could still excite people without music. There were some guests standing on the beach waiting for her. Thomas was also there in his swimsuit, with his towel laid out on a lounge chair.

Lydia took the lounge chair next to his, set down her backpack, took off her shirt, and walked into the water. It was refreshing. She dove under, trying to forget about the emails and the turbulent thoughts from earlier.

»Come on, everyone! Let's walk over there and form a large circle!«

The group followed her until they were shoulder-deep in the water. They formed a circle. Lydia demonstrated the exercise and explained what they had to do.

»Running on the spot! Let's go!« She grinned around at the group, her gaze lingering on Thomas. He had joined in and was participating just like the others.

The sand under their feet felt pleasant. The water was calm and only stirred by them. Young and old had come together.

»And now let's do jumping jacks!« She demonstrated the exercise, and everyone followed suit.

As they splashed their arms through the water, creating a spray that reached the others, Thomas seemed to particularly enjoy it. He watched the other guests attentively, his mind momentarily disengaged from thoughts of the women.

The blonde woman next to him seemed happy with her partner, and they displayed it openly. They formed a harmony that stirred something like longing in Thomas, something he wasn't familiar with.

Further down the beach, there were locals observing the group and enjoying the spectacle. They formed another circle and joined in the exercises. The circle grew larger, and the atmosphere became even more joyful, with some splashing around happening within the group.

Lydia couldn't help but think that sometimes the guests were a bit strange or perhaps had spent too long in the sun. She found it amusing how they were fooling around.

Everyone was having a great time, and that was the main thing. Otto, one of the guests, pretended to be the dying swan and joined in the water ballet. Otto thought he was doing great, but Lydia couldn't help but laugh. Seeing Otto dance around in the water with his imposing figure, it had nothing to do with a swan. He looked more like a dancing bear. He was a funny candidate who enjoyed putting on a show. As they hopped in a circle, the funny Isolde started singing, and everyone joined in. This water aerobics session not only trained their leg and arm muscles but also their laughing muscles.

»So, my dear people, now let's all swim a lap in a circle. And the last one attaches themselves to me at the back, then we'll continue with a polonaise.«

It was clear that Isolde started singing another song again. The train went once across the water and then back to the shore, where it dissolved.

»Thank you, that's it! The hour is over already, my goodness, how time flies. It was fun, I hope you enjoyed it too,« Lydia exclaimed.

All applauded and thanked Lydia.

Thomas emerged from the water right behind Lydia. »Is it always this much fun with you?« he asked.

»Yes, most of the time,« Lydia replied with a smile. »It's important for people to have fun, especially on vacation. How did you like it?«

»It was very good. Now I'm thirsty. Shall we go to the pool bar?« asked Thomas. Thomas picked up his things from the sun lounger and lay down in the sun to dry.

»That's a good idea. But let's dry off in the sun first,« Lydia said as she sat down on the lounger opposite.

Until the evening show, she had a break and therefore time for Thomas.

»After a while,« Lydia said, »Now that we're dry, we can go to the pool bar. I'm curious how your story is progressing. Has anything been clarified yet?«

He shook his head in denial as he gathered his belongings, and they walked up together.

With a smiling hello, she greeted every guest. They managed to secure the last two available seats on the terrace. They settled into the rattan chairs under the blue umbrella, making themselves comfortable.

During ordering, the waiter grinned suggestively, alluding to Thomas. She smiled, making a dismissive gesture, and ordered a bottle of water and a coffee for Thomas.

Lydia looked at Thomas. »Did you meet any women from the personal ads?« she asked.

»Of course! After I lost touch with Karina because my PC crashed and it took so much time to restore it, I didn't write to her anymore. Too bad, I would have liked to meet her. Then there was the relationship stress with Carmen, who kept complaining that I hardly had time for her and, and, and ... I didn't want to upset or hurt Carmen, but somehow it just wasn't fun anymore with her. I mean, even sex was never her hottest desire, so ultimately, I was looking for a purely sexual encounter and browsed through personal ads on the internet ...«

Lydia interrupted him. »But if things weren't going well with Carmen, you had Ute and Margit. Why were you looking for a purely physical relationship?«

The waiter brought the drinks. Thomas's gaze wandered over the terrace, observing all the vacationers and the bustling activity at the tables, accompanied by murmurs.

Then he leaned across the table towards Lydia. »That would have been too complicated. I was looking for a bit of variety. On the other hand, I didn't want to give my other lovers the impression that I suddenly had more desire for them just because Carmen wasn't interested. And if things had worked out with Carmen again, what would I have told the others? That suddenly I was busy again? No. I was looking for a woman with whom I could be together without any obligation.«

»Okay. Sounds logical!« Lydia said, adding, »Still, you're a cunning fox. Now you're looking for something for in between meals. Well done! You Casanova! Men are just... - they only want one thing, to enjoy the good life without any obligations! Well, I know that already too well.«

Lydia's ex seemed to have been one of those types. She tapped her fingers on the glass the whole time.

»What drives a man to act like that? Is it the primal instinct of men that needs to be satisfied? Are men not suited for relationships? Do they know what love means? Are men even capable of loving a woman or entering a relationship? I've read that women and men simply don't match or are from different planets. Women are from Venus; men are from Mars.«

Thomas took a sip of his coffee. He seemed embarrassed.

»If you think it's my primal urge! I don't know. But when I was out and about, there was always the opportunity... So, no problem! The out-of-town assignments became less frequent because I was only working in my local area.«

Lydia was horrified. Her own story came back to her. »Women are no better than men. Why? Equality. It's just that women have to be much more understanding. If both want the same thing, it's okay. I once had a relationship where, in my eyes, we were in a relationship, but not in his. He cheated.« Lydia nervously tapped her fingers on the table.

»Then, when we talked about it, he was completely surprised: ‚What, we‘re in a relationship? It‘s just friends with benefits. You don‘t have to think that I‘m in a relationship with you just because I sleep with you. That‘s something completely different.‘ I was shocked at the time. Okay, I assumed that if you end up in bed together, maybe there‘s more to it - like love, and spending leisure time together. How are you supposed to know if the other person feels the same way? The best thing is to ask. Are we together or not? It‘s like in school - isn‘t that silly?« Lydia looked at him questioningly but didn‘t get an answer.

Thomas was too preoccupied with his own story. He rummaged in his bag, took out his smartphone once again, and showed her the Emails.

»There, one day, I saw this personal ad on the internet that I found very interesting and appealing,« Thomas explained.

He handed Lydia the smartphone so she could read it more easily:

Username: Doreen

Marital Status: Divorced with daughter.
Age: 32 years
Height: 165 cm
Body type: Athletic
Eye color: Green
Hair color: Dark blond
Appearance: Elegant
Nationality: German
Occupation: Self-employed
Smoker: Yes
Car: Yes

I am looking for a partner in: NRW, Age: 30 – 45, Height: 170 – 185 cm, Athletic

Hello,
I am Doreen and I am looking for a romantic man for some tender moments by candlelight. You should be smart and educated, charming, brave and daring, wild, willing, and enduring, and completely captivated by me… If you also have class and are presentable in daylight, then why not write to me! Doreen.

Lydia put his phone aside.

»To his defense,« he said, »women want it just as much as men. Otherwise, there wouldn't be any women for men to go to bed with.«

Meanwhile, Thomas had become very thirsty. He ordered an apple spritzer.

Lydia watched him silently for a moment as he absentmindedly flipped through the emails.

»Naja. A bit of eroticism is good, since Carmen didn't want to, Ute was on vacation, and Margit had to attend a seminar at a bank on our weekend. So, I wrote the following back. Read it yourself.«

Hello Doreen,
your ad caught my attention. I think I'm presentable during daylight… Lydia skimmed through his email. But I would love to embark on an adventure with you. I like green eyes, sensual lips, have a fondness for candlelight and tenderness. If you're interested in a creative, lively, and hopefully enduring guy, then please get in touch. I look forward to hearing from you!!

Best regards, Thomas

Lydia looked visibly uncomfortable. She glanced around, feeling embarrassed, and leaned forward. »Thomas, you don't have to show me all the emails - just tell me how it went!«

Thomas took his smartphone.

»Her real name is Dorothea, but everyone calls her Doreen. She's more of a reserved person, very sweet and empathetic. Every other weekend, her ex-husband picks up their little daughter, and that's when we had time for each other. So, she was really a hot chick.«

»Aha. Reserved, yet a hot chick? How does that fit together?« Lydia was all ears.

»You know: Still waters run deep. She has a good dose of Rhineland humour, just like me. The romantic hours with her were beautiful.« He was lost in his thoughts.

»Where does she live?«

»She lives in Aachen.«

»It's not too far. About an hour's drive.«

»Düsseldorf and Aachen aren't too far apart. You just hop on the highway, and then it's quick. What do you want to know about Doreen?«

»What does she do?«

»Ironing, cleaning, the usual stuff, and she's self-employed. She has a small fashion boutique in Aachen, of course called ‚Boutique Doreen.' She's divorced and has a five-year-old daughter. Our first meeting was in Aachen near the Elisenbrunnen, we had a cup of coffee in a cozy atmosphere at the oldest café in town. I liked her right away. A woman to spoil.« Thomas grinned.

»I could spoil her very well... a massage feels really good there. In any case, I feel like I'm reborn after good lovemaking. A good red wine, good mood, a little magic... it was fantastic. She's a sweetheart with a lot of sex appeal, just amazing. I've thought about her for a long time...« He took a deep breath in and out again.

Lydia caught herself thinking, »Is he really that good in bed?« She shook off the thought immediately.

»Yeah, I really liked her a lot,« Thomas said as he rummaged through his emails again.

»Oh, here's a particularly lovely email I received from her. Let me read it to you,« he said.

He glanced around stealthily to see if anyone would overhear their conversation, but in the meantime, the tables around them were empty.

He read softly to her.

> „Dear Thomas,
> wow, I won't forget this wonderful, amazing evening. It was romantic, seductive, funny, amusing, simply superb!! I felt comfortable and haven't had so much fun in lovemaking for a long time. Thank you!
>
> „You are truly a special person. Your intelligence, tolerance, spontaneity, and zest for life have left me speechless! I would do anything for you. I always have time for you. I desire nothing more than a beautiful, romantic evening with you, and you should understand that and nothing more! Especially when I'm stressed, I know a good stress relief medication – it has three letters... That's why I think we should meet more often. I want you!! Above all, to feel and experience you!
>
> So, Thomas, if you want to see me, please get in touch!
> Best regards, Doreen.

»An enchanting woman. Very passionate and exhilarating …«

Lydia interrupted him. »So, a much hotter and more temperamental type than Margit, huh?«

He laughed. »Well, they're all like that, aren't they? On the other hand, I find that restraint in Margit so attractive and appealing. There should be a woman who has it all. A bit of a vamp, on the other hand, an angel, but they don't exist. That would be the dream woman.«

Lydia glanced at her watch. Slowly, she should start heading towards the bungalow.

»Sure, Thomas. Let's head towards the reception and the bungalow. You're checking the time?«

As they walked, Lydia nodded in agreement, her mind preoccupied with thoughts from their conversation.

As Thomas continued, he said, »That's all of them now. My four relationships. I can't decide to put all my eggs in one basket and end my affairs. I don't want to! I'd be left alone afterwards. That's not an option! I want to figure out which of these women I truly love, or which one fits with me. So, there's Ute, Carmen, and Margit. With Doreen, it's more of a friend with benefits situation, but it could develop into something more, if both of us want it.«

Lydia laughed. »Oh, just a casual acquaintance! Sure! No problem! I'm not saying you're a playboy or Casanova, but YOU just haven't found the right one yet. And now you're here to mourn over Ute and think about your other relationships before ending up alone. You're afraid of that. I totally understand!«

Lydia looked at Thomas sympathetically. It wasn't as simple for men as it might seem. Thomas didn't seem to be the happiest. Despite everything, she found him likable. She looked at him as research subject to find out how men who couldn't commit ticked. After all, her ex was such an example.

»You should bake your dream woman yourself?! By the way, it just occurred to me, there's a baking class tomorrow.«

She looked at him: »Maybe you really have to bake your dream partner. We find fault with everything and everyone. Does the dream partner even exist? Or does he, as the name suggests, only exist in dreams and not in real life? That would be a shame! Anyway, I haven't given up hope of finding the right man.«

She stretched her arms upward and made an expansive gesture as she continued, »He exists somewhere out there in the universe and just doesn't know his luck yet. With me, the superwoman!« She laughed out loud.

»What do you mean by baking class?« Thomas was a bit confused. »Are you making fun of me now?«

»No, I wouldn't dare. No, seriously! There's a baking class for kids on Sunday morning, and for adults, there's a discussion group. The discussion topics are posted on the bulletin board over there. And tomorrow, the current topic happens to be about loyalty and infidelity.«

They stopped, and she pointed to the blackboard at the entrance to the reception before they went in.

Surprised, he looked at the program sheet. »Do they have something like this here? Who attends these?«

»Well, normally this isn't typical. But in our club, you'll find a bit of everything,« she said enthusiastically.

»The entertainer Patricia, who leads this, is a psychology student and is writing her master's thesis on ‚Guest Behaviour in a Club Hotel.' Usually, there are between four and ten guests participating in the discussion to exchange their experiences. I think with such topics being highlighted again in the media, there's a big interest in it. Why not give it a try? It's surely very enlightening.«

»Thanks for the tip, I'll see what I'll do tomorrow morning.«

Lydia found herself undecided in front of the reception. She needed to get ready and organize some things for the Latin American dance evening. On the other hand, her stomach was growling, as time quickly passed listening to Thomas' love stories, which also made her hungry, regardless of whether for a man or food – but she opted for food, which was safer.

»Hey, Thomas, I don't have much time left, but there's still enough for a quick bite. I just need to throw on a dress because

I can't go in with my animation outfit.«

She disappeared in a flash through the »Staff Only« door behind the reception into the adjoining room, and promptly emerged wearing a beach dress.

Thomas looked down at himself, but his Bermuda shorts and shirt seemed suitable for the temperatures.

»I've worked up quite an appetite. Come on, let's quickly grab something to eat at the restaurant,« Lydia hurried off to the buffet to grab a quick bite.

»Tonight's the event, so I still need to prepare for that. You're coming, right?«

»Of course. One shouldn't let such a charming woman go out alone.«

»Ha, ha. Is that your typical pick-up line? Sorry, but that doesn't work on me, Maestro. Hasta la vista, baby, bang, bang!«

Lydia jumped up impatiently. »I have to go. See you later: Adiós, Thomas,« and hurriedly walked outside to the event tent.

She had to make the final preparations. But thankfully, she was skilled in organizing events, and she could rely on the others.

Juan and Alex stood by the tent with a bottle of beer, whispering to each other. »Ah, here comes Lydia. Finally! So, is that your potential type? You're only hanging out with him now,« they teased.

Lydia, annoyed, replied, »No! But I don't see how that's any of your business. Come on, let's get back to work! Vamos.«

The cocktail bar was beautifully decorated with vibrant colours. The musical group with their singer was positioned at one end of the bar, and the DJ was set up on the other side. Lydia greeted everyone and briefly went over the program once again.

The entertainers wore colourful attire for their performance.

The men donned black pants paired with red, orange, or green shirts, while the women wore black tops and short skirts matching the respective colours of the men's shirts. Lydia and the others briefly practiced their dance steps. Once everything was settled and the last questions were answered, Lydia headed back to her bungalow to take a long-awaited shower and prepare for the evening show.

Lydia felt determined to tease Thomas and provoke a reaction from him that evening. She wanted to playfully flirt with him and show off her seductive side, only to then reject him. She saw it as a vague experiment in direct confrontation, hoping it might open his eyes to his own behaviour. Lydia had nothing to lose and found the idea amusing. She intended to engage in some playful flirting, but with the intention of ultimately rejecting him. It was a game between man and woman, and she was ready to play.

Lydia was excited to see Thomas's reaction when she seductively danced with him. The Latin American evening was perfect for that. The music was lively, and people danced Lambada and Bachata, creating an ideal atmosphere for getting close and making flirting even more fun. It was all about dancing, nothing more.

After showering, Lydia carefully put on her, as she thought, hot black lace lingerie. Since she and Juan were the main performers at the dance evening, she chose to wear a fiery red sleeveless Carmen dress, unlike the other entertainers.

She imagined how Thomas would react when he saw her. She felt confident, sexy, and attractive in her floor-length figure-hugging dress. At each of these performances, she had received compliments from everyone.

Cleverly, she pinned her long hair up at the back, letting a strand fall across her face. She applied her red lipstick and took a spritz of her favourite perfume. Then, she quickly slipped into her dance pumps and headed towards the event tent.

Thomas sat at a small table right by the dance floor, sipping on his cocktail. Lydia entered the stage with her colleagues to welcome the guests for the dance evening. Murmurs spread through the tent. The DJ played music until the band was ready.

As Thomas saw her, he was taken aback by her appearance. His heart raced faster. He sat up straighter in his chair to get a better view of her. Wow, who was this? He felt proud that the other guests admired Lydia, but he, he had a special connection with her. At the same time, he hoped she would come sit with him later.

Her cheeks flushed with excitement as she wondered how the evening would unfold. With a swing in her step, she left the stage, greeted by applause from the guests. Matching her steps to the music, she danced her way through the crowd to Thomas's table with a smile on her face. »Is this seat taken?« she asked.

Thomas stood up and warmly greeted her with a smile, offering her the chair. »You are welcome to sit at my table. You look enchanting. Even more captivating than on the first evening,« he said.

She smiled at him and took her seat. He was lucky to have a table right by the stage because she always sat there. Thomas wondered if it was her professional demeanor that kept a smile on her lips. No matter what, always nice, always friendly. Just as one would expect from an entertainer. Where Lydia was, she spread joy everywhere and was highly valued by her colleagues.

»Oh, what a day it's been! You look absolutely stunning today, all dressed in black.«

»Thank you! You know, I'm quite thirsty myself. Shall I go over to the bar and bring back a cocktail for you too?« He smiled at Lydia.

»Good idea, but for me a non-alcoholic one, I still have to dance after all,« Lydia said amusedly.

As Thomas stood at the cocktail bar, another guest smiled

at Lydia, vying for her attention. He was about to ask her to dance, but then a flamenco performance began just at that moment.

On his way back to the table, Thomas observed the guest and Lydia, noticing how she smiled and talked to him.

Suddenly, a sense of possessiveness surged within him, prompting him to quicken his pace toward the table to assert his territory. As the guest moved away, Thomas arrived. He deliberately placed his cocktails on the table and seated himself comfortably, crossing his legs and leaning back.

Lydia was in a flirtatious mood. As she sucked on her straw, she winked at him and hummed along with the music. Thomas was somewhat puzzled – was she flirting with him, or was it just part of her job? As if by chance, Lydia tapped her foot to the rhythm with him and laughed. Thomas joined in, unsure where this was going to lead. Perhaps it was just a game, he wondered, noting the change in her tone and behaviour.

After the singing performance ended, the dance music started right away. The entertainers invited a few guests to dance or showed them the steps.

»Shall we dance?« Lydia took Thomas's hand.

»You want to dance?«

»Yes, or can't you dance at all?«

»Sure, I'd love to!« He let her pull him up.

First, they danced a Rumba to warm up. Thomas was a very good dancer, as Lydia noticed. He led Lydia confidently across the entire dance floor. After the Rumba came Salsa, then Bachata. They got closer and closer, and Thomas pressed his body more and more against hers. He was unsure whether she was flirting with him or simply dancing erotically with him. To find out, Thomas would have loved to kiss Lydia. But somehow, she always disappeared from his sight and evaded him. The dance was very body-focused, so you had to find the other person sympathetic. Despite this, he still couldn't figure out her behaviour.

»You have beautiful green eyes, Lydia.«

Sie grinned. His body felt ridiculously good, and his cologne was downright intoxicating. It reminded her of a crush, and she closed her eyes, revelling in the music. Suddenly, she couldn't help but think about the others. Surprised by the emotions overwhelming her, triggered by his cologne, she felt very cheerful and carefree.

»You have a beautiful smile; did you know that? And you dance well. It's lovely to glide across the dance floor with you!«

»That's because you haven't seen my solo performance yet, it's coming up later,« she said coyly, accustomed to receiving compliments.

The dance floor became increasingly crowded. The couple from water aerobics danced very passionately. Lydia was delighted whenever she could dance. It gave her a liberating feeling. They danced exuberantly and didn't stop. The cocktail was starting to affect him slowly. Thomas wished he could kiss her on the lips.

»May I kiss you? You're a very fascinating woman!«

She just grinned at him. »Thank you! No! Kissing animators is forbidden!«

He persisted. »I would love to kiss you on the mouth.«

Lydia brushed him off. She was relieved when their song started playing softly and said firmly, »I'm sorry. No, it really can't happen!« She grinned, wrapped her leg around his, and leaned her upper body backward. Now she was leading.

He didn't understand anything now and was momentarily stunned. Was this part of her performance?

The colourful lights dimmed, and a man in an elegant black suit stood in the white spotlight on the stage, looking around searchingly. This was the most thrilling moment for the guests: What would happen next?

Slowly, the melody grew louder, and the man began to sing. »Where are you tonight, baby? ...«

Lydia freed herself from Thomas' arms. »Now it's time for my performance,« she said.

She smiled at Juan, the man on the stage, and danced towards him under his singing, where she was welcomed with open arms.

Juan finished his solo and acted as if he was fascinated by Lydia. Through his gaze and gestures, he conveyed to her: »Hey, you are beautiful tonight!« and kissed her on the cheek, which was part of the performance.

Thomas was frozen. Surprised by his feelings, he felt his vanity wounded. Was that part of the performance? And she was allowed to kiss him? Was there something between them? She hadn't told him anything. Why was he suddenly feeling something for Lydia? He couldn't answer it with his head, but his body showed slight excitement.

The other guests formed a circle around the dancing couple and clapped to the beat.

The music changed again, and Mambo began to play. Juan and Lydia danced a hot Mambo reminiscent of ‚Dirty Dancing‘. The guests were thrilled, cheering, and moving exuberantly to the music.

After that, a musical mix followed, during which they danced closely entwined Bachata. Slowly, the other entertainers joined them on the dance floor, and, as in Dirty Dancing, the guests were invited to dance along.

Thomas was thrilled. He couldn't take his eyes off her body. Lydia and Juan simply danced very well, creating an electric atmosphere in the tent. The joy they spread was highly contagious.

Lydia needed a little breather. She bid farewell to Juan and danced over to Thomas. Exhausted, she collapsed into the chair.

»Phew, it's warm, that was exhausting. I need a drink first,« she said, taking a big sip.

So far, Thomas had been talking about his life, and he knew almost nothing about Lydia. He wanted clarity and to learn more about her. »Say, is there something going on between you two?«

Lydia looked at him surprised. »Juan? No! Men are so terribly boring, either taken or just ogling other women. Others have a huge fear of commitment. I danced with one of those ladies' men today. So, what do I need a man for? I would quite like to have a boyfriend, but on the other hand, I have far too much to do and no time for a man, really not.« She waved her hand dismissively.

Thomas looked at her but said nothing. He was relieved on one hand that she had nothing with Juan, but on the other hand, disappointed that he had misinterpreted their flirts while dancing.

»That's a shame. But saying you don't have time is just an excuse,« he remarked. Because he made time anyway. They watched the other guests dancing.

Lydia shrugged. She was tired. Tired from dancing and from all the conversations. She drank up her cocktail listlessly.

»Sure, Lydia. It was also a pleasure for me. I wish you a good night and good luck for tomorrow. Hasta luego!«

»Of course, Lydia. Can I take you home? Oh, what am I saying, ‚home' sounds good! So, to your bungalow? I'll also get my things.«

»Yes, Gracias.«

Thomas offered his arm to Lydia, she linked hers with his, and they walked out together. There were a few guests sitting on the terrace, and the other animators were nowhere to be seen. The moon shone brightly, and it was a wonderful, balmy, starry night. The music could still be heard faintly in the background.

At her door, Lydia stopped. »Yes, here we are! I wish you a good night with beautiful dreams! Buenas noches, Thomas!«

»Buenas noches, Lydia! I wish you a pleasant night with sweet dreams.«

In the moment, Thomas hugged Lydia tightly. She withdrew from his arms and climbed the last steps to her bungalow. Moving very slowly and gracefully, she looked back at Thomas and began to sing softly, »The look of love, it means so much... Just words could never say... I will feel my arms around you, and never will forget you...«

She quickly disappeared behind her door.

Thomas lit a cigarette, stood there for a while, watching as the light in her room turned on, his thoughts swirling around.

He couldn't decide between his women, and one was more beautiful and dreamier than the other. Each had their pros and cons; if only he could find a woman who embodied all his women in one person! But he hadn't found her yet, if she even existed. Nevertheless, he was looking forward to seeing Lydia again. With that thought, he slowly made his way back to his bungalow.

Alone, he arrived at his bungalow. He sat on his terrace with a drink from the minibar. The conversations with Lydia stirred something inside him.

He was starting to believe that he had fallen a bit in love with Lydia. Oh no, another woman! His problem wasn't getting smaller, it was getting bigger. Was it just the carefree atmosphere of a holiday flirt, or was it this wonderful woman?

It did him exceptionally well that she listened to him. He had her full attention, and she was interested in helping him solve his problem, to get to the bottom of his true feelings for his women. Was it love?

With these thoughts in mind, he undressed and went to bed. Sleepless, he tossed and turned for hours.

A gentle breeze played with her blue nightgown. The air was delightful. Since Lydia couldn't sleep, she stood on her terrace late at night, enjoying the warm summer night and having conversations with herself.

Do the conversations with Thomas unsettle me?! Didn't I say I'd never deal with a guy like him again?! It's been a long time since I had a real love relationship. Most interesting men are either married or commitment-phobic like Thomas. »Fri-

ends with benefits,« as they say. That's definitely not what I want. Did I really think in my last relationship: if I love HIM strongly enough, I'll be able to convince him - but no! I suffered for months because of that.

Lydia gazed out to the sea and softly sang a song to herself. »I'll explain women to you. I'll explain the world to you. But what you're looking for, you must seek yourself. ... I'm now by the sea. And if you want to be with me, bring your blanket to the beach ... Make your way to me, I have just as far to go to you! Every step I take in vain costs me time. It would be nice to see with you where the journey of life goes! If you don't come, I'll go alone - before it's too late for me ... what a mess!«

Just like Thomas, I hope for true love. The flirtation with him and the intense physical contact while dancing felt good to me, but there's nothing more there. The fact that he had the same perfume as my crush almost knocked me off my feet.

For today, she was too tired to continue thinking about the research project »how do men tick«. She went to bed. Tomorrow, she had to be back in old freshness and good spirits.

Roundtable discussion on the summer topic

The morning dawned. The sun emerged from behind the hotel complex, warming with its first rays and tickling Thomas' nose as he lay in bed.

As he got up, he thought about wanting to bring joy to Lydia, since she had supported him in his quest for clarity, but how? He put on his light blue jeans, a white shirt, and brown loafers. It surprised him a little that even on vacation, he shaved every day. A cloud of his aftershave surrounded him as he left his bungalow.

Thomas was keen to talk to Lydia about his current and past relationships, hoping that it would help him clarify what he wanted.

Lydia could empathize well with his quite different girlfriends and felt for them. Perhaps it was women's logic that a man wouldn't understand anyway!

After all, there were countless books about how women and men thought and acted differently. The man came from Mars and the woman from Venus. If people came together, it was because of sex, reproduction, or because they didn't want to be alone. His relationships were beautiful and exhilarating, but it became too stressful for Thomas under all circumstances.

He was starting to find it time-consuming, sometimes even annoying. It cost money, and the initial excitement gradually faded away. It was always exciting to get to know other women – and their bodies – intimately. It was nice to keep it casual, but it usually didn't stay that way.

Ultimately, it's nice to be able to enjoy everything with a woman, like his friend Ralf. Ralf had a charming wife, Constanze, and an adorable daughter – well, if only it were always so easy to find the right one! His friend was lucky. Ralf had met and fallen in love with her in the first semester at university, and she had been his constant ever since, as we jokingly called her.

Constanze looked fabulous, was intelligent, and they complemented each other. He also wanted a woman like Constanze. Ralf had an honest, profound relationship with her, often raved about her, and cherished her. He seemed balanced and happy.

Thomas was jealous of that. He observed when Ralf came to his office that he flirted with his assistant Monica. Ralf found her attractive, witty, and charming. A different type from his wife. But he would never seriously pursue anything with Monica or any other woman, as he loved Constanze.

Loyalty, love, and respect were important attributes in marriage for him, he always said. »Flirting is allowed… but meals are eaten at home.«

After breakfast, Thomas briefly considered what to do with the day.

He hadn't spotted Lydia. What a shame!

Then he remembered that today, on Sunday, the discussion group Lydia had told him about was supposed to take place.

He went to the information desk and looked at the bulletin board.

Immediately, he found the note.

»Discussion session on this year's summer theme: Loyalty

and Infidelity. Meeting point: Hotel beach café, Sunday from 10:30 a.m.«

»Exactly my topic,« thought Thomas, curious about what awaited him, and he set off.

As is customary, blue deck chairs and parasols were scattered around near the hotel's beach café. Those facing the lawn were occupied by some hotel guests.

Thomas took a seat on one of the deck chairs. He observed the others and greeted them with a smiling »Hello« to the group.

Therewere as many women as men present.

The entertainer distributed crepe tape. So that each guest could address the other by name, Thomas wrote his first name and stuck his name tag visibly on his shirt.

»Exactly the right topic for today,« Thomas said in a semi-loud voice, with a hint of irony in his tone, to the waiting group.

Patricia smiled at him with her big eyes. As the moderator, she sat in the middle of the circle on a chair. Her dark brown hair was tied back in a ponytail. Like all the entertainers, she wore dark blue shorts and a yellow polo shirt with the word »Animation« on it.

»Welcome to our circle. My name is Patricia, and I'm currently working on my master's thesis in psychology. Hence our topic today: fidelity and infidelity. The question is: Do men think about sex all the time? Do they cheat? How do we women feel about this topic? Is it better to go on vacation with your partner or with your lover?«

Patricia reclined in her beach chair, looking expectantly around the circle.

»Well then, fire away. I'm very curious,« Patricia said, encouraging the group to begin.

Next to Thomas sat Susan. She brushed her long blonde hair back with her right hand as she cleared her throat.

„I don‘t even know where to begin. I‘ve been wondering for a long time who defines and declares the rules of fidelity as valid. I‘m married and I promised my husband that I would always be there for him in good times and bad, and I am. „ Susan fiddled with her wedding ring with her fingers.

»Nevertheless, I didn‘t vow eternal fidelity to him. I think people evolve, and what fits today may be completely different tomorrow. However, I‘m against irresponsible one-night stands, and according to people, a bit of falling in love is required to engage in an affair. And what can you do against falling in love?! Sweating it out might be one way, but I believe that only leads to frustration. I would keep it to myself and add it to the other beautiful memories that one collects over the course of life.«

All eyes were on Susan as she shared her thoughts. Thomas found it interesting and listened intently to her.

»So just as you wouldn‘t tell a colleague out of tact that her new perm makes her look like a zombie, I wouldn‘t necessarily tell my husband that I‘m currently in the mood for something else. I don‘t like this double-edged hypocrisy. You don‘t have to live out every ego trip, you shouldn‘t lose sight of common interests, but in the end, you only have this one life, and it should be lived. If the butterflies flutter through your stomach again, then you should enjoy it quietly and take as much of it as you want. The women‘s quota among cheaters is steadily increasing. It‘s been a long time since it was solely a men‘s domain, but I think men are only slowly becoming aware of that now, aren‘t they?« She looked particularly at the men as she spoke.

Patricia and the others had listened attentively.

»Yes, you‘re right, Susan! There are more and more women who enjoy trying something new. That‘s why it‘s a very exciting and current topic. It‘s no longer just reserved for men. We women are right there with them,« Patricia responded.

Karin nodded in agreement. »I can only agree with every detail of what you said. However, one should never overestimate the whole thing. If one can, then one should separate desire and duty well. One should never take it for granted that there is someone else, but rather enjoy every minute.«

Patricia looked around the group. »Yes, now a man must take a stand on it! Please, Andy!«

Andy leaned forward. His short, light gray hair added to his allure. He wore a stylish pair of sunglasses and looked attractive for his age.

»If a man or a woman is unfaithful, the partner, if they ever find out, should ask themselves the question ‚Why?‘ Most of the time, one is ‚only‘ sexually unfaithful but still wants to stay with their partner. Sure, the allure of something new is tempting! Often, it‘s due to stale situations. The partner doesn‘t like this or that in bed, and so one seeks it elsewhere. That may be immoral. But what does immoral even mean? According to whose standards? Who sets the rules for morality? Fidelity is a delicate subject because everyone understands it differently. In any case, one should talk openly with their partner about it!«

Thomas could understand Andy well. He settled back comfortably to have a full view of everyone from his position.

Sandra, who was sitting directly in the lounge chair next to Andy, spoke up.

»That the concept of infidelity in general is always tied to sexuality, I already consider wrong. Without wanting to delve into the terms loyalty and infidelity here, because I think everyone knows what it means. In life, and especially in a partnership, things like love, trust, and reliability play an important role. I would include these aspects in the concept of loyalty.«

Sandra stretched out her long legs so that her tattoo could be seen clearly before continuing with her remarks.

»The sexuality can be directed towards one or more partners, without any of the mentioned three things needing to be present. So, anyone who has a casual relationship with one or more partners is making a deal, without being too offended if their partner does the same. If it bothers them, well, it‘s goodbye, and on to a new relationship!«

As she did so, she raised her right hand. In the background, there was murmuring of approval.

Someone opens a beverage can with a loud hiss, causing everyone to chuckle. Sandra looks annoyed at the person before continuing to speak and gesturing with her hands.

»If, however, I decide on a committed partnership, such as marriage or a similar relationship, and choose to be faithful in monogamy, to have no secrets from each other, and to support each other in difficult times, such as illness, poverty, and other challenges, then it‘s a different story. Because this often doesn‘t work out, many couples end up separating. The desire to engage in sexual relationships with other men or women surely exists in many partnerships, especially when expectations from one partner are not met or can no longer be met.«

Patricia looked interestedly over at her and made some notes. Andy and Susan, who were sitting next to each other, exchanged glances.

Sandra looked around the circle. Susan made circles in the sand with her feet, listening intently.

»If, however, in a partnership, one of the partners doesn‘t like this, for whatever reason, and the other one wants it, then the secrecy begins, the lies, the ugly suspicions, and with that, the breach of trust and the unreliability of the partner. That‘s the core of what we call infidelity. Most of the time, it‘s the secretary...!«

»So, about secretaries,« came the objection from Robert, who was wearing bright orange pants, »at least your own, I strongly advise against. They not only stop putting through calls from your girlfriends, but they might actively fight them off, for example, using your own schedule!!«

A few women whispered and giggled.

»Yes,« Patricia looked at Robert expectantly, »someone‘s speaking from personal experience. That can be relatable. It‘s quite fascinating to hear about your experiences!«

Thomas found it stimulating to hear the different opinions. Interested and eager, he sat on his lounge chair.

Patricia made eye contact with Uwe, who nervously tapped his feet. »Yes, Uwe, what do you have to say about the topic?«

Uwe ran his hand through his hair and cleared his throat.

»I think that when you're married, or let's say in a committed relationship, you should be faithful. For me, fidelity is about love. Whether I still love my partner, I decide that every day by standing by them. If I no longer love them, then I have to leave and stand by my feelings. But then I don't need to cheat.«

»Yes, that's true,« remarked Nadine, who had been silent until now but apparently hadn't missed a word. She was sitting next to Robert on a chair.

»I totally agree!«

She briefly touched her nose in embarrassment, as she wasn't used to being suddenly in the spotlight.

»If I love the other person, then loyalty is natural. Anything else isn't genuine love. In that case, it's better to end things. Just like Uwe sees it,« she said, smiling at him.

»That's more like it, that the person can't be alone. If you don't feel that the other person is our LOVE, then you should stay away. Being in bed with the wrong person is an emotionally costly affair, in the long run, it's not a trouble-free relationship. So, pay close attention to your feelings: Is this really the right partner? Then I can, or I am, loyal to him because I love him above all. It's that simple!«

Christian wore a light blue shirt. His blonde hair fell wildly onto his face. With his blue eyes, he looked expectantly at Patricia. Christian had been listening attentively the whole time, eager to finally express his opinion:

»It all depends on the circumstances you find yourself in. If you have a woman with whom you feel comfortable, in the broadest sense, and who appears to be faithful herself, perhaps a single affair could be forgiven. But if there are more, one should question whether it might have been better to remain single.«

Unexpectedly, a group of noisy children walked by with the

entertainer Tina. Tina waved apologetically to the group.

Christian waited until they were gone and continued speaking.

»Under certain circumstances, affairs can definitely be forgivable. It can spice up a relationship and even lead it out of crisis situations. It was the special moment or allure that led you astray, but the sexual aspect has nothing to do with deep love; it's purely physical.«

Andy's phone rang. Christian observed him as Andy took his phone out of his pocket, stood up, and moved away from the group while speaking.

Christian watched him as he continued speaking. »One should never confess to affairs! My experiences speak against it; such revelations burden a relationship. All in all, having an affair doesn't necessarily mean you're unfaithful!«

Patricia, holding her notepad on her knees, conceded, »With all affairs, one should protect oneself and, above all, one's partner, who usually knows nothing about it. Anything else is irresponsible!« She paused briefly, holding her pen to her mouth.

»…an unwanted child has already occurred. If one cheats, it must be with protection!« And she gestured with her pen, like a teacher addressing the group.

»Christian,« said Robert with a firm voice, who was sitting opposite Christian, »from your words, it sounds like occasionally it's permissible, but not always. As discussed here, there are many husbands who cheat regularly, some even with the knowledge of their wives, but otherwise the wife is better off not knowing anything about it. However, there's a big uproar if the woman does the same, suppose the man finds out. Of course, women can sometimes be very secretive. If it comes out, there's big trouble.«

Robert put on his sunglasses after the sun peeked through the umbrella.

»A friend of mine divorced his wife when he found out she had been unfaithful, even though he loved her very much.

When I told him, ‚Come on, Peter, if you still love her, why can‘t you forgive her? You‘ve been out with this and that woman several times yourself, you‘re no better,‘ his response was: ‚A man can do that, a woman can‘t!‘ What a ridiculous moral! I think this is nonsense! Love involves forgiveness.«

»I know a friend,« said Isolde, who had come with Robert, »who really wanted to have a child, but it never worked out with her husband. Out of sheer desperation, she placed a personal ad, something like: ‚Unfulfilled woman seeks man for intimate encounters.‘ It‘s hard to believe how men respond to that. She then met a nice man who met her criteria. He was educated, good-looking, and had a good character. After a short acquaintance, she decided to try to get pregnant by him. She met with him for several months, setting the time and place in a hotel. But unfortunately – or fortunately, as I see it – it was unsuccessful. What would have happened if it had worked? How could she have told her husband who the child was from? Certainly not from the Holy Spirit! There are various reasons why a woman cheats.«

Patricia rubbed her chin thoughtfully.

»I think not communicating with each other is often the key reason why a man or woman cheats in the first place. It should be possible to talk about your most intimate desires with your partner! Communication is very important. If that‘s not possible, there are always counselling services. Perhaps your friend could have adopted a child instead.«

Thomas sat tensely on his lounger, attentively following the discussion. As the various statements were made, he began to relax and found the courage to speak up.

Before he could say anything, Evelyn caught everyone‘s attention. She had long, curly blonde hair that cascaded over her shoulders, and she sat to Thomas‘s right.

»I think one should ask oneself: Where does infidelity begin? Is it cheating when you glance at another man? Or when you find someone attractive, meet them often, go out to eat, walk hand in hand, and even kiss them? I believe that‘s where a slight detachment from your own partner starts. Then, as Uwe just said, you should consider whether you still love your partner, or if you're looking for someone completely different.«

Evelyn played with her hair.

»Sometimes one doesn't even know it oneself, and a fling can be enlightening. Once I've realized that my partner is the one, I truly love, then that should remain unchanged. It becomes just a slip-up. Whether I confess this or not depends on how trustful the relationship is. I could tell my husband about it without him immediately filing for divorce,« Evelyn said, glancing at her friend Nadine, with whom she was vacationing here.

Patricia nodded, then she looked at Nadine, who was sitting next to Evelyn. Nadine glanced around the circle.

»As I mentioned earlier, I believe that anyone can be faithful if they are happy and feel desirable and sexually fulfilled in their relationship. It's only when one of these components is lacking or so severely affected that one seeks validation elsewhere that infidelity begins, and it's then not far from the breakdown of the actual relationship unless it's professionally addressed with outside help. I was able to save my relationship through couples counselling. I was surprised at how spontaneously my husband agreed to participate. For that, I thank him.«

Andy returned from his phone call and sat back down in his seat next to Susan.

Pierre, sitting next to Nadine, had been observing everything and spoke up.

»I don't think fidelity and infidelity are the issue here; it should be more about how I can best please my partner, and with what?«

This view caught Patricia's attention, and she began taking notes eagerly.

»Being happy is having a partner in the first place, and that's something we should take seriously and not for granted.

Just as seriously as our own happiness. In a way, we even owe it to our partners that we are happy ourselves. Because when we are happy, our partner is happy, after all, our happiness reflects onto our partner.«

It seems like Patricia was listening attentively. The group nodded in agreement. Thomas found it excellent to consider the various viewpoints.

»It's going well for all of us. Only when we lose our beloved partner, be it through separation or even death, do we realize - unfortunately often too late - that we were very happy together. When we ourselves are happy and know the feeling of happiness or contentment, we are only able to evoke this feeling in our partner. That's true love. I assume that one married their partner out of love and not for other reasons.«

Thomas was all ears, especially regarding the significance of »true love.« He overheard one of the guests telling another that Pierre is an expert in the field and knows what he's talking about.

»A relationship takes effort. I don't like the word ‚effort.' What I mean is, it doesn't just fall into your lap. Why shouldn't you involve your partner in everything you do? Only then do you understand the complete happiness of a relationship. I'm talking about intense communication, exchanging feelings and thoughts. I completely agree with the words of the previous speakers,« he said, making eye contact with Nadine and Evelyn.

»If I'm not willing to do that, my partner may not even know what I need, what I'm missing, or what makes me happy. Even after years in a relationship, you can't read your partner's mind,« he added.

Pierre looked around the group, and the two friends who were whispering to each other immediately stopped, feeling caught.

»Furthermore, behaviours change over time and with increasing age. Therefore, intensive communication and engagement with our partner are indispensable.«

Uwe nodded in agreement.

»So, our partner feels blessed when we give them attention or affection. It cannot be that one cheats, as it ruins the relationship. It breaks trust and destroys love. People need social recognition, affection, affirmation, love – plus sex, to be happy. This is especially true in times of uncertainty, or when a change is imminent, be it in career or personal life. When children come into the picture or leave the nest, a relationship undergoes exceptional changes. We hunger for a loving relationship, for beloved partners, wives, children, for a place in the family. Who doesn't yearn for love and a wonderful partnership, characterized by harmony and a hint of adventure?« With a smile and a grateful wave, he looked around the group.

Spontaneously, some guests applauded.

»Thank you, Pierre, for this insightful contribution!«

»Indeed, considering the time, I can only take one more comment,« Patricia said, glancing briefly at her watch.

Nadine also glanced at the clock and nudged her friend, prompting Evelyn to leave. As they got up, they briefly bid farewell and hurried away from the group toward the main entrance.

After everyone had the opportunity to contribute to the discussion, Thomas raised his hand to say something in conclusion.

Patricia smiled at him. »I see a raised hand, please go ahead, Thomas, you have the floor!«

Thomas straightened up.

»I believe that Pierre's question ‚How can I best delight my partner, and with what?!' has been very aptly portrayed. Discrepancies arise when moral values drift apart, when values do not match, and when communication is lacking. These should be disclosed by both partners. Therefore, it's important to discuss in the relationship how to handle such situations. Apparently, achieving complete happiness in a relationship requires some work,« Thomas said, grinning at Pierre.

Patricia stood up.

»Indeed, that was a concluding statement. Thank you, Thomas! I want to extend my heartfelt thanks for this incredibly enlightening discussion and hope it has helped you all progress a bit—or at the very least, prompted some reflection. Personally, I've enjoyed it, and I appreciate everyone contributing to this intriguing topic of fidelity and infidelity. Thank you for your attention!«

All applauded and expressed their gratitude. Slowly, the guests rose from their seats. Some stretched, while others immediately started to walk away.

Patricia called out to the group, »So, what's next on the agenda? First, let's have some food, and after the siesta, we'll continue with beach volleyball at 3 o'clock with Alex and me. You're all welcome to join.«

Pierre turned to Patricia and handed her his business card, mentioning that if she needed any support for her master's thesis, she should contact him. He was a trained psychologist and found her work commendable.

Thomas settled comfortably into his lounge chair under the umbrella, deep in thought. He didn't feel unfaithful; after all, he maintained relationships with everyone.

Pierre was right about true love and being loyal to that person. But which of his women was the TRUE LOVE?! He had to figure this out by the end of his vacation.

Lydia had been a great help to him. Undoubtedly, it had been a great tip from Lydia to participate in this discussion round. Seeing how others were doing was invaluable.

He closed his eyes and lingered in his thoughts. He felt a pleasant sensation and a perfume in the air. Someone was emitting a pleasant flow of energy. He opened his eyes, and there stood Lydia before him.

In the first moment, the sunlight was so bright that he shielded his eyes with his hand.

»Hello, Lydia. Nice to see you! I didn't expect to run into you. Although I must admit, I've missed you. It's even more delightful to see you.«

Lydia grinned at him and looked at him expectantly. »I hope you had a pleasant evening and an engaging discussion this morning?«

»Oh yes,« Thomas grinned.

»I can't complain. Last night was very enjoyable. I haven't had that much fun in a long time. Thank you, Lydia!«

»No problem,« Lydia said, running her fingers through her hair.

»I spent last night with a very charming young woman. She's simply unbeatable, as she immediately gave me the tip to participate in this discussion round ‚How do I envision my dream relationship‘,« Thomas said.

He took a seat and gestured for Lydia to sit as well. Lydia pulled a lounge chair closer to him and took a seat opposite him.

»As I can see, my student has obediently followed my advice. And have you made any progress in terms of relationships?«

»I must say, the discussion round was highly interesting. But before I continue, my stomach could use a little something. How about you?«

»Yeah, great. I'm starving. Then that was a good tip from me. I'm curious.«

They walked over to the beach café and grabbed some food and drinks. Together, they strolled to the nearest bench and sat downside by side.

»And are you a faithful or unfaithful tomato?« Lydia asked Thomas.

»Well, hard to say! The situation I'm in wasn't discussed today. I'm in three relationships at the same time – does that count as cheating? I think I'm faithful to the relationships. Overall, a little affair isn't that serious. It's just physical, you know! But I love Margit, Carmen, and Ute. With Doreen, it's more of a friends-with-benefits situation. Although that's truly enjoyable. However, if I think about it longer, I haven't seen or heard from Doreen in two months.«

»Are you just realizing this now? After all this time thinking about it?!« She looked at him incredulously.

»Well, I'm constantly on the move, so I lose track of time. Here today, gone tomorrow, barely in one place before I'm off again! That's how my life goes. Lately, I've been working for two, so I haven't had any time for anyone or anything else.«

Thomas stared ahead. »Oh, just taking a vacation alone is really something. The last trip was almost a disaster.«

»Where were you? And with whom?« Lydia took a bite of her baguette and looked challengingly at Thomas.

»I was in Mexico last year with Margit. It was a hell of a trip.«

»Why Margit? And what about Carmen? Have you been on vacation with Margit more often or not?«

Thomas and Lydia were repeatedly greeted by hotel guests coming from the beach and passing by them. Thomas felt honored that some of them addressed him by name from the morning session. Lydia took note of it.

»I told Carmen first that I had to go to America for work. She understood. Being the head of the department, I can arrange my vacation whenever I want, sometimes very spontaneously. I just need to clear it with the top boss. Of course, I schedule my vacation so that Carmen is busy herself, so she couldn't come along. It was staged by me that she couldn't take a vacation at short notice. With Margit, it was planned long in advance. It was supposed to be an adventure trip through Mexico.«

Lydia made a face and asked incredulously, »With Margit, an adventure trip? After everything you've told me, I can't imagine that at all.« Lydia looked at him in astonishment.

»Oh, really? Well, we had plenty of adventures. We traveled across Mexico with the Rolling Hotel. Have you heard of it?

Those are those red buses with sleeping cabins attached, quite adventurous. It was organized down to the smallest detail. We flew from Frankfurt via Paris to Mexico City and then to Cancun. Everything was fine until we arrived at the Cancun airport at two in the morning, and her suitcase was missing.«

»No, that's a disaster!« Lydia covered her mouth with her hand.

»Yeah, exactly! And from then on, the dilemma with her began. She had hardly any belongings, just her backpack. Thank goodness, she had a few clothes in there. It was really unfortunate! You can't imagine. Margit made a huge fuss when she saw the small cabins where we were supposed to sleep on the first evening. Ours was one in the middle, so she didn't have to climb too much. Each had a small window on the outside of the bus, which you could open with a small curtain in front of it. She calmed down immediately because we got a double cabin, and I thought we had plenty of space for 1.40 meters width. It was hot, and she complained that I was too close to her.«

Thomas shook his head at the thought.

Lydia had to laugh inwardly but remained serious towards Thomas. She thought to herself, »I wouldn't have gone on an adventure trip with Margit; she was the wrong type for that. Men never seem to understand which woman is best suited for which vacation. If you have a few options to choose from... I would have taken Carmen. Mexico is beautiful!«

»The worst part for me, you can't imagine, was when we were at a campsite, and she hates camping. I didn't know that, otherwise I wouldn't have done the tour with the Rolling Hotel with her. On the first day, there was the shopping spree. She needed everything new. The tour guide helped with everything – without him, I would have had a nervous breakdown.«

Now Lydia couldn't hold back her laughter any longer.

»I can't believe it. You really have it tough. One thing I don't understand: If you choose a country like Mexico, want to have an adventure vacation there, and you have the choice between three women, why did you choose Margit?«

Thomas looked at her with a puzzled expression.

»Why not? I thought it would be fine. After all, it wasn't a hut-to-hut trek in the Himalayas, but a bus tour, especially suggested by her friend. She's a different type though. I have to admit, I just booked it without really knowing what I was getting into, as did Margit.«

Lydia shook her head.

»How could you just book a vacation like that?« She gestured incredulously with her hands.

»Well, if someone suggests something to me and thinks it's great, I don't ask too many questions. I'm easy-going. I can sleep anywhere, and I want to see a lot of the country without spending hours in the car driving myself.«

»But camping wasn't Margit's thing, was it?« Lydia asked cynically.

»Where did you hear that from? Did I already tell you?! That's right. Thank goodness it was a tour with some hotels, so we could occasionally book an extra room instead of sleeping in the bus hotel. That was an extra cost. The beds weren't any better, but at least we could sleep together. In one hotel, she had a fit because she had no space to put her suitcase at the foot of the bed. The room was so small that you could fall directly into the bed. Other than that, everything was great.«

»How long were you in Mexico and where did you go?«

Lydia was interested in learning more about this colourful country. So far, she hadn't managed to fly there herself. Even more impressive to her was how Thomas told her about his adventure vacation. If she had gone with him, he would have had less stress. He just had the wrong woman with him ...

»As I said, it was a fantastic tour. If you stick to the schedule tightly, you can see everything in 15 days. We went from Cancún to Campeche, Oaxaca, and then to Mexico City. It was amazing. I recommend you check it out if you travel to Mexico.«

Lydia nodded. »What did you visit? Did you go to Chichén Itzá too?« She looked at him eagerly.

Thomas enthusiastically recounted his trip.

»We first explored the Mayan ruins at Tulum and were able to swim in the Caribbean Sea. After soaking up so much culture, adjusting to the time difference, and traveling, we were glad to enjoy the sunset on the Caribbean coast at Playa del Carmen. From there, we ventured through the rainforest to Chichén Itzá. Then, we traveled through the state of Yucatan, passing through Mayan villages to the state of Campeche and the coast of the Gulf of Mexico. From San Cristóbal, we explored the mountainous landscape of Chiapas, the land of the Tzotil and Chamula Indians.«

Lydia was impressed and listened attentively.

»The route continued from San Cristóbal to Oaxaca. It was a beautiful landscape of cactus valleys, often referred to as the dream road of the world. Absolutely stunning! And of course, we had to try the Mezcal!«

»What is that?« Lydia asked.

»Mezcal is distilled from agave in the Mexican highlands. There's a worm in every bottle,« Thomas explained.

Lydia grimaced at that.

»I drank a glass with a worm in it and got a hat as a reward for my courage! Margit hated it, but you couldn't taste the worm at all. It was just a weird thought, eating a worm. There are huge fields of agave plants. In Monte Alban, we learned about the Zapotec cultures.«

»Man, you know a lot and remember a lot. I would be completely confused with all those Zapotec cultures, ascetics, pharmacies, and discos,« Lydia joked, laughing.

»Margit is very well-read. Sometimes it's terrible! It was fortunate that the tour guide could tell us a lot and answer all her questions,« Thomas grinned.

»Yeah, it was quite a packed itinerary! We tried to see as much as possible during our time there,« Thomas replied.

Thomas was completely in his element.

»The Popocatépetl volcano was cloudless. Simply fantastic! The sites are very impressive and extensive, so good footwear is important. It's really amazing to think about what human hands have created. In the end, we spent two more days in Mexico City before boarding the flight back home.«

»My goodness, it sounds absolutely beautiful. Mexico! All the places you've been. Fantastic! Thomas, I envy you, I would have loved to join you on that trip. It's no wonder you know so much, with all your travels and experiences with different cultures. An adventure trip is an experience, isn't it? Hats off to you, Margit had quite an extraordinary vacation with you! Except for the camping story, everything else seems to have turned out wonderfully.«

Thomas drank his water and placed the bottle on the ground.

»That's what I mean. I wouldn't have the time to organize such a trip myself, it's better to travel with a tour group. Otherwise, we had disagreements from time to time, but overall, it was a beautiful journey.«

»I'm thrilled. The trip was last spring, and now you're only going on vacation again!« sighed Lydia.

»Yes, usually after such a trip, you need another vacation right away. You spend the whole day on the bus and get culturally enriched. But that wasn't possible. Only now am I taking a relaxing vacation. It's a change of scenery, for a specific reason, as you know, to get clarity in my relationship situation. I wouldn't have minded if everything had just continued. But after Ute broke up with me and I don't get along with Margit one hundred percent, plus the stress at work, I got scared. I don't want to end up alone later without a woman by my side! That makes you think. And I'm getting older, not younger. Plus, I'm worried about my work. Not everything is going smoothly. It would be more stressful without my great team. It's one thing after another.«

Lydia looked at him sympathetically.

»Man, you poor thing! Is it all piling up on you right now? Relationship stress, and then work stress on top of that. Ooooh – a round of sympathy,« she said, patting his shoulder.

»Thomas looked puzzled. Was Lydia making fun of him? He glanced at her with a serious expression and continued.«

»Yes, that adds to the difficulty. Slowly, I don't know where my head is anymore. I'm glad to have such an assistant as Monica.«

Lydia took a sip from her bottle.

»Does she support you in your work?«

»Of course! She does everything. Monica supports me in all my endeavors, creates presentations, researches new topics, and does acquisition. Without her, I'd be really lost, and of course without my secretary, who coordinates all my appointments.«

Suddenly, Thomas fell silent and stared into space.

Lydia looked at him intently, wondering where his thoughts had wandered off to. Something seemed to have triggered him during the reflection on Monica.

After a short pause, he continues, »In principle, Monica organizes all the tasks in the office. She contacts the clients and handles the acquisitions, which are crucial in this business. She revises my marketing concepts and provides input and ideas.«

He touches his head.

»Man, and here I am attending the seminar on ‚The Employee of the Future‘ and I completely overlook that without my loyal assistant Monica, nothing runs smoothly! I haven't paid her enough attention. I haven't thanked her for the documents she prepared for me so quickly for the meeting last Thursday. Well! Hmm, and I've turned off WhatsApp now. I'm on vacation.«

»Well, if she can support and relieve you in all areas, that's worth a lot,« said Lydia.

Thomas nodded in agreement.

»Lydia, it's just hitting me now how utterly dependent I am on my assistant. I can't believe I didn't realize this sooner. Essentially, I'm just the face of things. I'm the star getting all the credit, while she does all the real work behind the scenes. And I don't even praise her for her outstanding performance!«

Angry at himself, Thomas stomped his foot on the ground. Lydia tapped him on the shoulder as he stood up.

»Yeah, realization is the first step to improvement. Hey, I've got to go, my next activity is calling. I've got kids club this afternoon.«

Thomas hung his head low.

»Oh, too bad I'm not a kid anymore. I'll head down to the beach. See you later.«

Lydia headed to the Kids' Club. Since it wasn't vacation time, there were few children. Most of them participated in the morning care, and in the afternoon, they played on the beach with their parents. After half an hour passed with no children arriving, Lydia closed the Kids' Club and went down to the beach.

Lydia greeted a few guests as she looked for Thomas. Sometimes, she found it fascinating to immerse herself in someone else's life. Now, she wanted to know what was next for Thomas.

When she spotted him on the sun lounger, she walked straight to him. She stopped in front of his sun lounger.

»Would you like an ice cream too?«

Thomas looked at her in surprise. »Back already?«

»Yes, unfortunately no children showed up. So, I'm back. You won't get rid of me that easily,« Lydia replied with a smile.

Thomas blinked over his sunglasses.

»Oh, I didn't mean to get rid of you either. Thanks for letting me selfishly enjoy your company,« Thomas replied.

Lydia gestured with her outstretched arm towards Jorge.

»I'm craving a big ice cream with lots of fruit and plenty of whipped cream. Shall we sit at Jorge's and have one? He has the best ice cream, and of course baguettes, but we already had those today.«

Thomas welcomed this decision.

He stood up, grabbed his backpack, and they walked over to the beach café. Lydia ordered a large sundae with lots of exotic fruits, while Thomas opted for a small cup.

On the terrace, there was thankfully space in the shade of a parasol. They sat facing each other. It was hot again in the sun today, so a refreshing ice cream worked wonders.

While enjoying their ice cream, Lydia thought about Mexico. »Last spring, you were in Mexico with Margit. Where else have you been on vacation with each of your women?«

Lydia glanced over to the neighbouring table where a child had spilled its glass. The mother quickly jumped up to put the glass back in place and avoid getting dirty.

Thomas followed her gaze.

»Nun, I only went on vacation with Carmen and Margit. Not with Doreen, no question about it! With Ute, I always wanted to, but it never really worked out. She simply had too much work and no time. Because whenever she had time, I was already committed with Margit or Carmen.«

Lydia glanced over at him.

»That's a shame! Wasn't Ute disappointed?«

Thomas leaned his elbow on the table and rested his head on his hands. He had already finished his ice cream.

»She might have been disappointed. Out of frustration, she went on vacation alone with her friend during the summer. And when I was away for several weeks again, she bought herself a watch for comfort. She said she could delight in this beautiful watch and that time would pass a bit faster, but it would surely make time more beautiful until I came back.«

»A real romantic, your Ute!«

Lydia caught a dripping drop of ice cream with her tongue. She was curious. »Where did you go with Carmen?«

»Oh, Carmen and I are pure adventurers. I feel like a teenager, like I'm twenty again,« Thomas replied.

Lydia became attentive. »Like when you were twenty? What did you two get up to?« She leaned in towards him.

Thomas laughed. »What do you do for a holiday when you're twenty? You go camping. Last summer, Carmen and I went to Normandy. Packed everything into her camper van, and off we went! That's romance and adventure at its finest.

Oh, it brings back memories of my old scouting days, and with Carmen, I can relive them! Isn't that wonderful?«

»Yes, I used to go camping at that time, but not anymore. If I were to experience nature again, I'd prefer a bit more comfort. But go ahead, tell me about Carmen.«

Thomas leaned back again, crossing his legs.

»It's always a blast when I'm on tour with Carmen. We make a great team. I drive, and she takes care of the food.«

He chuckled at the thought.

»We drove along the coast and settled in at a nice spot that we liked. That's the beauty of it! You can decide freely how long you want to stay at a campsite, otherwise you just move on.«

»Do you cook yourselves, or do you go out to eat?« She pushed her empty ice cream cup to the centre of the table.

»Oh, Carmen is an excellent cook. Italian pasta always tastes good. You must know how to help yourself. I find it great to make a campfire in the evenings with the other campers. I could stare into the fire for hours. Occasionally, I bring my guitar on trips, and then we sing campfire songs.«

Lydia marvelled. »Wow, what mega things you do! How long have you been playing guitar?«

»Oh, since I was about twelve years old. It's fun, especially because it's very social and attracts people,« replied Thomas.

He grinned. »Especially women.«

Lydia laughed. »Are you trying to be the king?«

»No, I don't think so,« Thomas replied.

»It's strange, isn't it? You're away for a few weeks, barely back home, and the routine sets in again. Kind of a shame! Do you have any ideas on how to maintain that holiday mood all the time?«

Lydia looked at him. »I think you have that holiday mood when it's warm, the sun is shining, and you're near water. For me, it's simple. I don't know exactly why, but I don't have that problem.«

She raised her arms up, made a half-circle motion, and laughed.

»Haha, sure, you always have that vacation vibe when you work at a holiday destination, but you won't stay here forever, right? So, what will you do to capture those experiences and memories? That's what I want to know.«

»Yeah, that's definitely a valid question. One possibility could be to create a certain mood through typical music, then maybe use vacation photos, souvenirs, etc., to reinforce the memories.«

»Yeah, that sounds pretty good already. But there must be something else.«

Lydia shrugged. »I don't know. It's difficult to bring home all the different things, impressions, and experiences so that they continue to be present there. You could cook various exotic dishes at home, but it will never be the same as being there, or it tastes completely different. The landscape, the people, the food, the culture, even the air is different there. You can't really bring the beach and the sea home with you. I find it sad when my time here is up, and I have to go back home, especially when winter is starting again for us.«

She grimaced. »I think I'll hang up an oversized poster of my most beautiful sunset to capture the mood.«

Thomas scratched his neck and contemplated.

»Hey, do you have to work tonight? I hope not, then we can keep chatting.«

Indignantly, she responds to him. »I always have to work and take care of the guests' well-being. What am I doing right now? I'm taking care of your well-being so you can go home worry-free. That's the beauty of my job.« And tiring, she added in her thoughts.

Both sat on the terrace, looking down at the beach from the hotel premises.

On Sundays, many locals were out and about, and it was bustling with activity. Most guests wanted peace and quiet. A group was playing bocce, while other hotel guests were playing beach volleyball with the locals, alongside Tina and Alex.

»Something else, Thomas! You told me yesterday about this shoe-thinking model of the Indians. In connection with how you met Margit.«

»Hmm, I did, and what about it now?«

Thomas gestured to order a coffee. In the background, the music was turned up. Some guests pushed tables and chairs to the side and danced. Two older couples moved rhythmically to the music.

Lydia briefly observed the scene as the waiter served the coffee, then turned back to Thomas.

»Actually, one could apply this to any problem. Why not also to your relationship crisis? To the fundamental decision of which woman is right for you.«

Lydia provocatively looked at him.

Thomas was curious about what Lydia was about to say as she continued to develop her thought.

»Let's say you put on the summer shoe! If I remember correctly, it's yellow. Then this shoe represents sunshine and optimism and helps you see the advantages of a situation. Which of your women, quite rationally, brings you the greatest advantage?«

Thomas shook his head, dropped a sugar cube into his coffee, stirred slowly, and set the spoon aside.

»Indeed, you've remembered quite well what I've told you. I haven't looked at my relationships from that perspective yet.«

He took a big sip of coffee.

»For me, it's always sunshine, no matter which of my women I see. They're always in a good mood, and so am I. Hm, when I really think about it, there's no financial advantage with any of them anyway. They all earn quite well, just like me. So, I'm absolutely independent in that regard.«

He set his cup down and pondered.

»It's hard to say which of my women brings me the greatest advantage. I don't know. They're all optimists, love life, are in good spirits, and all three have equally good ideas, so honestly,

I wouldn't know.«

His gaze wandered out to sea. On the horizon, a large steamer sailed by.

Lydia absentmindedly scratched her left upper arm. It seemed she had been bitten by a mosquito, but she didn't pay it much attention.

»Ah, it seems your relationships are more complex than I thought. Somehow all your women seem very similar to me. You must have a thing for the same type, huh? So, they all seem to be favourable to you, and there's no significant difference. Okay, let's accept that for now. Let's move on to the green hiking shoe! That represents creativity, new proposals, ideas, suggestions, growth, energy, and life. Right?«

He nodded in surprise.

»Absolutely right! I'm amazed at how well you've remembered everything in such a short time. But as for my women, I have to say that they're all very creative.«

Lydia countered, »That can't be right, Thomas! There must be some differences, otherwise we'll be just as clueless tomorrow as we are today. Isn't Carmen more creative than Ute? Or than Margit? Go into detail!«

Thomas furrowed his brow.

»I don't know. Carmen is very creative when it comes to writing texts. Margit always has good ideas when I'm not sure what else to include in presentations. Ute paints pictures and is unbeatable in the architectural field. Even Doreen is creative in her own way, with her fashion. They all contribute to my creativity, without a doubt. When I'm searching for a new topic, I call Ute and Margit, who are more than willing to share their ideas with me.«

He took another sip of coffee.

»Furthermore, Carmen always supports me. Since she is nearby, she often prepares presentations for me or helps with the elaboration. She is a great help. She keeps track of all my appointments, only the travel ones though. But of course, Carmen doesn't know everything. She is also very busy with her job, and in the evenings, she's out with her horse. Sometimes that annoys me.«

»Why? Isn't it normal to work overtime in one's job? Or spend time with one's horse?« Lydia wanted to know. She works more than eight hours every day. And listening to the guests' joys and sorrows for hours can be exhausting at times.

»Carmen often works on Saturdays and Sundays. It wasn't like that before; we used to spend more time together. Suddenly, our weekends together became less frequent. Now we only meet on some evenings, mostly on Thursdays and Fridays.«

Thomas looked at her, concerned. »Lydia, what's wrong? You seem a bit confused.«

»Could it be that you didn't have time on weekends at some point? You must have a lot to do, like organizing marketing events, preparations, etc. They often take place on weekends, don't they?«

»Sure! There was a time when there were many marketing presentations that took place on weekends and were also further away.« Thomas nodded in agreement.

»Then you wonder why Carmen might have eventually thrown herself more into her work? That's obvious. If a man doesn't have time for someone, then a woman finds another occupation. Unlike men, women at least still concern themselves with fundamental things,« Lydia remarked somewhat sarcastically.

»If women were neglecting their men, it would be a different story,« Thomas replied.

»Aha, how so?« Thomas asked, surprised.

»It's obvious! Either men are sitting in front of the TV, in the pub, or having fun with another woman,« Lydia replied.

She was right, thought Thomas. Some men don't even notice when their wife is absent. It's true that he had neglected Carmen. During the week, he had a lot to do, and also on weekends. He understood that. In reality, he was fortunate to have Carmen. While his work sometimes overwhelmed him, he often socialized with others. Despite spending little time with Carmen, she remained loyal to him. Instead of looking for another man who had more time, she also threw herself into work and was very successful in her job. No one could match her. This, in turn, filled him with pride to have such a successful career woman as his girlfriend!

»Who knows, maybe Carmen is having an affair,« joked Lydia, but Thomas was startled and snapped out of his thoughts.

»Carmen, having an affair? I don't believe it, no! Absolutely absurd!« He finished his coffee.

»Who knows? What you can do, women can do too, when suddenly they don't have time for you,« she teased him, leaning back.

Thomas became thoughtful. Could Lydia be right, and Carmen had a lover beside him? This thought hadn't occurred to him before. But on the other hand, he couldn't imagine it with his Carmen, not in the slightest. No, she was faithful!

»Carmen is fine and a faithful woman. She's ambitious. Within a year, she's worked her way up to the top.«

»I'm saying exactly that. Women usually dive into their careers when things aren't going well with the man. As long as there's no family planning coming from your side, or if you block it otherwise, women seek fulfilment and validation in their jobs.«

Thomas remained silent, affected by Lydia's words, and pondered what could have triggered Carmen's behavior. He couldn't think of anything. »She's a real career woman,« he said, sounding lost.

Lydia leaned forward again and slapped the table with her hand in confirmation.

»Alright, then we got that sorted. Carmen is definitely a career woman whom you value highly. Margit and Ute are also holding their own.«

Thomas nodded in agreement and looked at her. Their attention was diverted by loud applause and cheering. The two older couples from the dance floor sat down to take a break from dancing. The man was attentive to his wife, and both were brimming with fun and energy.

After observing the dancers, Lydia's gaze returned to Thomas. She leaned towards him and spoke almost in a whisper.

»Let's continue with our shoe models. Let's say we're going barefoot, which represents emotions, sensations, feelings, etc. Hmm, now comes a very intimate question, but with whom do you prefer to be with and have sex with? That's an important factor for you men, isn't it?«

Thomas raised his eyebrow. »Am I supposed to answer that? Of course, sex is important. Very important, and it has to be right.«

Thomas spoke openly about this topic.

»Well, Carmen and Margit aren't exactly enthusiastic about sex. I mean, they enjoy it, but it's more or less the usual routine. Margit is even more modest, once a month is enough for her. But then there's my dear Doreen, who takes care of that.«

»You mean, she takes care of your unsatisfied desires?« Lydia admitted, playing with her earring.

Thomas cleared his throat.

»Doreen is simply a sex goddess. It's a lot of fun. She manages her child and her professional independence remarkably well. Hats off to her, as a single parent! She's a passionate woman in bed. I'd like to do more with her: movies, theatre, etc., but she's not into a serious relationship, just a passionate affair.«

»That's even a bit unusual for me. Doreen is an intelligent, attractive woman. She's great, feels good, and you can talk openly about everything with her. But unfortunately, she doesn't want anything serious.«

At the neighbouring table, a middle-aged couple sat down. They greeted the two with a smile.

Lydia was astonished. »Are there women who only want

sex and nothing else from a man? On the other hand, it doesn't surprise me. What's the use of a man anyway? Nowadays, as a woman, you must do everything yourself: build shelves, wallpaper, handle a drill, mow the lawn, earn your own money. When you really need a man for something substantial, he's either not there, or he's suddenly too busy. Thomas, what does a woman need a man for? Except for tender moments together?«

Thomas pondered. His gaze wandered over the premises, observing the couples and how they interacted with each other.

From all the talking, they had developed a dry mouth and ordered a large bottle of water, which the waiter promptly brought over.

»Your relationships are strange, don't you think? You have Carmen, Margit, and Ute, who love you and want to share everything with you, whom you don't really love, and then there's Doreen, who doesn't want you, whom you want to have.«

Lydia shook her head.

»Men are like little children, they only want what they can't have. Or boys never become real men, just better toys! Doreen just turned the tables. Now she takes men the way she needs them. Well, life is sometimes strange. How is the sex with Ute? Come on, spill the beans!«

Lydia wanted to know everything in detail. To cool down, they drank the cold water.

»Ute is adventurous. She's open to everything, whether I come up with tantra or try a new position from the Kama Sutra!« Thomas smiled slyly.

Lydia became attentive. »You seem to me like a wonderful specimen of a man who enjoys trying new things. Am I right? Speaking of which, do you have a preference for special places or even a favourite place?«

Thomas glanced at her appraisingly from the side.

»It seems to me that I have an expert sitting next to me here. You don't seem to be entirely ‚without,‘ am I right?« He flirted with her.

Lydia hesitated. »No, I... - oh well! Alright, I'm not a blank slate, that's true. But that's beside the point here, as it's about you.«

She laughed at him as their eyes met.

»Too bad, one less alternative! Where were we? My favourite places? Where one can engage in all sorts of activities,« said Thomas, looking at Lydia with a wide grin.

»In the bathtub, in bed, on the couch. The floor carpet can be hard on the back, depending on who's underneath, and the other might end up with sore knees. So, the desk seems more appealing, or on a chair, there are plenty of options. I've heard sitting on the washing machine can be quite appealing for the woman, is that true?« He looked at Lydia questioningly.

She laughed. »Oh really?! But only during the spin cycle.« Then she became serious again. »No, honestly, I have no idea!«

She tried to get some air by waving her T-shirt. Restlessness spread; the dance group seemed to be saying goodbye. Chairs were shuffled around, air kisses exchanged, and the group dispersed.

As it became quieter, Thomas turned to Lydia with confidence.

»Well, I prefer it most in summer, on a green meadow. That's where I get the best ideas,« Thomas said.

Lydia raised an eyebrow. »Oh really? Like what, for example?«

»If you're lying there on a big picnic blanket, the sun shining, holding your girlfriend in your arms, that's something fine!«

He sighed and stretched his arms upwards to stretch.

»Which girlfriend? Come on, don't keep me in suspense! And where exactly?«

»My goodness, you're not curious at all! Why do you want to know every little detail?! Well then, I guess I'll have to tell you all about it in vivid detail,« Thomas chuckled mischievously.

»Of course, what else!« She leaned forward.

Thomas continued to indulge in his explanations. »In the summer, I like to go swimming at a gravel pit. It's wonderfully refreshing. Depending on which of my dear friends is with me, things can be quite civilized or not at all. With Margit, I don't go to the gravel pit, we're more likely to go to the public pool.«

»That doesn't surprise me; I didn't expect anything else from Margit. She's a bit particular. Not a big deal, just an observation!«

Thomas frowned. »Don't interrupt me constantly. I was just about to tell you that I enjoy going swimming at the gravel pit with Carmen or Ute.«

Lydia felt scolded, as if by her mother, and pouted for a moment.

He waited until he had her full attention.

»With Ute, it was the best. She didn't mind, later after sunbathing, finding a spot on a meadow... And then one thing led to another. You know...«

Lydia looked at Thomas with wide eyes. »Tell me more.«

Thomas didn't need to be told twice. »We would find a secluded spot in the greenery or elsewhere, but always in the sunlight. Sometimes, even a stubble field had to do.«

»A stubble field pricks, though.« Lydia grimaced.

»Doesn't matter. We spread out our red-green checkered picnic blanket and lay down. Ute could undress so charmingly. That really got me going. I, on the other hand, always undressed quickly.«

Thomas almost said it in defence. »But men never wear as much as women do. Then we made love shamelessly in the setting sun, forgetting everything around us.«

Lydia nodded. »How romantic!«

»Come on, you've surely done something like that too. And - how was it for you? What's your story? Hey, tell me something about you! I'm curious!«

Thomas rocked back and forth on his chair, shifting from one side to the other.

Lydia became embarrassed. »As for me? The grass was green, the sky was blue, and the man was horny,« she laughed.

He looked at her with puppy dog eyes. »But seriously, I've been talking about myself this whole time, and I haven't heard anything about you.«

She sat up straight, her expression turning serious.

»There are a few stories, and it's tempting to lie in the sun and make love. Just like skinny dipping in the lake! But this isn't about me, it's about you, and figuring out which woman you want to be with.«

»Looks like my Lydia isn't prudish. I like that! Okay, you're right, primarily it's about me!«

For a moment, Lydia was lost in her thoughts. Then she looked directly into Thomas's eyes.

»Have you ever taken nude photographs of your girlfriends?«

»Of course! No question about it! Carmen wasn't open to it at first, but eventually she came around. With Doreen, it was a blast. She really enjoyed posing in front of the camera. Even with Ute, we could spontaneously pack up the photography gear and head out into nature. Amazing pictures! It's incredible what I can do with Ute that I can't with the others!« He shook his head in amazement.

As they sat comfortably, they ordered a strawberry milkshake. Today, they seemed to be regulars, but they weren't the only ones. The young couple at the next table had been there just as long.

»From Margit, you probably couldn't take any nude photos, at most in a swimsuit, right?« Lydia's question sounded somewhat ironic.

The waiter brought the drinks with a smile.

»They certainly have their charm, no doubt about it! Sad but true, I'm not with Ute anymore,« Thomas bit his lower lip.

Lydia sipped on her straw. »What was your most erotic love

adventure?«

»There are some with Ute, but also with Doreen. Should I tell you?«

Lydia made an inviting hand gesture. »Of course.«

Thomas didn't tire of talking about his women.

»Alright. First, Ute. - Ute had invited me to her place in Hamburg. After a delicious candlelit dinner at one of those boat restaurants on the Alster, we drove to her apartment in my car. Ute made it exciting when she unlocked the front door. In the hallway, she asked me to sit on a bench and wait. I had to close my eyes and only open them again when she led me into the living room. It was amazing when I finally opened my eyes! Everything was bathed in red. The light was warm, yellowish orange. I think it was on my 44th birthday. There were lots of red, thornless roses on the floor, and she sang: ‚For you, it shall rain red roses...' She was like Sleeping Beauty, wanting to be awakened from her dream. The roses were sort of like guides; they led us to the bathroom first. The bathroom, illuminated by candlelight, was incredibly romantic. We relaxed our bodies and minds in the floral scent of the water. We splashed around in the bath until we couldn't stand it any longer and followed the rose path to the bedroom. Even the bedding was in rose design. It was a beautiful staging!«

Lydia hung on his every word.

Thomas sighed and continued with his story.

»Another time, Ute surprised me with the theme ‚Queen of the Night!' since I had called her that the first time, we were together. She was waiting for me in her apartment. When she greeted me, I was absolutely speechless. The whole apartment resembled an oriental bazaar, like something out of Arabian Nights! Instead of doors, there were sheer curtains in various colours layered everywhere. The kitchen was decorated in red, orange, and yellow, where she served me various delicacies. Ute looked very seductive. She was wearing dark red lace lingerie, and over that, she had a kimono. She danced around me. The entire apartment was illuminated only by tea lights.

Incense and oriental music added the final touch. The highlight was her self-designed canopy bed, where she placed me and performed her belly dance for me. From the ceiling hung a violet-coloured mosquito net embroidered with blue and red beads; I was enchanted by everything. Beautiful!«

Lydia had come up with many things, but Ute was creative. She rested her head on her hands and thought.

Who should she seduce? There was no one around. She would have liked to have a boyfriend. Her last relationship ended, and she had suffered for a long time because of it. Through Thomas's stories, she felt a longing for all these experiences. The best ideas often come when you're in love, and unfortunately, she wasn't at the moment. Thomas was enviable, being adored by his women like that! He certainly didn't need to complain.

She sat up straight again.

»I want to know more about Doreen. You said you had a purely sexual relationship with her, right?«

»Doreen, as I said, is an exciting woman. She challenged me to a game of pool,« he chuckled.

»Pocket billiards?« They laughed.

»No, even better! A friend of hers owns a pub with, how should it be otherwise, a pool table. She arranged for us to be there outside of business hours. Just the two of us. It was on a late summer day. She was wearing a very provocative, form-fitting, black dress, short, very short, with an interesting deep back cut. Simply sexy, and then her high heels to go with it!«

»Wow, how do you remember all of that? You have a demanding job, then four women, and all of those stories on top of it. Insane!« She looked at him fascinated.

Thomas scratched his chin awkwardly.

»Truth be told, I attended a memory training course and I have a photographic memory. It seems to have been in my nature from the start,« Thomas admitted.

»Okay,« she rolled her eyes. She couldn't believe all the

things he came up with.

»To Doreen… First, she explained the rules to me in detail. Although I knew them, I enjoyed hearing them from her. The game started with the solids, so it was her turn. She knocked me out with how she leaned over the table, giving me a clear view of her ample bosom. Doreen focused intently on the ball, the cue between her long fingers, then she smoothly slid the cue back and forth until she struck, another hit and a ball sunk! Her posture was very aesthetic, her buttocks slightly arched back, her legs stretched by her high heels. It looked seductive, the way she half lay on the pool table, that I couldn't help but give her a slap on her behind. When it was my turn, all she said was: ‚Shake your Popo for me.‘ She ran her hand over my shoulder and slid it down my back to my buttocks, giving them a firm squeeze. I could hardly concentrate on the game and stood in front of her. She unbuttoned my shirt, ran her hand over my stomach, further down, undid my pants… I was blown away! Well, I can say, the pool table held up!«

Lydia grinned.

Thomas cleared his throat, pulled out his cigarettes, and placed the pack on the table. He took one cigarette and lit it with a match before continuing to speak with the cigarette in his mouth.

»And did you have such an adventure? I don't want to keep talking about myself all the time!«

»No, I haven't had such extravagant love adventures. I'm sorry, I can't compete with that. But it sounds very erotic.«

»That's okay. It may still happen!«

Lydia saw Tina coming up from the beach. When Tina spotted Lydia, she waved from afar, indicating that she was taking a break. Lydia signalled to her that she was staying put.

»But back to the point,« she cleared her throat to regain her focus.

»Which shoe were we at now? The yellow summer shoe, the green hiking shoe, and we were barefoot. We're missing the blue sports shoe, that's me. The sports shoe represents critical observation. The street shoe represents factual information, which is quite difficult to apply with women. Or are you keeping any statistics?«

Thomas laughed.

»Not that I know of. Just in the phone calendar, when I was where, with whom, and what we did. Otherwise? I don't know, there's nothing informative to tell you that I haven't already reported!«

Lydia paused briefly. Then she adopted a soft, sensual tone.

»So, Thomas, let's summarize everything factually once again! Girlfriend number one,« she said, placing the cigarettes in the centre of the table in her place.

»There's the somewhat reserved, petite, imaginative Margit, with whom you prefer to have a relaxing hotel vacation rather than trekking through the jungle with her.«

Beside the cigarettes, she places the box of matches.

»Let's move on to candidate number two. A spirited Carmen, who can whip up a magically delicious soup even from water, with whom you can go horseback riding and embark on adventure vacations, and who is always there for you with advice and support.«

Lydia glanced briefly at him. »Girlfriend number three.« As a representation of Ute, she placed her straw there, which she had licked before.

»The colourful, creative Ute, also known as the ‚Queen of the Night,‘ who has a sense of humour and can stage any kind of performance, can research and work well, but unfortunately broke up with you.«

Interested and reverent, he followed her voice.

»And last but not least, candidate number four,« she said, placing her keychain with a stuffed animal hanging from it on the table as a representation of Doreen.

»Doreen, the sex goddess Aphrodite, who is up for an erotic adventure at any unusual place and on any occasion but isn't seeking a committed relationship. Now, dear Thomas, make your choice.« And she tapped on each item corresponding to each number.

»One, two, three, or four?«

Thomas looked at her with a wide grin.

»Lydia, sorry, but you forgot the black lace-up shoe; we're not done yet, although I must say I've enjoyed this performance of yours.«

Lydia sighed. »Ah, the black lace-up shoe, meant to prevent you from doing things that harm you. Quite challenging with so many relationships! Somehow, one of the women always misses out. That was the notorious black thinker. For risks, side effects, and complaints, consult your doctor or pharmacist,« she joked.

»I'm glad to have contributed to your entertainment!«

Lydia responded with a quick comeback, »Thank you, likewise! I hope you can start thinking more about what or who you want eventually.«

»Thank you very much, I'll think about it,« he replied warmly, then proceeded to put away his cigarettes and matches.

Lydia tucked away her keys.

»And when another problem arises, you can solve it quite nicely and quickly by incorporating the shoe game, can't you? It certainly provides a lot of fun, excitement, and entertainment!«

Suddenly, a fresh wind picked up, causing the umbrellas to sway vigorously. She got goosebumps.

She rose from the chair, her pants clinging to her. She had become stiff from sitting. Quickly, she loosened her legs.

Thomas's jaw dropped. Suddenly, he felt an inner restlessness. He jumped up immediately. Surveying the situation, he called out to the older guests, urging them to run over to the building. The attendees fled to the hotel.

The two waiters hurried back and forth. One closed the shutters of the beach bar while the other cleared away the cups and glasses.

Lydia assisted the waiter. Before the umbrellas could topple over, Thomas helped by closing and securing them tightly.

The sky turned black.

»Something's brewing. We should hurry to get to the hotel!«

The rain poured down on them. In a flash, guests could be seen running towards the hotel complex with their beach bags.

The waiters had closed the shutters tightly and secured the umbrellas.

Suddenly, a strong gust of wind-swept in. The palm trees swayed vigorously, and the sand was whipped up. Lydia pulled her scarf over her face. The rain intensified, and the wet clothes clung to her skin.

They ran through the wet sandstorm as fast as they could, making their way to the hotel lobby.

Soaking wet, they stood in a corner of the lobby, peering out.

Inside, there was a loud murmur accompanied by children's laughter and a hustle and bustle of people moving back and forth.

Thomas breathed heavily. He knew he needed to work on his fitness again.

»Wow, what was that?! I'm completely out of breath. How about you? Are you okay?«

He looked around for Lydia, who was squinting her eye.

»No. A grain of sand got into my eye. Otherwise, I'm okay,« she replied.

She took off her glasses and rubbed her eye with her hand until it was gone.

Outside, it was pouring rain. The wind lifted chairs, sending them into the pool. Several umbrellas were also knocked over by the storm. Guests watched the spectacle from the hotel entrance hall. The temperatures dropped significantly. The storm lasted less than 15 minutes before it was over. Immediately, hotel staff began cleaning up.

Until Lydia's evening event and the dinner buffet, there was still time. What should they do for the next two hours? Their late afternoon activity literally fell through. They couldn't enthuse any of the guests for games like Battleship or City-Country-River. They preferred to relax in their rooms.

In fact, Lydia felt like treating herself to some pampering. Since the weather outside was unfavourable, she pointed out the hotel's wellness area. If she could recruit one or two guests to go to the massage area, the entertainers would receive complimentary treatments. She immediately motivated a few guests, and Thomas was also thrilled right away.

She took him by the hand and led him into the oasis for relaxation and rejuvenation.

»In this hotel, there are many luxury wellness offerings! Did you know that? Some guests come here just for the wellness options. You can book individual treatments on-site.«

His eyes widened. »What can you recommend to me from the luxury wellness offerings?«

»Where should I start? There's aromatherapy, Ayurveda, colour light and LaStone therapy, Lomi Lomi massage, Qi Gong, Reiki, Tai Chi, Shiatsu, and yoga!«

»My goodness, that sounds amazing. Do you have friendly Asian practitioners who are knowledgeable about the Chinese arts? What are these specifically, and what are they suitable for? Please enlighten me, I'm clueless about all of this.«

Lydia glanced at him with a smile.

»That's usually the case with things we don't deal with on a daily basis! I'll start with aromatherapy. This involves baths and massages with essential oils, which are meant to relax or stimulate. Citrus scents, lavender, or floral oils like rose are used here. Ayurveda is a 5,000-year-old Indian healing art and lifestyle. It aims to stimulate metabolism and detoxify the body with forehead oil pouring, full-body wraps, or facial masks. Tai Chi, Yoga, and Qi Gong are meditation, breathing, and movement exercises.«

Thomas was interested in a relaxing massage.

»I would like a relaxing massage, where I can sort out my thoughts after telling you everything this afternoon!«

»Of course, there are massages that soothe body and soul. Lomi Lomi is a sensual and gentle massage from Hawaii. Masseurs use their palms and forearms for this. With rhythmic movements, they circle over the neck, back, shoulders, and legs. Calming music is usually played in the background to enhance the effect. In the end, the whole body is swayed back and forth. This type of massage is recommended. It usually lasts for at least an hour, as the body typically begins to relax only after about fifteen minutes. I think we should go for this one before I continue giving you a lecture on massages.«

Lydia danced impatiently in front of the wellness entrance. She wanted to take off her wet clothes.

»You're right. Besides, it sounds wonderful to be pampered by gentle hands for an hour. Which way do we go?«

Looking around, he searched for direction, and she pulled him into the nearest door.

»Right this way. Here, everyone can find towels and a bathrobe, and over there are the individual cabins.«

Armed with their towels, they didn't have to wait long before two masseuses arrived.

»Then I'll see you shortly, but afterwards, I'll definitely be more relaxed,« called Thomas before disappearing behind the masseuse through the door.

The walls of the aroma steam bath were painted in orange hues. Thomas found it cozy to first enjoy a pleasantly warm steam bath by candlelight. He was served a delicious fruit cocktail to complement the experience. The rooms were designed in various colours, and accordingly, the lighting was adjusted, as the primary colours of red, green, yellow, and blue are said to influence the brain through the eyes and affect the psyche, either calming, relaxing, or activating. He received his full-body massage in a room decorated in red to induce complete relaxation.

With soft music playing and a massage underway, Thomas became increasingly relaxed and liberated. He was able to organize his thoughts and reflect on the conversation from the afternoon.

Lydia enjoyed the time for herself, without guests or other entertainers. Relaxed, she listened to the melody.

After a comprehensive wellness program, Lydia and Thomas met at the wellness bar, refreshed and dressed in fresh clothes.

»Well, how was it? Did I promise too much?« asked Lydia, smiling at Thomas.

With a wide grin, he beamed at her.

»No, it was wonderful! I feel relaxed and at ease. The hour flew by so quickly. I was able to truly unwind and pamper myself. The ambiance has clear echoes of Asian culture, combined with modern yet thematically fitting accents. You didn‘t promise too much! It‘s just what we needed on a rainy day! Now, how about a freshly squeezed orange juice? We‘re doing well!«

»You look refreshed. That‘s great. Thomas, I‘m afraid I have to leave you again,« she grinned as she patted his shoulder, »duty calls. Enjoy your orange juice. Hasta luego!«

Thomas sighed. »Ah, really? Well, see you later then!«

The evening program featured a musical performance. Lydia was excited, hoping the costumes had come back from the cleaners on time. She went to the costume room, where Tina, her colleague, was already checking everything.

Tina greeted her with a wide smile. »Hey Lydia, great to see you. Patricia has a severe migraine and can‘t play the lead role today. You‘ll have to take over. Unfortunately, there‘s no substitute candidate, except YOU!«

Startled, Lydia flinched. »Me? Oh dear.«

Excitedly, she ran her right hand through her hair and took a deep breath in and out. Tina looked at her expectantly.

Lydia shook her head. »Even if you show me the choreography, Tina, I can‘t learn the whole piece in such a short time. Absolutely impossible!«

»What do we do then? You can improvise,« she said, clapping her hands as if the solution had just fallen from the sky.

Lydia rummaged through the clothes. She pulled out her favourite dresses, one after another.

Suddenly, she turned to Tina. »I‘ve got it! A medley of different musicals.«

Tina applauded, and they gave each other a high-five.

»Everyone will showcase the performance they excel at. Just one song from *Cats, Phantom of the Opera, Grease, Hair, Saturday Night Fever, ABBA, Evita, Elisabeth,* and for the grand finale: all together, *The Rocky Horror Picture Show.*«

As she listed, they successively brought out the respective costumes for their fellow performers. During the performance, everything had to move quickly. Therefore, they sorted by musical and costume, hanging them on racks. They were a well-coordinated team.

In the WhatsApp group, they informed their colleagues about their roles for the evening and why they had to improvise. Everyone took it lightly, as they had frequently performed the pieces before.

Backstage, they could observe the lively hustle and bustle of the guests. Everyone wanted to have the best seat.

Lydia entered the backstage area.

»Hey everyone. Please check if your costume is here and you have everything you need.«

Tina did the makeup and hair for each one of them in turn. Lights, music, and technical aspects were all set. Just before the performance, nerves spiked backstage. Then, the intro played, the announcement came, and off they went.

The show began with Cats. Three cats prowled on stage to the song »Memory,« sung by Lydia. Nervously, she emerged from behind the curtain. However, as soon as she stood in front of the stage and her music started playing, the nervousness vanished.

Then followed one performance after another. Phantom of the Opera, Grease, Hair, Saturday Night Fever, where the entertainers Alex, Juan, Lydia, and Tina alternated on stage.

During ABBA's performance, Lydia sang »How Deep is Your Love« together with Juan. She looked into the audience, searching for Thomas, but blinded by the lights, she couldn't see him. Tina sang »Evita« alone.

Then Lydia stepped onto the stage in darkness, illuminated by the spotlight, portraying Elisabeth in a turquoise dress.

At the sight, Thomas was left with his mouth agape. Lydia wasn't a trained singer, but she had a distinctive voice. Her singing lessons had paid off. She captivated the guests, and that was what mattered. The piece Lydia sang resonated with him; he could identify with it.

»I don't want to be obedient, tamed, and constrained... I am not your property, because I belong only to myself.«

Just like me. I want to be free and unattached, not bound by any woman. I need absolute freedom to do as I please. That includes being able to act like a child, but above all, only being responsible for myself! Women have no problem taking on responsibility. They bear full responsibility for their children, without struggling with their role. That's what I admire about Doreen. Sometimes I wonder how she manages it all. Doreen is a perfect manager, juggling child-rearing and a career. Plus, she has time... Doreen entered into an erotic relationship with me.

»If you want to convert me, then I'll break free... If I want the stars, then I'll find my own way there...«

A woman is only bothersome - when she tries to dictate to me or convert me. They want children and a family right away - I'm busy with my career. That doesn't work. I'm constantly on the go, what woman wants a man who's never home? None!

»... If you want to find me, don't hold me back. I won't give up my freedom. ... If you want to bind me, I'll leave your nest ...«

Before I commit, I have to be sure. I've never been sure before. That's why I can't get married. Now, one after another is breaking up with me. The fear of being alone is suffocating. That's the only reason I have multiple girlfriends. They give me exactly what I need: enough freedom, tenderness, and love.

»... I share the joy; I share the sadness. But don't demand my life, I can't give you that. Because I only belong to myself! ...«

I must not forget that I am getting older. All my friends are married and have families. I would like to have security! The way things are going, it can't continue like this. Too exhausting in the long run! When I think about it, quite unsatisfactory. Yes, I only belong to myself. Sooner or later, I have to choose one before they choose me. I don't like to be alone. There's something to be said for feeling secure, for feeling the warmth of the other...

Thomas lost himself in his thoughts.

The applause from the audience and the cheering snapped him out of his thoughts. As others stood up, Thomas followed suit, he was blown away by her performance. Then she disappeared behind the curtain.

Juan made the closing announcement and called one performer after another onto the stage, introducing each briefly.

For the grand finale, everyone danced together to The Rocky Horror Picture Show, encouraging the guests to join in as well. It turned into a general disco dance, but Thomas didn't feel like participating.

The older guests bid farewell and headed back to their rooms. Thomas followed suit, waving goodbye to Lydia, who couldn't see him through the lighting.

He had become tired from the many constructive conversations with Lydia. The discussions had done him a lot of good. He felt more organized, as if his relationships were gaining structure. Slowly, he gained clarity. He lay down on his bed. Eventually, happy and content, he fell asleep.

What does astrology say?

TThomas was sitting at the pool bar when Lydia approached after her morning workout to order a bottle of water. Upon seeing him, she made her way over to his table.

»How come you‘re still at breakfast?« she asked, placing her backpack on one of the empty chairs.

Thomas gestured with his hand, inviting her to sit down.

»Oh, I overslept, or maybe I just didn‘t feel like the breakfast buffet. The food here tastes much better, and being served makes it worth staying a bit longer in bed. I couldn‘t fall asleep last night,« Lydia explained.

Lydia sank exhausted into a chair opposite him. The long night of dancing followed by an early morning workout had been exhausting.

»I didn‘t see you; you left early. The air in the room feels stuffy. I can‘t sleep with a fan,« Lydia said.

Thomas nodded as he chewed. »True. You were great yesterday,« he said, giving her a thumbs up in appreciation.

»My thoughts were racing in my head. But then I slept like a log. Thank goodness I‘m on vacation, so I can sleep in. That‘s what I‘ve been doing, as you can see,« Lydia replied.

Lydia took a sip from her water bottle. »So, how‘s your art with women going?« she asked, looking at him expectantly.

»Nothing new,« Thomas said, inviting her to join his breakfast.

Lydia looked at him and then glanced at the croissant.

»Here, take it, go ahead. Butter? Jam? Everything's here,« Thomas offered.

She tore off a piece of the croissant.

»Yes! It's coming together slowly,« Lydia replied.

»Have things changed? Or have you sorted out your feelings and thoughts?« She took the torn piece into her mouth.

Thomas, meanwhile, spread some cheese on a roll.

»I have come to the realization that I either have commitment issues or have not yet found true love, and I cannot solve this problem, no, this challenge, by being in multiple relationships at the same time,« Thomas explained.

Lydia nodded in agreement. »That's great. Acknowledgment is the first step towards improvement. And what conclusion have you come to?«

He set his knife aside and picked up the glass of orange juice.

»I've come to the conclusion that my relationship with Doreen is the most senseless one, as it exists purely on a sexual basis but has no future, at least since she doesn't want a committed relationship with me. I'm afraid that if I focus too much on a relationship, the eroticism will fade away.« He drank half the glass and set it back down.

»Exactly! Doreen was sort of my validation that I'm still useful as a man and not completely past my prime.« He took a few bites of his cheese sandwich.

Thomas wasn't entirely satisfied with Lydia's choice of words, but she had hit the nail on the head.

»Yes, exactly. Moreover, I find a woman I've known for years no longer stimulating, and her erotic appeal is fading. That's my problem. On the other hand, women don't let me go.«

Lydia understood him. From her own experiences, it was the excessive closeness with a person that changed everything, and initial infatuation turned into a familiar relationship, which often led to routine. If there were no children or shared hobbies, the relationship and one's own life just drifted along.

»I believe that both parties are responsible for maintaining a certain level of tension in the relationship so that the eroticism lasts longer,« Lydia said.

»My experience has shown, dear Lydia, that it's not always possible. I was with my girlfriend at the time for over three years, everything was wonderful, and after we got married, everything suddenly changed,« Thomas explained.

He took a roll from the breadbasket and spread some jam on it as he continued speaking.

»It didn't take long before we were divorced again. She was looking for someone who comes home at the same time every day. She didn't understand that I had to continue studying at home on weekends, and these problems also affected our sex life. Can you imagine?« he looked into Lydia's eyes as he said this.

»With multiple parallel relationships, you're not obligated to any one woman. Because you don't see each other often or get too close, the eroticism remains.«

Thomas waved to the waiter and ordered a cappuccino.

»So, I think that your first marriage didn't work out because you were too different and too young. You had different outlooks on life. I don't think you're really in a relationship. You can't take care of your women's concerns or be genuinely interested in them.«

Lydia looked at the waiter as he brought the cappuccino.

»If you were interested in a deep partnership relationship, you would spend your leisure time with a woman. You don't have the opportunity to develop a culture of argumentation because you don't see each other.«

Before Thomas could object, she continued.

»I think it's about looking forward to each other, forgetting about the annoyance. Perhaps the erotic aspect plays a predominant role.«

Thomas dabbed his mouth with the napkin.

»That's what I'm saying! Don't think there are no problems! Women see problems everywhere!«

He took a sip of his cappuccino.

Lydia made a serious expression and gestured with her hands.

»Thomas, I have to say, in the long run, it's unsatisfying for everyone involved, don't you think? Because you don't commit to ONE proper relationship, you end up losing them again. You're afraid of yourself! Women can tell, and boom, they start complaining, and there's the problem! The man only sees that the woman is nagging. And why? Because she's unhappy in the relationship, because she doesn't get enough attention. She feels misunderstood by the man. But look, the problem is YOU. You do what pleases you and have multiple relationships at the same time. Women don't make up problems, but the problems are pre-programmed. Caused by you.«

Thomas looked away, feeling affected.

»That's not entirely true,« he countered. »I have a problem with a woman when the relationship becomes too close and one-sided.«

»That's what I mean,« Lydia responded firmly.

»A relationship stays fresh only as long as both are willing to put in the effort. Every relationship requires work and willingness to compromise. It's up to you whether you maintain the excitement or not. Of course, routine sets in. It depends on the person how stuck or open they are to the world. You are an open-minded person and need an equally extroverted woman; all others don't fit your type. I am convinced that with the right woman by your side, whom you love and who loves you, you won't get bored. The eroticism will also be maintained. If that's not the case, you haven't found the right woman yet. Or you weren't ready to commit to her.«

Thomas finished his breakfast and leaned back as the waiter cleared the table. He ordered water, and she ordered a Milkshake.

»That could be,« Thomas remarked.

The waiter first wiped the table clean and then brought the drinks.

»It raises the question of which of my favorite women is the best match for me?«

Lydia leaned forward.

»After what you told me, I can summarize that only Carmen and Margit remain. Doreen was never a relationship, as you just said. Ute has bid farewell to herself. Ultimately, it's two women who significantly simplify a decision,« she concluded.

She sipped her milkshake and wondered if she should start her own practice as a psychologist.

Lydia and Thomas ignored the other guests on the terrace. Lost in thought, they observed and noticed that the same scene unfolded every morning. At the adjacent table, John and Frank played backgammon all day long.

She was glad to work where others vacationed.

Patricia walked through the hotel grounds to recruit guests for her next activity. She stopped at her colleague's table and tapped her on the shoulder.

»Hey, Lydia, are you ready?«

»Don't worry, I still have my schedule for today, and there were enough guests participating in the morning sports activity.«

Patricia nodded and walked to the next table.

Lydia turned back to her favourite guest.

»Okay, it's still helpful to thoroughly examine all relationships. On one hand, you can gain distance, and on the other hand, you can get closer to your dream woman. What zodiac sign are you? I'm interested in astrology.«

»For astrology, Thomas had little interest so far. He was surprised at what his zodiac sign had to do with his girlfriend, but if Lydia wanted to know, why not. „I'm an Aries.«

»Hm, I thought so,« Lydia said triumphantly.

»The Aries is indeed a charmer and captivates people,« Lydia explained.

Mischievously, he leaned over to her. »Aha. Tell me more

about me and my zodiac sign!« Thomas asked with a smile.

She gladly complied with this request and immediately got into her element.

»What can I say? The Aries is someone who manages to captivate and motivate a variety of people. They excel at bringing diverse groups together in the business world. Therefore, your profession as a marketing manager suits you well,« she explained.

Thomas looked at her invitingly, and she continued.

»Widows are spirited, energetic beings with a strong willpower and full of drive. The Aries likes to travel and embark on adventures. Currently, you are making a big exception when it comes to your vacation; you prefer individual travel. Japan will surely appeal to you, and you are certainly interested in the Japanese tea ceremony, but even more so in the samurai tradition. Surely, you would feel great enthusiasm during a trekking tour in the Himalayas! You prefer to hike off the beaten path, which makes you happy!«

Thomas looked at Lydia with wide eyes. Was all of that typical for an Aries? In astrology, she seemed well-versed. He hadn't considered his relationships from this perspective before. Perhaps there was more to astrology than he had realized. Maybe he had been with the wrong zodiac signs, those who didn't have a sense for these things, which is why he clashed.

Meanwhile, Lydia continued talking.

»The Aries is very optimistic, but he wants to go through the wall with his head. His biggest weakness is his great selfishness, the word ‚I' is written super large.« Thomas felt caught.

»Well, you're absolutely right. I'm ruthlessly selfish, but very helpful. I'm like a child and never want to grow up. That keeps me young and promotes creativity,« he said with a self-deprecating grin.

Lydia added, »Well, men who never grow up? That's a problem for women - having a big kid around!«

Thomas replied, »But the Aries is an eternally youthful, passionate lover! No woman can resist that,« and winked.

Lydia laughed heartily. »At least you believe that about yourself, don't you? I think a relationship with you will never be boring, but it will be challenging when it comes to love.«

She ran her hand through her hair and glanced over at Patricia, who was playing bocce with some guests.

»It's hard for you to rein in your sense of adventure, isn't it? Your sense of duty is limited, and in exchange, you have a very strong desire for freedom. I believe the one-night stand is not foreign to you. You're a connoisseur in all areas. Nevertheless, I can imagine that you remain a gentleman, sometimes maybe a Casanova, pleasing your numerous lovers. Perhaps it's because of your ascendant. This influences character traits.«

»Wow! And now I'm curious, do you know about the other zodiac signs as well? Then you can surely tell me about the zodiac signs of my dear women.«

Lydia surprised him once again. A curious woman. She was constantly on the move from morning till evening as a guest relations manager, with a seemingly inexhaustible supply of good cheer and a readiness to deal with physical and mental stress.

Slowly, Thomas began to see the demands of an entertainer's job. While he had initially envied her for working at a vacation destination, his envy diminished. The sun was hot and scorching from morning till late evening. He didn't envy her for constantly dealing with new guests each week, listening to their problems all the time.

Thomas found himself in an enviable position this week. Lydia remained cheerful and had never indicated that she was tired of discussing his relationship issues. Was she doing it out of a sense of duty, or did she like him? That was something he couldn't quite grasp.

Lydia continued chatting. »Okay. I'm very interested in astrology and its implications, especially in romantic relationonships. However, there are exceptions even here. It heavily depends on the ascendant, which is calculated from the birthplace and exact birth time—it can differ down to the minute.

For some, everything aligns perfectly, for others not so much, but you can generally go by it. So, what are the zodiac signs of your women?« She looked at him expectantly.

Thomas leaned back, crossed his legs, and pondered for a moment.

Carmen's zodiac sign would be Taurus, as she has a birthday in early May.

Her brows furrow.

»Early May, Carmen is a Taurus. Oh, Aries and Taurus are not well-suited. The Taurus is a peaceful and balanced person, whereas the Aries is too temperamental. Also, the Taurus is not spontaneous for a wild night and passionate sex. They are jealous. Faithfulness is highly valued. And especially sex and a sense of adventure play a big role for you. I think the relationship with Carmen wasn't perfect, and you looked around because something was missing. Bulls like Carmen want to start a family and get married, understand!«

»The waiter cleared the dishes from the neighbouring table, and they ordered themselves a juice spritzer.«

„Juan carried his full duffel bag over his shoulder and came over to them. ‚Do you have the key to the Kids Club? I need to do some laundry and I forgot mine, but' he gestured toward the bungalows, ‚before I go all the way back up to the room.',,

»Sure thing. I'll unlock it for you.«

Immediately she jumped up and turned to Thomas. »Don't run away.«

Together, they walked around the corner where the Kids Club was located. She took the opportunity to freshen up.

After a short while, Lydia returned. She adjusted the parasol, so they were back in the shade and then sat down. In the meantime, their drinks had arrived.

»How about Margit?«

He frowned. »Margit is, I believe, Pisces. How does a fish match with an Aries?«

She hesitated before continuing. »Pisces and Aries are like fire and water. The Aries will have difficulties with the Pisces.« She took a hearty sip and searched for words.

»Between Pisces and Aries, there can be a short-term romance, a brief, intense flare-up of passion and fascination. This bond will be difficult to sustain for a lifetime. The two worlds are too different to provide the basis for a long-term relationship. Well, Thomas, here you have bad cards. When is Ute's birthday?«

Thomas quickly checked his phone.

Ute has her birthday at the end of May, probably also a Taurus?

She thought for a moment. »No. At the end of May is Gemini.«

»Yes, I'm sure,« she replied confidently.

»Yes, I'm quite sure. Geminis are open-minded, flexible, and interested in many things. Sometimes they struggle with inner conflicts that prevent them from finding peace, fluctuating between extreme highs and lows.«

Thomas nodded in agreement.

»They find it challenging to pursue a goal consistently due to their restless mind. However, their flexibility and creativity often surprise others, as they come up with solutions that nobody else considers. Geminis question everything to expand their knowledge and understand connections. On the other hand, they love endless discussions.«

Thomas waved his hand dismissively. »Oh dear, yes, endless discussions with Ute,« Thomas sighed. »Night after night. Everything had to be questioned. It was nerve-wracking! No matter what it was, she had something to say about everything.«

Lydia rolled her eyes. »Well, now you know that this is typical for her. She can't help it, it's in her nature. Their sociability, refreshing humour, and entertaining nature make Gemini popular companions. So, as you described Ute to me, the air sign fits.«

Thomas nodded. »Yes, the sociability and her humour are exactly the points I liked about Ute. That's why we got along wonderfully. We were a dream couple,« he said, stroking his chin.

Lydia smiled. »I'm starting to believe that too,« she said. »It's a shame it's too late. But better late than never. The Aries and Gemini are a good match. Yes, let me guess, your Doreen is probably also an Aries, just like you?«

Thomas looked surprised. »Yes, that's right, our birthdays are two days apart. How did you guess? I'm really impressed by your knowledge!«

Lydia joked, »I just know it. Doreen loves romantic adventures just like you. She's certainly not prudish, from what I've gathered from your stories. She's open to all kinds of temptations and sexual adventures. In every sense of the word, she's the fiery lover. So, what's more natural than attracting an Aries?«

Thomas felt validated. He sat back in his chair, relaxed, hanging on Lydia's every word.

»Moreover, the Aries woman is sexy, seductive, imaginative, and charming. Thus, Doreen fulfills your ideal woman's image. She embodies the role of the mistress, the full-blooded woman who takes charge when it comes to sex. You two probably match perfectly in the bedroom, like attracts like, but only in passion.«

Thomas covered his mouth with his hand.

»Oh, now I'm an open book for you,« Thomas said.

„He ignored her statement and continued. ‚On the other hand, Aries and Aries can be a difficult constellation, leading to conflicts. It gives me the impression that you're meeting the wrong women,'„ she said.

Thomas leaned back and watched the activity at the bar.

»Yeah, that seems to be the case. Except for Ute, that was the best match. Too bad, it's over!«

He leaned forward to Lydia and asked, »What's your zodiac sign? I'm curious.«

She grinned. »I have to disappoint you. I'm a Capricorn. Capricorn and Aries don't typically match. Although… there's a chance if they accept each other and give each other space, it could be enriching for both in the long run.«

Thomas felt hopeful. »So, wouldn't it be doomed to failure right away, that's a good condition, isn't it? Don't you think? What does Capricorn have to offer?«

She refused to be pigeonholed. He was fascinated by people who were not easily defined. He wanted to understand why, how, and what made them the way they were. He found it intriguing, so he intended to get to know Lydia better.

Lydia nervously shifted in her seat. »Well, what do you want to know? Capricorn is ambitious and conscientious, diligently fulfilling life's tasks. They possess a sharp and critical observational ability. I think I could show you that.«

With a start, she looked at her watch.

»Oh dear, I've talked too much again. I wanted to go to the weekly market and buy a few things. I wanted to use my lunch break for that, otherwise it'll be too late. Would you like to come with me? Let's go!«

They got up and headed towards the village. They walked down the road to the weekly market. The village was close to the hotel complex and worth a visit. There were many colourful stands offering fruits and vegetables, fish, cheese, tapas, flowers, fabrics, and clothes. It was a bustling scene.

Thomas accompanied Lydia and enjoyed the wonderful atmosphere. He loved strolling through a market. Lydia knew some of the stallholders who greeted her warmly.

»Señora. ¿Cómo está usted?«

»Bien, gracias.«

»I'm impressed by your language skills!«

Thomas trotted along a step behind her.

She turned to him. »Me? No! I learned the most important words in a crash course at the hotel. Upon arrival, everyone received a little booklet. A language course was supposed to be offered for guests, but since none of us can speak flawlessly, that initiative was scrapped from the program.«

Lydia bought a leather belt and walked over to the flower stand.

»Buenos días, señora!«

»Buenos días, Raphael.«

Lydia looked at one bouquet after another. They were all beautiful.

Thomas held a fragrant bouquet in shades of orange under her nose. »If you like it, I'll buy it for you. After all, I need to repay you for your time.«

She didn't say no and let him proceed.

»I enjoy shopping at the market. It's a piece of vacation, even though I'm working here.« They slowly strolled back towards the hotel.

Thomas agreed with her. »I can understand that. I also enjoy going shopping at the market occasionally, unfortunately I don't have time for it very often.«

»Oh, not enough time? Time is relative. If you really enjoy doing something, you'll find the time, it's that simple! Otherwise, it's not important to you and you prefer other things. You surely have time. After all, you manage your time with women just fine. If you spent all your time with just one, I'm sure you'd feel much better about it.«

Thomas looked at her from the side. »Do you really think so?«

Lydia pushed small stones along as they walked. »Well, if you ask me, the first thing you should do to end your affair with Doreen. Then you'll have time for yourself.«

Thomas grimaced. Over time, he had come to see the truth in Lydia's words. If he focused on Margit or Carmen, he would have more time for himself and his hobbies. Moreover, his hobbies provided him with the opportunity to unwind. He relaxed during sex, but there remained a dissatisfying feeling of emptiness.

Thomas walked silently lost in thought beside her. Lydia looked at him appraisingly.

»Do you know that men are much more efficient when they are in a stable and happy relationship? This is scientifically proven, and besides, they live longer. Others who are forever searching for a suitable partner are usually not successful in their careers.«

Thomas stopped at a bench and set the flowers down as a gecko quickly disappeared. »And you think that's true? Well, I'm on the right track to choose a suitable partner, but it's not easy. Even according to zodiac signs, if you believe in them, Ute was the suitable partner. But she doesn't want me anymore, there's nothing I can do about that. Between Carmen and Margit, I still can't decide properly.«

Lydia sighed, took the bouquet from him, and continued walking. He followed her. In the sun, he was melting away, causing beads of sweat to form on his forehead.

Between the village and the hotel, there was the beach promenade. Along the way, there were scattered palm trees and benches.

She set the pace. Thomas had to walk faster. Three cars drove by. Further ahead of them, a couple from their hotel was walking, otherwise the street was empty.

Lydia turned to him. »Unfortunately, I can't help you with that, you'll have to figure it out yourself. I understand that both women have their merits. I advise against a three-way relationship. I must say, you've chosen completely the wrong cast for that, especially with those two!«

He was surprised. He hadn't even dreamed of such a relationship construction. And the fact that this remark came from a woman surprised him even more!

»Do you think that would have worked? I don't believe so. Women rarely get along with each other, can they?«

Lydia smelled her fragrant bouquet of flowers.

»I'm not sure, based on what I've experienced and seen. There was once a couple who obviously had no problem with it. He always travelled with two women, one on his right arm and the other on his left. So, it does happen that two women like each other and share the same man. You know how it is: Some men have their wife at home cooking, and a mistress they take out. I would find that terrible, so why not just have a three-way relationship?«

Thomas glanced furtively at her.

»There must be true love out there!« she said, shrugging her shoulders.

They were moving so quickly that they caught up with the couple. They greeted them and passed by, leaving the couple standing there, lost in love, gazing out at the sea.

»Come on, Thomas, look at yourself. You're in multiple relationships at the same time. Now imagine if the women knew about each other and that you're involved with both. There are two possibilities, but most often the following happens: They both break up with you, but not before giving you a piece of their mind. Then you're single again. That's the likely outcome given your current relationship setup. The alternative is that you have two women who are very open to everything, and you have an open relationship with both. If the women get along well, a three-way relationship might work.«

Thomas argued, »That won't happen. I can't imagine that working. I admit, I like the idea. I think you might be the first woman who would tolerate it.«

Perplexed, she looks at him. »Why? Did I say I'm in for that? Definitely not! Some men are like Casanova and already have a mistress, only it's hidden. Or do you think you're practicing something different with your relationships right now? In my opinion, you're not doing anything different. That's too stressful for me in the long run.«

They walked through the hotel grounds to their bungalow. »What do you think I'm here for? Because these part-time relationships are starting to wear me out. But I don't believe in a three-way relationship, plus it's socially complicated in my situation.«

Lydia shook her head. »But having multiple relationships or a mistress is legitimate?! Ha, ha! Okay, let's leave it at that.«

They had arrived at their bungalow. Thomas said goodbye at the door.

The rest of her break time was spent resting.

Thomas briefly stopped by his apartment to freshen up. With a large beach towel in hand, he headed to the beach.

Smiling, he greeted the guests he passed by, some of whom he recognized from previous encounters. At the beach, he found an adjustable lounge chair under a parasol, offering him a view of everything around. He made his way there and laid out his towel. The parasol provided shade, shielding him from the sun.

He took off his pants and his yellow shirt, folding them neatly. Placing them at the head end of his lounge chair, he turned them into a makeshift pillow. Then, he adjusted the chair to a semi-reclined position.

In his swim trunks, he lay back on the lounge chair. The sun was shining in the blue sky. He reflected once again on everything that had happened.

He lit a cigarette and pondered. What should I do? A threesome is out of the question. Continuing the relationships as before is not an option. Margit? I must find a way to compromise in every relationship...

In the afternoon, Lydia had the kids' club. She gathered the children to build a big sandcastle together on the beach. First, she found a good spot and distributed the sand toys she had brought along.

Thomas watched Lydia with her group of children from his beach chair. When she smiled and glanced over at him, he waved to her.

So, she could get some colour, she changed out of her animation clothes. She looked great in her bikini, showing off her figure.

At the sight, Thomas whistled after her. When she glanced over at him, he pushed his sunglasses down. She couldn't help but grin, thinking what a macho man he was.

The children were eager to participate. He could tell by their faces that they were all having a great time playing in the sand.

Trenches were dug, and wet sand was brought in from the sea in buckets. The little ones were assisted by the big builders, and after a short while, two young fathers joined their offspring. It was hard to tell whether the fathers were having more fun with the architecture and construction or their kids.

If Thomas had a child, he would have gone over to Lydia. He envied the fathers, being at his age.

The mound of sand that the children had gathered formed into a large water castle with a park. Lydia sat in the middle, and the others followed her instructions. Large stones bordered the castle, and the entrance was a bridge made of bushes.

Thomas had never raised the question of starting a family. If he wanted children, then only Carmen would be an option, as she was much younger. Margit also did not want any. For him, it felt like a never-ending story. So far, it had never come about. On one hand, he left it to chance, but on the other hand, he made sure that something could have happened. Suddenly, he saw it from a different perspective. The question was, who would be the mother of his children?

That's the right question. Because he was going through his midlife crisis and ultimately didn't want to reproduce or spend his daily life alone. Children not only bring life into the house but also a new life task. And it was a task that one could not simply get rid of – depending on needs and desires. It meant duty and responsibility. Children were enriching, sometimes stressful, but that was more due to parenting.

As he lay on his lounger, he watched the fathers with their children. He felt a longing he had never felt before. To take responsibility for a new life and contribute something to the world. Some children looked very much like their fathers. He wanted that too, a little likeness of himself.

This thought arose from his encounter with Lydia. He could see that she liked children.

If he weighs the pros and cons, he decided on Carmen. With her, he could have children. Additionally, Carmen was open to new ideas and visions. He had also been in the longest relationship with Carmen, and after several attempts at an on-off relationship, she was the right one.

In the long run, the part-time relationship with Margit was too stressful for him. With her, there were always heated discussions. Moreover, she was jealous and made a scene whenever he met other women; then the plates flew low. Oddly enough, she felt that others could outrank her!

With Ute, she hadn't felt that way back then. Ute was more the one who suspected that he was in a relationship with Margit. Carmen was the less stressful option.

The mother of his children would be Carmen. Did he love her unconditionally? Slowly, he warmed up to the idea of staying exclusively with Carmen. The last six years had been good. Yes, Carmen was his chosen one. All the thinking and discussing had served a purpose, and he could fly home feeling relaxed.

As he arrived for dinner, Lydia was sitting with other guests. Not that it bothered him, but he was disappointed. He sat alone at a table.

He didn't bother with the evening karaoke event.

After dinner, he strolled back to his bungalow. He would have liked to take a walk with Lydia to share his thoughts with her, but being alone, he wasn't in the mood. Instead, he picked up a book and went to bed early.

Campfire Romance

Tuesday morning, Lydia was busy with her job. She moved from one sun lounger to another, encouraging guests to join in.

She stood next to Thomas, who was sunbathing on a lounge chair.

»Would you like to join?« She looked at him expectantly.

Thomas blinked up at her. »No, thank you! I'm waiting for the excursion bus to César Manrique's house.«

»Too bad! But a great alternative. Have fun!«

His gaze directed at the bus stop. „Tomorrow I can join in again. „

Lydia made a face. »I'm sorry, but tomorrow is my day off, so I won't be here.«

»Too bad! Then we'll say goodbye tonight. I'll be back at five p.m. I'll pick you up,« Thomas replied.

Lydia stood rooted to the spot beside his sun lounger. »Why, are you flying back home?« she asked.

»Yes, my flight is Thursday morning at four o'clock,« he replied.

»Yes, then we only have tonight indeed. That's a pity!«

It seems like Lydia's mood instantly dropped. She liked Thomas. Having constantly changing guests was exhausting. Just when she got used to them, they flew back home.

»May I invite you to dinner at Pedro's? I know you usually have to eat with the guests at the hotel. But can you make an exception for the farewell? Besides, I really need to share my thoughts with you,« Thomas asked.

Lydia was delighted. »I'd love to! By the way, after four months, I can't stand the food at the hotel anymore. It's the same every week, so a change will be nice. Oh, I'm curious about your news,« she replied.

»Great, that makes me happy! We'll be back in time for the evening event,« Thomas responded.

As his bus arrived, the other guests waited at the bus stop to board.

»Oh. Tonight, we have musicians with guitar music at the hotel, we have a Spanish folklore evening. I can come a little later, that's fine. We are a great team. The main thing is that everything goes well, and then it's okay. I'll just let the others know.«

»Great. Yes, it's evident to guests when your team works well together and gets along,« said Thomas.

Thomas hurried to catch the bus. The others had boarded, but the tour guide was still chatting with the driver.

Lydia called out to him as he headed for the bus. »Have fun on the excursion! See you tonight!«

Thomas wanted to at least get a glimpse of the local culture and scenery before flying home. He didn't have much time to spare, so he spontaneously signed up for the excursion. He had heard a lot about the artist they were visiting. Now that he had solved his problem, he could focus on other things. The heavy burden on his shoulders was lifted, and a sense of relief washed over him.

Palm trees lined the road leading to the sea and the cafes on the opposite side. Everywhere, Spanish music filled the air from the local establishments. How wonderfully light everything felt! The Spanish women were dressed in scanty clothing, with their long black hair and big eyes, looking seductive. But the people from the south had a different temperament – that was exactly his Carmen.

Thomas enjoyed his last evening with Lydia over a delicious

meal and candlelight at Pedro's. She had grown close to his heart. He felt he owed her something. Thanks to Lydia's help, he had gone on a journey through different worlds of women. He found her lovable. The dance evening lingered in his mind. If she lived in Germany, he wouldn't be opposed. But that wasn't an option, with her on Lanzarote and him in Düsseldorf!

Lydia put on her favourite music before getting ready in the bathroom. She was in high spirits. Singing loudly to the lyrics, she showered. Let's see what the evening brings. She felt a bit melancholic thinking about saying goodbye to Thomas. The time had been fleeting, just five days – not long! Yet, she felt like they had known each other for ages. She was eager to hear his thoughts and couldn't wait.

Just in time, she was ready when there was a knock on her door. Thomas stood there with a bottle of wine to pick her up.

She smiled at him.

»Hello, dear Lydia! Here's a little token of appreciation.«

He handed her the wine.

»Thank you, for later! I'm glad! Come in, I'll put the wine in the fridge,« she said.

She disappeared around the corner, with Thomas following her.

»Nice place you have here, cozy,« he said, looking around. On her table was the beautiful bouquet of flowers, filling the room with their scent.

„She had a small refrigerator, in which she stored everything. ‚So, now we can go!'„

„Yes, gladly. Vamos. Let's go!'„ She grabbed her handbag, and together they left the apartment and walked down the street to Pedro's.

Lydia looked at him expectantly. »I'm curious about your thoughts.«

He continued to tease her. »Yes, about that later. For now, let's enjoy the beautiful evening atmosphere.«

Upon arriving at Pedro's restaurant, they looked for a spot on the terrace where they could both have a view of the sea. Once they found it, they headed over to take their seats.

They ordered tortillas and each a cocktail. It was a pleasantly warm summer evening. Thomas and Lydia absentmindedly watched the hustle and bustle on the beach promenade as they waited for their food. Families with their children were out for their evening stroll on the beach.

The waiter brought the cocktails.

Lydia was eager to hear Thomas's thoughts and smiled at him encouragingly.

Thomas ran both hands through his hair at the same time.

»Hard to believe that I'm flying back home the day after tomorrow. Seven days go by so quickly. Just as soon as you arrive, you're already leaving again!«

Lydia sighed. »You're right about that. You're welcome to stay here a few more days.«

Thomas sat up straight in his chair. »No, that's not possible. I still have a lot of preparations to make, and then my full schedule continues. In two weeks, I have a tour across Germany for a big company, introducing a new product - and I'll be presenting it, so I have a lot of work to do!«

He took Lydia's hand. Both looked into each other's eyes. »Tomorrow is tomorrow and shouldn't concern us today. I have something to tell you.«

Smiling, she withdrew her hand from his. Tension made her breathless. She couldn't prevent her heart from racing faster. Then it burst out of her. »Shoot, finally tell me, how have you decided?«

Thomas took a deep breath. »I have come to a decision, Lydia.«

Slowly, he reached into his pocket, took out his cigarettes, and lit one, placing the pack on the table in front of him.

»Come on, you're driving me crazy!« and clapped his hands.

Thomas took a drag from his cigarette and slowly exhaled the smoke to the side so Lydia wouldn't get it. »I think Carmen is the right one.«

Relieved, Lydia slumped into her chair. »Well, thank goodness. Carmen!«

Grinning, he calmly put his cigarette pack back into his pocket.

»Right. Carmen! I think that's a good decision. I came to this conclusion this afternoon. After all our conversations this week, I've been reflecting on everything. I think I love her.«

Lydia looked at him indignantly. »I hope so for you. I'm glad. And Margit? How will you break it to her that you want to break up?«

Thomas looked into the distance, out to the sea.

»I'm not sure. Do you have any ideas? I don't want to offend her or hurt her feelings,« Thomas replied.

Lydia nodded. She couldn't give an answer to his question. She shrugged her shoulders.

»Separation always involves pain. I don't know how you can solve this problem, but I'm sure you'll come up with something. At least I'm glad you've come to a decision.«

He crushed his cigarette as the food arrived. It smelled delicious. Both of them had a big appetite.

Chewing, he said, »Yeah, I've been bothering you with my problem all these days! Not my style to bore women in this way! There's certainly more exciting stuff from my life to talk about, but how about you? How was your day today?«

Lydia smiled. »Thanks, it was pretty good. There was a lot to do. The entertainer Patricia was sick, so I had to handle the kids' activities alone in the afternoon.«

»Sounds interesting. What did you do with the kids? Was it fun, or did they get on your nerves too much?«

Lydia laughed. »No, children are something beautiful. From other mothers, I like them the most. We collected lava stones and then painted them.«

Thomas looked over approvingly. »Very nice.«

He took a sip of his cocktail and pondered.

»Does that mean you don't like having your own children?«

Thomas laughed. »Our parents survived it too, so it can‘t be that bad.«

Lydia made a dismissive gesture. »No, it isn‘t! That was a joke.«

Thomas teased her and looked horrified, as if he had taken her seriously.

Lydia rolled her eyes. »I like children. They are enthusiastic, curious, funny, laugh a lot. You can‘t even be mad at them when they‘ve done something wrong. They just look at you with such an incredibly sweet smile that they can easily wrap you around their finger without you even noticing. I think children are an enrichment to life.«

Thomas had finished eating and pushed his plate aside.

Lydia raised her eyebrows. »And what about you, do you like children too?«

»Of course, I like children. However, I‘m not sure if I want to have any yet, I haven‘t decided. It depends on the mother.«

»You can still think about what you ultimately want to do ... For that, you first need the right woman! One thing at a time, right?« She smiled at Thomas and took her last bite.

Thomas sat across from her, relaxed. He enjoyed her company. However, the thought of having to sort things out at home weighed on him. After all, each of his women had contributed to his professional success through their creativity. It was like losing a whole team of potential. He wanted to part ways amicably. That was at least his intention.

The waiter cleared the table. At the next opportunity, they paid the bill.

Thomas gazed thoughtfully out to the sea, appreciating Lydia‘s understanding of his situation. She was in good spirits and sought solutions with him. He couldn‘t talk as openly about his problems with any other woman. Despite being fifteen years younger, Lydia brought life experience to the table. Surprisingly, he realized he could discuss many things with

Carmen, which he found important.

Lydia had opened his heart without a doubt! Now he wanted to travel home quickly and observe the further developments that would arise with Carmen and Margit. He intended to keep the planned meetings as they were discussed before his vacation. Carmen was supposed to pick him up from the airport. But that was scheduled for the day after tomorrow. Tonight, he wanted to enjoy the last evening with Lydia.

Suddenly he clapped his hands on his thighs. »Yes, that's it!«

»Irritated, Lydia looked at him from the side.«

»May I give you a beach walk as a farewell gift? It's a wonderful evening.«

„With a glance at her watch. ‚Ok! That's a good idea. I still have time.'„

He took her right hand and hurriedly led her to the sea.

Arriving at the beach, they took off their shoes and strolled along the water's edge, holding them in their hands.

Lydia ran her hand over Thomas's back. Saying goodbye was certainly not easy; she had grown accustomed to him! Could he be faithful when the right woman was in front of him? Whether it was Carmen, she didn't know.

Thomas put his arm around her shoulder, and they strolled along the beach together.

Nearby, a few teenagers sat around a bonfire grilling sausages. Two of them played guitar while the others sang songs.

Thomas and Lydia stopped to watch the group, one of them waved at them invitingly.

Thomas spontaneously suggested, »Should we join them? What do you think?«

Lydia looked at him. »Why not? If he's inviting us kindly. It'll bring back campfire romance, like in the old scout days!«

Thomas laughed. »Yeah, you're right. Are you an old scout, just like me? Really nice!«

As they approached the group, they noticed that there were German and Spanish exchange students. A young woman greeted them and invited them to sit down. It was a nice social gathering, with lively music being sung. After a while, one of the guitarists asked if Thomas played and handed him his instrument.

Thomas didn't miss the opportunity and enthusiastically started singing the song »Über den Wolken« by Reinhard Mey ...

After finishing the song, they said goodbye and continued their way.

Suddenly, Thomas began running with his arms outstretched, circling around Lydia, who came to a sudden stop.

»Indeed! In two days, I'll be sitting on the plane, soaring above the clouds. Boundless expanse, above me the blue sky, beneath me beautiful cloud formations that constantly invite me to dream! There, freedom knows no bounds ...«

»Wait a moment,« said Lydia, laughing.

Thomas stopped in front of her.

»I have something in my handbag!« She looked inside and pulled out a small bottle, opened it, and what came out?

Thomas looked surprised as Lydia let soap bubbles rise. »You're a bit crazy!« he laughed.

»That should be an answer to your daydreaming, Thomas! Dreams are sometimes like soap bubbles. Some last longer than others and fly quite far. Other dreams burst, just like soap bubbles burst, because they've come too close to the sun. When one dream is fulfilled, there are instantly new ones.« She blew some soap bubbles towards his face, then closed the lid to seal the bottle.

»Do you know, I got this bottle from a dear guest,« Lydia said, running her hand through her hair.

„It contains a beautiful poem about dreaming, author , which goes like this:

Never forget to dream,
to envision a world,
where love has more space,

where hope never ceases,
and peace is the deepest longing of all people.
To dream is a gift,
Your energy awaits.
To be harnessed towards your dreams.
Stand up for what you believe.
Just as you are your dreams at night,
so are you your waking dreams,
no one dreams like you do,
and no one realizes your dreams Like you do."„

Thomas had been listening attentively.

»Indeed, you're right. Everyone should live their dreams! I believe those were the first words of our encounter. Should they also be our last?«

Lydia put the bottle back into her handbag.

»Let's just keep moving and see if we can fulfill some dreams together! Here we go!«

She took Thomas by the arm and pulled him along.

The music of the Spanish folklore evening grew louder as they approached the hotel grounds.

At the stairs leading from the beach to the hotel, Thomas stopped.

»I'm not in the mood for the folklore evening, but duty calls for you, of course!«

He stood in front of Lydia and looked directly into her eyes. »I don't like long farewell scenes. One should leave when it's most beautiful.«

He pulled her into his arms and kissed her on the mouth without warning. Perplexed, she stood there.

Thomas found words first.

»I think it's time for you to go. Thanks again for your patience. Your team is probably waiting. It's gotten later than expected!« he said, glancing at his watch.

»It won't be a problem. Tomorrow you can have a sunba-thing day,« he suggested.

»I actually thought about that. It's a pity I won't see you anymore. My flight leaves Thursday in the wee hours of the morning. Lydia!« He took a deep breath. »I have to thank you for your pleasant company, which delighted me immensely. You're a great woman, almost a pity that you're so far away.«

Lydia laughed and made a dismissive hand gesture.

»No, no, not with me. Otherwise, you might end up having another one of your numerous relationships with me. So, I'm not going for that! It's either all in or nothing at all.«

Thomas nodded. »Alright - don't be mad at me, there's no reason for that. I'll be gone tomorrow, and who knows, may-be you're a bit glad to be rid of me again. Then you'll forget about me quickly. But what do you think - I could keep you updated on how things are going for me, provided you're inte-rested. And of course, I'd be interested in how things are going for you.«

»Of course! Very much so! I'm excited - I believe we should cut short our farewell. I'll just say: See you soon! Hasta lue-go!«

Thomas says goodbye with kisses on the cheek and a big hug.

»Hasta luego! You'll hear from me. Goodbye, Lydia.« Lydia bounded up the steps to the hotel and mingled with the guests.

Thomas walked whistling to his bungalow. He was in a good mood, as Lydia had given him an unforgettable evening, even a vacation.

End of vacation

Thomas's last day of vacation. It was Wednesday. After a morning swim alone in the pool at sunrise, he looked forward to the delicious breakfast buffet.

At home, he never took the time. He entered the breakfast room, apart from a young couple sitting at the other end of the room, he was one of the first guests. He wore a long T-shirt over his quickly drying swim shorts, and his towel was draped over his shoulder. Outside, he found a seat at the entrance to the terrace and laid down his towel.

The waitstaff greeted him as they set up the buffet. The rolls came out freshly smelling from the oven, just the way he liked them: crispy and warm. He grabbed a freshly squeezed juice and ordered a fresh omelette with peppers, mushrooms, cheese, and ham at the counter. Butter, jam, honey, and some cold cuts he took on a plate. He went back and forth between his table and the buffet several times.

As he finally sat down, he ordered a large cappuccino from the waitress. Thomas was looking forward to sitting on the terrace in the warm morning sun and enjoying breakfast with a view of the sea. It's a pity I don't have this at home in Düsseldorf. Last day, my short trip is coming to an end. Unfortunately!

After his hearty breakfast, he walked down the stairs to the beach. He went for a windsurfing session.

During his walk with Lydia, he had seen a surf school with

rental services. It was run by a German expatriate who had fulfilled his dream. After renting a perfect yellow board with a white sail, he surfed in the sea, letting himself be carried by the waves.

As the morning progressed, a few guests joined him. They communicated with each other through facial expressions and hand gestures. After a while, he laboriously pulled his board with sail out of the water back to the sports rental. As a young lad, he couldn't get enough of it, but without fitness, his arms and legs felt like lead.

After returning his equipment to the surf instructor, he retrieved his towel and settled down on a lounge chair under a parasol near the surf school.

The warm wind dried his body. He had solved his problem, rested, and was full of energy to fly home and sort everything out. Before he could dwell on it any further, his eyes grew heavier, and he fell asleep.

When he woke up, many guests had already left their sunbeds. The beach was deserted in the midday hours. Everywhere was silent.

Thomas rolled up his beach towel and headed back to the hotel. Along the way, he greeted several guests. At the beach bar, Patricia was sitting with a guest, engaged in an intense conversation. He bought a bottle of water and a baguette before making his way to his bungalow. After surfing and sunbathing, he looked forward to a refreshing shower.

On his terrace behind his bungalow, he sat down comfortably. He took a pleasurable bite of his baguette and drank his water. He observed a few geckos climbing on the wall, seeking shade. Even they found it too warm. After the last bite, he crumpled up the paper in which the baguette was wrapped and tried to throw it into the trash can next to the bed. But he missed! Laboriously, he got up from his chair, shuffled over to the bed, bent down to pick up the paper, and threw it into the trash can. Tiredly, he collapsed onto his bed and stretched out.

As he pondered, it occurred to him that he didn't have Lydia's email, nor did she have his. How could he provide her with his email address, hoping she would reach out to him?

He pondered how he could do it most skillfully. He sat down at his desk, took the hotel notepad that was there, and began to write a poem.

On his way to dinner, he passed by Lydia's bungalow with the letter in hand and his jacket over his shoulder. He stopped at her door to slide his letter under the door. Whistling, buoyant, hands in his pockets, he continued on his way.

Wednesdays and Thursdays were the days of arrival and departure. Many new guests had arrived at the hotel, creating a wild and loud atmosphere. The new guests had to find their way around. In the far corner, Thomas found a free table and took off his jacket. He had learned early on that it was best to secure a seat first by leaving something there. That's why he always had his jacket with him, even though it was warm. He squeezed past the other tables, greeting everyone with a »Good evening.«

At the buffet, he queued up for the first time. There, he met Robert, who was the last in line. They chatted until it was their turn. Thomas learned that Robert and his wife came from Düsseldorf and that they were also flying home tomorrow. Robert had ordered a wake-up call at the reception. Thomas found that to be a useful idea.

With an overloaded plate, as he didn't want to make a second trip, he arrived at his table. He quickly finished his food before it got cold. In the background, there was a loud murmur.

The entertainers went from table to table, soliciting guests for their evening program. It was supposed to be bingo night. He could do without that, especially since he usually woke up in the middle of the night.

At the reception, he ordered a wake-up call to ensure he wouldn't oversleep. At the bar, he had a nightcap. Before the bingo game started, he was back in his bungalow. His suitcase was quickly packed before he went to bed.

Their day off was spent by Lydia together with her colleague Tina. Late at night, they returned to the hotel from their trip around the island. The resort was quiet, with the guests sleeping.

She regretted not exchanging phone numbers with Thomas. As she unlocked the door to her apartment, she noticed a note lying on the floor.:

Those were indescribably beautiful days,
and last night...
It was just a moment,
yet it was very beautiful.
It was good that nothing happened,
We both wanted it.
We stood united and walked together,
Yet each of us was alone,
And wanted it that way.
I felt very good in that moment—
In that tiny moment of our lives—
Very good indeed!
And I'll remember not having done anything,
That little moment will remain precious to me!
And if you want to write to me,
I would be happy,
Then I'll get your address all by myself.
And if you're reading this,
Quiet and alone,
And if you feel a little heartache or
You feel a little smile,
Well, then just get in touch with
Your Tom@Thomas.Freimut.de!

She folded the note with a smile. She missed him a bit, this Thomas.

Back home

At the airport, Thomas encountered yet another surprise. His luggage wasn't with him, as the cargo taxi in the Canary Islands had not brought his travel bag. After waiting for an hour, the airline informed him that his luggage had mistakenly been loaded onto another plane. They promised to deliver it to him the next morning.

Thomas tried to reach Carmen on his phone but received the message: »The person you called is unavailable!«

Carmen was supposed to pick up Thomas from Düsseldorf Airport, but she was nowhere to be seen when he finally arrived at the exit, with an hour delay.

Unsuspectingly, Thomas took a taxi home without his luggage and without Carmen. How foolish! Had Carmen forgotten about him? She was always reliable, which worried him.

Arriving home, he tried once again to reach Carmen by phone, but she wasn't home, and her voicemail picked up. Her phone was still switched off.

Usually, Carmen would respond promptly, but not today. Anxious, he paced back and forth in his room. Had Carmen lost interest in him? Could something has happened to her? She knew he was back home!

He cleaned up, filled his washing machine, and kept trying to reach Carmen.

In the afternoon, Thomas tried again. Carmen couldn't be reached! They were supposed to spend Thursday to Friday together. Now he was worried, that couldn't be. He grabbed his car keys and decided to drive to her. Something was wrong.

Arriving at her front door, he rang the bell frantically. Carmen opened the door as if she had been expecting him for a long time.

She looked serious. »Oh, hello Thomas! How are you?«

Somewhat concerned and relieved that she was at home, he asked, puzzled.

»Why didn't you pick me up, and why aren't you answering the phone or returning calls? That's not like you,« Thomas looked at her with concern. »Are you sick?«

»Sick?« Carmen laughed, but it sounded forced.

»I don't know who of us is sick. Apparently, I must be sick to not have realized all this time that you're leading a double life and have another woman beside me, and I, silly me, really loved you...!«

Thomas was momentarily confused.

»I don't know what you're talking about,« he said, wanting to calm her down and preferring to continue the discussion with her inside the apartment rather than in the hallway where everyone could hear.

»What do you mean you don't know what I'm talking about? Don't act so hypocritical,« she said, standing in the doorway and not letting him in.

Thomas realized that something must have happened here. He became serious.

»Okay, let's discuss this inside calmly,« he said, gently removing her hand from the door frame and guiding her inside. Then he closed the door behind them.

Quietly, he asked, »What's going on?«

Carmen was upset.

»What's going on? Pronto, I accidentally found out that you've been in a relationship with Margit for two years. What do you have to say about that?«

He felt like a little caught boy who, in the first moment, tried to get out of the situation. »Margit? - Okay. - Yeah. Let's talk.« He took a deep breath, but before he could say anything, Carmen spoke up.

She stamped her foot on the ground energetically. »No, I'm talking now! And I can tell you that I met Margit. I was with my friend Fernando last weekend...« she couldn't finish her sentence as Thomas Interrupt her.

»Oh, you visited your friend Fernando last week. Just like that? Barely a week into my vacation, you're off visiting your old friends. That's strange!«

Thomas felt rejected. He wasn't used to that.

Carmen was in her element. »Yes, last week I visited Fernando in Frankfurt. Fernando works at a bank that was hosting a summer party. He took me to the party and introduced me to his boss. Guess what her name is? That's right, Margit Waldmann! An incredibly elegant person with a lot of style and tact! Actually, you could learn a thing or two from her.«

Thomas remained silent, feeling affected and listening intently. His thoughts were racing. Carmen didn't give him a chance to respond.

»We started talking, and after a short while, we were surprised to realize that we love the same man. Crazy, right? I was completely shocked. It was something else, you can't even imagine!«

Angry, she slammed her fist on her wardrobe.

»So, at first we were really pleased, thinking that we and our friends shared the same interests. Eventually, it became more and more puzzling, the similarities were too astonishing. Then I showed her a photo of you and said that was my Thomas. She paused, then said, ‚Yes, that's my Thomas too.‘ We were completely stunned. It knocked me off my feet. And here YOU come asking how I'M doing? I feel awful ... Heartbreak always hurts – and it's terrible to be so hurt. But, as you can imagine, I'm ending the relationship right now!«

Tears streamed down her cheeks.

He hadn't expected that. He handed her a tissue.

Thomas endured her anger. For the first time, he found himself at a loss with a woman. He had already planned to end things with Margit anyway. Now Carmen had thwarted his plans. The decision he had originally intended to make was taken out of his hands. It was another sign that fate was making it clear to him that he needed to change his life.

Thomas raised his hands in a conciliatory gesture. »I'm truly sorry,« he said. He couldn't bear to see her cry. »I didn't mean to hurt you! I love you.«

Thomas stepped closer to Carmen, offering her comfort as she cried.

Carefully, he continued speaking. »Carmen, you're right. I've been a jerk. For years, I've been playing a game. But that's over now! I finally realize that it's not okay. I'm sorry! You didn't deserve to be cheated on. You're an amazing, wonderful woman!«

He tried to hug her, but she pushed him away.

»I will break up with Margit. That's what I was planning to do anyway, and then let's give it another try. Yes? I will change. I promise! You're the woman by my side whom I love. I'm serious about this! It became so clear to me during the vacation. I need you. Please, give us a chance!« He pleaded with her.

Contemplating, she leaned against her hallway closet.

Now he finally noticed the music emanating from her living room—a song by Andrea Berg, »Du hast mich tausendmal belogen« (You've lied to me a thousand times).

Carmen shook her head vigorously. Her tears smudged the eye makeup on her face.

»Too late. You should have thought about that earlier. I'm sorry. Goodbye.«

»All his belongings she had thrown into a bag. Carmen flung open the front door, tossed the bag in a high arc outside, and then Thomas followed.«

»Goodbye. Leave me alone! It's over for good!« The door slammed shut hard. That was final!

It was the weekend, and thus his last vacation days were approaching. As planned before his vacation, he intended to meet with Margit over the weekend. However, that would be it for them. Since he was planning to end things anyway, he had nothing to fear either way.

He called Margit without mentioning what he had learned from Carmen. Instead, he waited to see how she would react.

»Hello, dear Margit. It's Thomas. How are you? I wanted to check if our meeting this weekend is still on?« His voice sounded as lively and strong as usual.

»Hello, Thomas! Sweet? - not always! Thanks for asking, I'm doing fine considering the circumstances. And yes, it's okay, I think we still have a lot to discuss.«

Thomas swallowed. He had expected accusations, but not this peaceful tone. He gathered his courage.

»I'm glad you didn't hang up right away. But after everything that happened, do you really want to see me again?«

Silence on the other end of the line.

After a deep sigh, then. »Well, you know, Thomas, I am indeed hurt, but not as hurt as Carmen. I never deluded myself. I never wanted to marry you anyway. I never thought about children – unlike Carmen. I must confess that I sort of had a feeling that I was just your mistress!«

Thomas cleared his throat; he had a lump in his throat. He hadn't expected that. She felt like a mistress. He felt relieved that Margit kept her composure.

»Then we'll see each other tomorrow. I'll come by car,« he said, slightly excited.

»I'll keep the meeting as agreed and promised, and I'll prepare a delicious meal. But I think you'll have to stay in the living room. I'm telling you that straight away,« he said.

»Oh, what delicious treats are in store?«

»It's roast pork,« Margit chuckled to herself, »filled with prunes and apricots, served with potatoes and savoy cabbage. A delicious meal for our last meeting, don't you think?«

»Yep, delicious. Okay, see you then.« They ended the call.

Margit warmly welcomed him and had everything prepared for their dinner together.

After dinner, over a glass of wine, Margit unloaded all her grievances on him.

Thomas endured it all. In the end, he felt sorry for hurting her because that was not his intention.

After their conversation, they slept together. It was a kind of reconciliation sex, with the understanding that it was going to end in the future. That was clear to both.

The next morning, they sat down for a leisurely breakfast and talked about old times.

»We can still be friends,« she suggested as Thomas was about to leave. »If you're ever in Frankfurt on business, just let me know!«

With such a farewell, he hadn't expected. He was relieved that Margit wasn't grumpy. Apparently, he wasn't such a heartless guy after all. With renewed hope, he drove back home.

The work calls

Full of energy, he drove to the office early on Monday morning. After the weekend, he felt relieved. Nevertheless, the separation from Carmen and Margit weighed on his mind. Things had turned out differently than expected once again.

His assistant Monica had not arrived yet when he entered his office, whistling. There was some backlog of mail, so he started sorting through it, grateful for a task that didn't require much thought.

He spent the morning working on his signature folder, which had been placed on his desk by his team assistant Stefanie.

Even in the afternoon, he barely glanced at his entire inbox. The amount of work that had piled up during a week of vacation was incredible! At least 300 emails had come in during that time. With responding to those, he had plenty to do for the next few days. Then he needed to prepare the presentation for the Berlin company. In the meantime, they had finally sent him the missing documents. He was so busy with organizational tasks that he didn't notice his assistant Monica hadn't shown up.

Even on the following day, her absence wasn't immediately noticed. It wasn't until Thomas was searching for important documents for his presentation that he realized Monica wasn't there.

He asked Stefanie when she came into his office, »Where is Monica, by the way? Is she sick?«

Stefanie looked at him bewilderedly. »Hasn't she informed you that she wants to take a break? Otherwise, she's handing in her resignation, unless it just arrived by registered mail. Here, see for yourself.« She handed him the registered letter.

Thomas read:

Dear Mr. Thomas Freimut,
I hereby resign from my position as Assistant to the
Management ...

Thomas sank into his chair, feeling a mix of surprise and disappointment. It seemed Monica had decided to leave her position without much prior notice.

»Indeed, why is she leaving?«

»Dear Mr. Freimut, you really shouldn't ask me that. I've been her team assistant for years now and I don't interfere with her leadership style. But, if I may, allow me to say something: If you had shown Monica a bit more appreciation, she would surely have stayed, I think.«

Deep in thought, Thomas repeated her last words. »A bit more appreciation.«

»Ja, you two really make a strong team. Monica takes care of customer service, preparations, and presentations, while you shine with your speaking skills. Excuse me for saying so, but I'm sure we'll struggle without Monica!«

He was bewildered. As if that wasn't enough, everything went haywire during his absence of just one week. While on vacation, he realized several things. Likewise, he became aware of Monica, his ambitious assistant, who supported him and had his back.

»I am aware of everything she does for me. Then we agree on that point.«

Stefanie remained standing in the doorway.

»Excuse me, that didn't come across from your assistant.

She worked tirelessly from morning till night, and now...«

Thomas' thoughts were racing.

»Does she have something new lined up?« He played with his pen, feeling anxious.

»Well, she wanted to move to the competition. Call Monica. Increase her salary! Bring her back, with her charm and everything that comes with it! Otherwise, we might as well close the shop soon. I can't handle her workload! I'm already fully occupied with the usual administrative tasks. Please! And you won't be able to manage it alone either!«

Resigned, he nodded. This was the last thing he needed. His assistant gone! He had to win her back! He had some leeway for a salary increase, but he would have to discuss everything else with his boss. He didn't want to leave any stone unturned.

Thomas made the decision to call Monica without hesitation.

»Hello, dear Monica! It's Thomas Freimut.«

Back came a short, cool, ‚Hello, what's up?‘

»Monica, I was quite shocked when I found out that you submitted your resignation. What's going on? No, what I mean is ...«

He took a short pause. He couldn't afford to make a mistake now. No clichés. He decided to be honest.

»I need you here. You are an organizational talent, and your work is perfect! I'm sorry I didn't tell you this earlier. And more often. Of course, there will be a salary increase for such excellent work.«

Resigned, she replied, »I'm not really keen on a salary increase.«

Thomas sat at his desk, feeling tense.

»Frankly, Monica, I haven't appreciated your work enough. You deserve proper recognition for your contributions. I deeply regret having neglected that so far. Please accept my apology!«

Thomas realized he was stuttering. The silence from Monica made him uncomfortable. If she refused – what should he do?

For what felt like minutes, there was tense silence.

Then she cleared her throat.

»Okay! Apology accepted,« she said.

He took a deep breath. A burden was lifted off his shoulders. Encouraged for a fresh start, he felt euphoric. »So, are you coming back?!«

One could have heard a pin drop.

Then she said, »Yes, but only because I personally like you.«

Thomas would have loved to do a little dance of joy, but he restrained himself. With deliberate calmness, he said, »I expect you to start work again next Monday. Until then, take some time off, go on vacation, or do whatever you want. You're on leave. I'll see you back here in the office next Monday!«

He heard in her voice that she was relieved, and unexpectedly, he felt warmth in his heart when she said.

»Sure thing, boss! Thank you! See you on Monday, ready to roll again!«

Thomas hung up the phone with a sense of relief. Would everything turn out for the better now? At least he had solved his work problem and regained his assistant!

In the following days, Thomas focused entirely on his work, living in the present moment. The week with Lydia had brought him some insights. He was ready for a fresh start! He wanted a relationship, that was clear, but with a woman who embodied everything he was looking for. Following Lydia's advice, he had compiled a list of what his dream woman should be like, which values were important to him, common interests, and so on ...

He looked through his vacation photos one by one, printed two photos of Lydia that were particularly striking, and placed them on his desk. So far, she hadn't contacted him. Did she not have any interest in him? It was a pity he didn't have her email address or even her phone number! He would have liked to tell her about his eventful week!

Several days passed, and just when he had stopped expecting it, an email from Lydia appeared in his inbox.

Hi Thomas,

How are you and your ladies? Finally, I find the time to get in touch with you. Today is my day off. Many new guests with children have arrived. I think it's holiday season.

Thank you for your poem and your email address, otherwise I wouldn't have been able to get in touch. I enjoyed having you here. It brought some variety to my everyday life.

The end of the season is approaching, and who knows, maybe we'll see each other again? Until then, I'm looking forward to your report.
Sunny greetings, Lydia

Thomas was glad to hear from her at last. Since he didn't have much time, he replied only briefly.

Dear Lydia,

Guess what? My women problem has evaporated. Both favourites bid me farewell. As always, you were right... strangely enough, Carmen and Margit did indeed cross paths. And just as you said, they decided to break up with me afterward. Well, that happened. Carmen made a scene and kicked me out of the apartment with all my belongings. On the other hand, I'm truthfully alone, and strangely enough, I feel relieved.

Thomas sent Lydia a bouquet of flowers through Fleurop. He felt relieved. Subsequently, he received a message.

Slowly, peace and tranquility returned to his office. Everyone was looking forward to Monica's return. On her first day back, she was greeted by Thomas with flowers, which both surprised and delighted her.

»Yes,« he said. »From now on, things are going to change.«

Monica raised an eyebrow. »I'm curious to see what you have in mind.«

If she was honest with herself, she hadn't come back for a raise. She liked Thomas, and in a spontaneous mood, she had bought a new dress just for this day.

Thomas clapped his hands. »Then let's get started!«

He returned to his desk, sat down, and looked at the photo of Lydia. A remarkable woman! Perhaps he would like to see her again. No, he definitely wanted to see her again!

He watched Monica as she entered with a smile, carrying the presentation folder.

»Here's the presentation for Berlin, by the way!«

»She placed the folder on the desk, and her smile froze as her eyes fell on Lydia's photo. She had never seen a photo of a woman on his desk before. Was this the change? Had her boss fallen in love? He was acting differently suddenly. She tried not to show anything but couldn't hide her disappointment.«

»Great job, Monica! Superb presentation! Where would I be without you? Why do you look so down?«

Thomas looked up at her. »I don't say that just like that. By the way, you're wearing a nice dress today.«

Thomas noticed her gaze fixed on the photo. »You're looking at the photo. It's my vacation acquaintance – Lydia.«

She felt caught and took a step back.

»Oh, sure. No problem,« she said quickly, trying to compose herself. »The documents are ready for forwarding.«

»Yes, exactly! That's great if you do that, excellent!«

Thomas was glad that everything was going well. He owed it all to Monica! It was good that she had come back. In doing so, she had changed. Previously, he hadn't noticed that Monica had such a feminine figure. Apparently, the dress emphasized her exceptional figure!

He had a thought. »Oh, Monica, wait!«

Startled, she turned around. »Yes, Thomas?«

»With all the work you've put into it, you probably know more about it than I do. Would you like to accompany me to the meeting?«

Monica couldn't believe her ears. Accompany?

»Yes, that would be nice!« she stammered. »When?«

»Wonderful. The presentation was postponed earlier by a month. But then – let's look forward to our first business trip together!« And smiled at her.

Thomas was amazed at how happy he was.

Wanderlust – It's nice to have friends

The fact that the date for the presentation had been postponed suited him well. The separation of Carmen and Margit, the new collaboration with Monica, had shaken up his emotional life enormously and turned it upside down. Lately he had been dreaming of Lydia at night.

After a few emails and phone calls with Lydia, he realized that he obviously missed her. On the spur of the moment, he wanted to get to the bottom of his feelings. He needed to see Lydia again to get clarity. The photo on the desk, his changed mood, had been positively perceived by everyone in the office. So he spontaneously booked online for a weekend trip.

Lydia was sitting at the pool bar with a guest when Thomas arrived by taxi. Beaming with joy, he waved to her.

Astonished, she saw Thomas coming. He hadn't announced his visit. She apologized to the other and ran to meet him.

»What, what are you doing here? Solve another woman's problem?« She laughed and stopped in front of Thomas. He greeted her with a kiss right and left on the cheek, like between old friends.

»Let's see, I hope there won't be a problem with women.«
He took a deep breath. »I'm here because of you!«
She looked at him with wide eyes in disbelief.
»Because of me?« And took a step back.

Thomas ran his hand through his hair. »I couldn't email you everything. I'm on a roller coaster with my emotions right now.«

Lydia put her right hand in front of her mouth.

»When I left here, I was still euphoric in thinking it was Carmen. But then they both broke up with me. Monica irritates me, and then I have to think about you a lot.«

He looked at her expectantly. »I don't know why, but my feelings are in complete chaos. I need to talk to you, you understand me, that's why I'm here.«

Lydia was speechless.

A lot had happened in the three weeks since Thomas' visit. Life went on with changing guests.

Now there was again an extraordinarily handsome male guest in the club hotel. Thankfully, he didn't have any problems with women, looked honest and faithful, was Austrian and his name was Markus. He was a country doctor and went on vacation with his friend. Markus was looking for a serious relationship and swarmed around Lydia, which she liked. He was very different from the other men she had met here at the hotel. Unlike Thomas, he knew exactly what he wanted.

Now she stood in front of Thomas, stunned that he missed her as his interlocutor, honored her, or did he want more?

»Please, Lydia, don't disappoint me now. I'd like to talk to you about everything at dinner tonight.«

Lydia didn't know what to say. »You really don't have another woman by your side right now?«

»No, not really! I'm single,« he suddenly realized, and smiled at her.

Irritated, she looked at him. After everything she had experienced so far, she was cautious. What did Thomas want from her?

»So, you're single. And now you're in a state of emotional turmoil because there's no woman left in your life?«

»Exactly!« Thomas took her in his arms and hugged her warmly.

»I think I'm ready for a new relationship, but this time it's going to be very different from everyone else. Just ONE woman by my side, and no more infidelities!«

Lydia freed herself from the embrace. She didn't like it. He was nice, but she never wanted anything from him.

She shook her head, »Well, if you came especially for me… – then we'll see you tonight at the hotel restaurant for dinner. Let's see!« Smiling, she ran back to her waiting guest.

Lydia was blown away.

Suddenly, Thomas stood in front of her. Did he want a relationship with her? She took a deep breath and absolutely wanted to listen to her femininity, her inner voice. Her gut feeling had never let her down. Intuitively, she always knew right away what was right or wrong, when she listened deep inside herself, it didn't feel like it with Thomas.

She put on her royal blue dress, which looked particularly good on her. She glanced at her watch. To be on time, she had to hurry.

On the way to the restaurant, they bumped into each other in the hotel lobby.

When he saw her, he made an inviting gesture towards the restaurant. »Hola, Lydia! You look adorable!«

»Yes, thank you, but so do you!« She smiled at him and together they entered the room. They were among the first.

They got their food from the buffet and went to a table that was a little apart. During the meal, they sat opposite each other in silence.

Her silence unsettled Thomas, because he didn't know that she didn't say anything at all.

»I don't know, I mean, I didn't mean to attack you, but do you like me at all? At least a little bit? Or do you have a friend?«

He looked at Lydia trustingly. If she knew his love stories very well, he hardly knew anything about her in principle.

She pushed her empty plate aside.

»No, not at the moment! That's because I'm sick and tired of men!« And he looked sadly into his eyes.

»You've been disappointed? Of such a scoundrel as I was? Mind you: Was! I'm not anymore and I'm going to change my life completely,« his voice sounded decisive.

While the waiter was taking away their empty plates, he asked if they wanted a drink. They ordered a juice spritzer.

She leaned back in her chair and looked at him sideways.

»Oh, yes?! I'm curious about that. You know, my ex promised me the blue of the sky. I would be the love of his life and so on... And? We even wanted to get married—but then-« and made a farewell gesture with his hand.

Interested, he leaned over to her. »Yes, and what happened? Why didn't you get married?«

Annoyed, Lydia shifted back and forth in her chair.

»For an unavoidable professional reason, I had to go to another city for a long time. You won't believe it: Then he announced to me that love had been lost, because of the distance, and so on. Just excuses!« She slammed her hand on the table.

Thomas shook his head. »First the great love, and then suddenly everything is gone?«

The waiter brought the drinks and winked encouragingly at Lydia. She smiled back tiredly.

Then she turned to Thomas. »The affection and feelings were still there, but the butterflies in the stomach were missing.« Lydia sighed, »This man had been the only person I had ever really been in love with, and whom I would have married.«

»Did he have another one?« asked Thomas.

Lydia hunched her shoulders.

»I don't know. I wished we could have talked about everything. It happens that when you live together for a while, you are so familiar with each other that there are no butterflies in your stomach again, as is the case at the beginning of a relationship. But he blocked everything.«

Thomas looked at her sympathetically. »It must have been very hard for you! Has it been a long time?«

She poked around in the drink with the straw. Her thoughts were spinning. She had spent a great day with Markus and was now thinking of him. Was he serious? When do you know? Thomas even came by in person to clarify his feelings.

Thomas misinterpreted her silence. »I'm sorry I probed like that.«

She sighed. »Oh, what is love? Love is, after all, being attracted to the other. Feel comfortable when the other person is there, radiate harmony! To have a longing! Or not? That's love, isn't it? I don't need the butterflies in my stomach, you have that at the beginning of a relationship. Most of the time it evaporates. A different feeling spreads. Maybe the certainty that you have the other, that you want to be together! Love means understanding each other in silence! Knowing what the other person likes, being able to listen, tenderness and sex, of course!«

Thomas looked at her the whole time. How right she was! What was love? Everyone had a different definition, and yet this feeling of affection was the same. To feel safe with the other, to love him! She was right, butterflies are only there at the beginning of a relationship, then this feeling wears off rapidly. After a while, you ask yourself: Was that it? Is this love?

Then he muttered to himself, »Exactly! What is love really?«

She watched the other guests who were sitting a little further away. Some got up and walked towards the evening event.

»As I said, for me, at least in the beginning, there have to be butterflies in the stomach. Then there's the longing for the other person, feeling drawn to them, being able to smell each other. But...« She made an open-handed gesture. »I don't have that right now!«

Could he have been mistaken that Lydia thought he was nice, but nothing more? Thomas cleared his throat. »That's a pity! And—« he faltered, »there's nothing wrong with us?« he asked cautiously.

She looked at him.

»If I'm honest, I don't really get a feeling. It's rather oppressive when you hug me. It was all good the way it was, but I didn't have any feelings for you, and nothing will happen.« She was relieved that it was finally out!

Thomas hadn't expected that and wanted to get to the bottom of it all.

He looked into her eyes. »Okay! Didn't you tell me about happiness? Isn't love also happiness that doesn't fall into your lap every day? Still, Lydia! I've grown fond of you!«

Thomas could see from her face that she was hesitating. »Don't you think we had a lot of fun together? Laughter is healthy! Not only that, but it also helps solve problems. Even the Greeks said that laughter was a gift from the gods. Laugh at yourself, and it will fill your life. Then there is no room for worry and fear. No matter what problem we have!«

Lydia waved her hand away. »Easier said than done, I can tell you a thing or two about that. Here you always have to laugh and be in a good mood. Your contingent of good mood must never run dry. But the sorrow remains!«

»That's right. If you take a closer look... Who knows, a new love will change your life at the same time. Or? „Mine, at any rate, has changed since the holiday.«

A smile crossed Lydia's face. He didn't seem to give up that easily. She drank her juices in large gulps.

»Okay! You're right, we had a lot of fun together.« She laughed, and her eyes sparkled. »It was nice to have you there! I enjoyed it consciously. We flirted together, too, but that's it...«

He interrupted her. »Yes, then I interpreted it correctly, or is that part of the professional context?«

Lydia snorted. »Thomas,« she took a deep breath, »there's just something missing... I like you, but it is not love, and never will be.«

Thomas swallowed. He understood and nodded silently.

Lydia looked at him sceptically. »I'm sorry to disappoint you. Men fall in love differently than women. Honestly, if there is no feeling of infatuation with a woman, nothing will come. Do you understand?!« She rubbed her forehead quickly.

Thomas looked thoughtfully into space. If it wasn't Lydia, why was he always in a good mood?!

„I've had a lot going on in the last few weeks. That's what I told you. The separations with Carmen and Margit. The stress with Monica when she suddenly didn't want to work anymore ... „

Lydia sank into her chair, relieved that the conversation was taking a different direction.

»Exactly, what's next for Monica? How are things going for you? Tell me how you were able to win her back, she didn't want to work for you anymore, did she?«

Thomas stroked his hair. He spoke very euphorically about his success in winning Monica back. »It wasn't easy. With the tongues of angels and a raise, I finally made it.«

He looked at Lydia a little complacently.

»I don't know what I would have done without Monica,« he continued. »She's such a fantastic woman. Lately, she's been wearing dresses, in which she looks stunningly sexy. I never consciously noticed it before. When I told her that we were going to the customer in Berlin together, she wanted to throw her arms around my neck. Yes, really! „ he insisted as Lydia looked at him doubtfully. It was only to the photo that she reacted strangely.«

»What kind of photo?« asked Lydia in astonishment.

»Ok, I've put a photo of you on my desk. When I looked at you, I felt better.«

Lydia interrupted him. »A photo of me? On your desk?! That's not possible! We're not together,« she was really indignant.

Thomas looked at her apologetically. »I know, but we had such a great time together that I thought you would do me good.«

She looked at him sceptically. »It's okay. But what did you really feel when you looked at my photo?«

»You'll laugh, but I've always asked you what you'd say now.«

»You mean, if you had a problem, did you think how I was going to solve it now?«

Thomas nodded.

Lydia smirked. »So I'm your coach?! I like that. But this has nothing to do with love. When I watch you as you enthusiastically talk about Monica, your eyes really light up. Maybe you should think about it?«

Incredulously, Thomas looked at her. »I like her as a person. During the week when she wasn't here, I really noticed everything she does for me. I missed Monica a lot. I was so relieved when she came back, you wouldn't believe it! We celebrated with champagne. My secretary had told me her favourite flowers, so I presented her with a bouquet as a welcome. Monica was amazed. She said she only came back because I'm such a nice boss and I had earnestly asked her to come back.«

Lydia looked at him triumphantly. »You say she reacted a little strangely to my photo?«

Thomas justified himself. »I've never had a photo of a woman on my desk. No one knew if I was in a relationship or not. But—when your photograph was there, there was tension on her face.«

Lydia's ears perked up and she leaned over to him. »Is she jealous?«

»Monica? Jealous? What makes you think so?« He rested his chin with his hand.

»Perhaps she had high hopes. You want her back, and all of a sudden she sees the photo after your vacation, so she was disappointed.«

»Monica!« Thomas pondered. »We get along quite well.«

»Hmm—when I hear you like that, you'd think you'd rave about her.«

Thomas refused. »No, I thought I felt something for you.«

»I'm just your coach. You just said that you take my photo to ask me how you solve your problems. Or how do you feel about it?«

»Feeling?« Thomas was overwhelmed, should he talk about his feelings now? He didn't know himself, so he'd flown to Lydia in the first place.

Lydia looked at him intently. »Thomas! What do you feel when we talk?«

He pondered. »Like you're a longtime friend.«

»Ok. What thoughts do you have when you think of Monica?«

He leaned back thoughtfully.

»Hmmm, when I think of Monica ... – She is a very attractive woman, she is self-confident, her perfume is stunning, she has recently started wearing figure-hugging clothes, she is always in a good mood, has great ideas. She never ceases to amaze me with great presentations. Together, we are an unbeatable team. But most of all, I appreciate her honesty and that she says what she thinks.«

Lydia leaned back. Her gaze scanned him. »Could it be that you are in love with Monica?«

He felt like a boy who had been caught. »In Monica? I? No, indeed. We're a good team, nothing more.«

She continued to look at him incredulously. His posture spoke volumes.

»Thomas, I know you quite well, and how you talk about women. But you've never talked about a woman like that before and you have this sparkle in your eyes. Anyway, I'm not the one you're in love with. I'm just a good friend, like you just said. More of a coach. You didn't rave about me.«

He ran his hands through his hair. »You mean I'm in love with Monica? Oh God, what am I going to do again?!« Puzzled, he looked at Lydia, who had a fit of laughter.

When she had calmed down, she continued. »You think you've fallen in love with me because you're very comfortable in my presence. I'm still the one who helps you with words and deeds, listens to you and is just a very good buddy, or like a good friend. You've had this good feeling since you're back home. Couldn't it be that the feeling has something to do with Monica?« And looked at him cheekily from the side.

It took his mind a little time to sort it all out. »To be honest, I couldn't place it. I'm in a good mood, I'm flirting with Monica, it's all relaxed and cheerful. After all, we've been working together for a long time, so I never noticed her. But, speaking of it, the time without her was terrible!«

»You never noticed her because you weren't free. You still had your other relationships, maybe you didn't want to do anything with your colleague. Do you think it really got you this time?«

He looked at her incredulously. »Do you think, Lydia, that Monica is interested in me at all?«

»Oh, I think so, if she was a little jealous of my photo. Does she know you're here now?«

»No, I didn't tell anyone about it. When she asked who the woman in the photo was, I said it was a holiday acquaintance. After all, I wasn't sure if and how and what I felt for you.«

»So, so, a holiday acquaintance! Well, there you have the answer.«

»What do you mean?«

»Well, if you acted intuitively, it was that I'm really just a holiday acquaintance. You noticed her jealousy, and you didn't want to scare her away because she meant something to you. If I had meant more to you, you would have reacted differently, but it was only superficial. However, you didn't want to hurt Monica's feelings. It shows that it means more to you than you want to realize.«

Thomas nodded. »You're right, I like her figure, her eyes, her mannerisms, things I never noticed before. I find myself always looking at her backside when she leaves my office. I'm interested in her favourite flowers, how she's doing. It pleases me when I can make her happy and see her eyes light up. Her way of thinking and her work have always fascinated me.

I know her weaknesses, but also her strengths. In terms of work, we understand each other perfectly, maybe she's even my soulmate.«

Lydia claps her hands enthusiastically. »Wow, you're totally in love. Well, maybe you had to get my okay for that. You came to the island to get clarity, and now, Thomas, I can tell you: I think you've found the right one. Congratulations!«

She looked at the clock with horror to see that it was time to leave. Immediately she got up and was about to go.

Thomas remained seated and held her by the arm for a moment. »Lydia, thank you for your frankness. I wish you all the best, maybe you will soon have found the right one. Thank you for giving me your precious time. What's on tonight?«

»Tonight is a musical evening. I have to go. As always, we talked each other up again. See you! See you later!«

Lydia waved to him and hurried away.

It was the musical »Saturday Night Fever« being performed. The entertainers danced and sang. Lydia felt as if the musical reflected her life. A young woman who fell in love with a man she couldn't have. Then he comes back to her and falls in love. Should Markus be this, Toni? She was more nervous than usual. Surely because Thomas and Markus were there watching. Both were impressed by her performance.

When she came down from the stage to Thomas after the show, he hugged her warmly and gave her a kiss on the cheek. Markus, who was sitting at the next table, asked her to sit down at his table.

Humorously, she took Thomas by the hand and pulled him over with her. »If I can bring Thomas with me?«

Markus couldn't argue at all because there they sat down.

»I'm thrilled with you, Lydia! Perhaps you have the time and inclination to come to me in a month or two, when this is all over.« Markus confidently put his arm around her shoulder and beamed at her with a smile. He didn't know what role Thomas played, but he wanted to at least stake out his territory.

Lydia didn't find it uncomfortable and continued to flirt with him. »Yes, perhaps I will come to see you. How long are you going to leave here?«

»I'll be here for another ten days. I'm sure we'll have one or two more evenings together ahead of us.« and grinned broadly at her.

Then she looks over at Thomas, who was sitting right next to her on the other side. »And how long are you staying, Thomas?« asked Lydia.

Thomas watched the goings-on.

„Well, not for long! Honestly, just the weekend. I negotiated a special rate with the hotel and went there via Düsseldorf in the morning and my return flight goes via Munich on Sunday afternoon. It wasn't possible otherwise! I really had to see you. And as we now know, it was exactly the right decision! „

He sat there relaxed and looked at the two of them.

»Oh, yes?!« Lydia had a big grin.

Jealously, Markus looked over at them.

Thomas leaned over to Markus to talk to him better.

»Nothing works without my coach. Lydia is an excellent adviser, and since I only have this evening, may I take her away from you?«

After Markus realized that Thomas was no competition, he let go of Lydia and joked. »Only if you leave it to me afterwards. I find her very sympathetic and don't like to share her with other men.« He winked at the two of them.

Thomas ran down to the beach with Lydia. They sat down on their lava rocks and looked at the stars. It was a wonderful, clear night. Lydia saw a shooting star and wished that she would finally find the love of her life – maybe it was Markus, whom she found quite sympathetic.

Thomas looked at Lydia mischievously. »We should be real friends. I'm happy about that.«

Lydia took him by the shoulder. »As I have come to know you, you will soon be courting Monica. Then you can tell me, and I'll be there to help you if you have any questions.«

She smiled at Thomas. »It's an offer, isn't it? Everything has a purpose in life.«

With a big grin on his face, he nudged her. »Yes, you're right, as always. Everything has a purpose in life ... You should sort out my life. It's an honour for me to have you as a friend.«

Lydia's eyes soon closed. She yawned loudly. She stood up with difficulty.

»Let's go to our bungalows. I need to sleep; it was a super exhausting day today!«

»Yes, of course! I'll accompany you. It's a pity that I'm flying home tomorrow, but I'll write to you when something new happens with me. Conversely, I'm also curious. Now a new life begins for me!« and winked at her.

„I'm glad for you. „

The Dream Woman –
The Wild Years Are Over

Monday morning

He was so early that he unlocked the offices himself. First, he aired, then he put on coffee, which he never usually did. Fit and cheerful, he did his job. Full of vigour, he looked through his e-mails. He even tidied up his desk.

The sky cleared, and a few sunbeams streamed in, he felt the energy flowing. Finally, he hung up his painted acrylic picture from the vacation. It looked good to have a splash of blue on the white wall. Immediately, he thought of Lydia and grinned to himself. She had managed to bring order into his life. Her photo went into the drawer. He had a strange feeling about having a photo of a woman on his desk who wasn't his.

Monica, who was again wearing a colourful, summery dress, brought him the Berlin documents. Normally, she always had her hair pinned up, but today it was open, which immediately captivated him.

»Where should I put the documents now?«

His gaze was glued to her. Something was different. »It's best to sit here on the desk, there's plenty of room there.«

With a wave of his hand, he pointed to his empty desk and grinned at her.

She immediately noticed that the photo was gone. But she didn't dare to say anything.

Thomas watched her. His gaze was fixed on her body. »I like your dress very much to-day,« Thomas remarked. »They should also wear their hair down much more often, then they look even younger.«

In the past, he hadn't even noticed his assistant. On the contrary, he had had the feeling that she looked like a gray mouse. But that didn't matter, after all, he had hired her because of her exorbitantly good work, not because she looked good. He hadn't been aware of that, like his friend Ralf, who had always had a look at Monica. Suddenly, he seemed to see everything through a new pair of glasses.

»Thank you for the documents, I'll look over them in a moment. Monica, how long have you been working for me?«

Undecided, she stopped after placing the papers on his table.

»A little more than a year. I started the job the spring before last. Why?«

Thomas leaned back in his desk chair and clasped his hands behind his head. »Well, I'm very happy to work with you. I'm looking forward to our advertising campaign on Thursday and Friday in Berlin. Do you know Berlin?«

Monica shook her head. »No, I don't know Berlin, but I'm very glad to go there with you.«

Thomas thought for a moment. With a smile, he said. »Do you have any plans for the weekend?«

»At the weekend? No!« She looked at him expectantly.

»If you'd like, I can show you Berlin. Then we book two more nights until Sunday or in another hotel. What do you think of that?«

She looked at him in surprise. »Yes! Of course! That's great!«

»Then book the weekend. You know what to do.«

Monica hardly recognized her boss. Prancing lightly, she left his office.

The enforced time-out had made him think. He was transformed. Much more cordial than before. The looks, his smile, his compliments – it was all for her! Monica couldn't believe it, but surely the long weekend together would bring the answer.

Thomas was surprised at himself for making this proposal to her. He knew Berlin well. He immediately started researching what he wanted to experience with her on Saturday. Sunday was the return trip in all comfort. He was immensely pleased that she had reacted enthusiastically. Did Monica find him attractive? Anyway, now he had a chance to find out.

After his vacation, he thought a lot about Lydia's words. He wanted to change, fundamentally change. He followed her advice and created a list of all the things and ideas about how his future relationship should be. Essentially, he wanted to get along well with his future partner, to find each other sympathetic, and to pursue the same values and goals. Professionally, Monica fulfilled at least these points. He enjoyed working with her because he could completely rely on her. She was talented at organizing, and they shared jokes they laughed about. He was excited and impatient to get to know Monica better. Whether she could cook didn't matter to him. If not, he could present her with his cooking skills. He looked forward to showing her Berlin.

His presentation and speech at his client's company party was a marginal phenomenon.

The trip to Berlin went without any problems. Time flew by. They talked animatedly about God and the world. Thomas felt it was time to be on a first-name basis. They understood each other and laughed. Monica talked about her life and Thomas listened.

After checking into the hotel, they went to their rooms to

get ready for the evening. Around 5 p.m., they planned to meet in the hotel lobby.

Thomas waited comfortably in an armchair downstairs in a suit and bow tie. He jumped up immediately when he saw Monica in the gallery. He stood there rooted. He couldn't help but stare at her. He felt like he was seeing her for the first time.

Her dress was simple, elegant, and only bright and striking because of the colour. Her long hair swings to her shoulders in time as she slowly descended the stairs like a diva. Her eyes lit up and came out even larger with make-up. The lipstick was the same colour as her red dress. A pair of black pumps and a small leather bag completed her outfit. Was that his Monica?

With pleasure, Thomas took her in his arms and kissed her gently on the cheek.

»My lady in red. Monica. May I beg you—hook up!« He held out his arm to her. Together they climbed into the shuttle car that drove them to the gala event. The company they were working with had invited them to do so. There was a new product launch with a musical performance by the Berliner Philharmonic.

After the first speech, the appetizer was set. They chatted animatedly with the people sitting next to them. Everything was festively decorated. The men wore black suits and the women were the eye-catchers in their colourful evening dresses. In red, Monica was the only one.

Thomas was invited on stage for the main speech. He presented his lecture with humour and suspense. It wasn't just Monica who hung on his lips. She admired how easy it was for him to present. He was escorted to his seat with great applause. With a kiss he lovingly thanked Monica for her work.

At the same time, the waiters served the main course in the hall. There was fish. Monica didn't like fish and only ate the side dishes.

Out of the corner of his eye, Thomas watched her and whispered in her ear. »Don't you like fish?«

Embarrassed, she grimaced in denial.

»Never mind. Then you'll eat the side dishes, I'll eat the fish, and then we'll swap plates.«

Relieved, she ate the side dishes, and he ate his fish, and then they quickly swapped plates. No one seemed to notice. Inwardly, they both grinned at how familiar they had been.

The dessert was decorative with fruits, ice cream and chocolate mousse. Both were two cuties who emptied the plate. Again, and again their eyes met. The others were engaged in conversation, but because the music was too loud, they couldn't understand anything. They focused only on themselves.

Thomas was bursting with pride to have such a beautiful partner by his side. While dancing, they were followed by many admiring glances. Thomas was a good dancer. He had a lot of fun with Monica. Only now did he realize that he didn't dance so well with every woman.

Monica floated with him over the floor. She felt superior and found it pleasant to have a dancer to guide her. Her boss didn't just look good, he had an insanely charismatic charisma when he entered the room or the podium. She felt like Cinderella. While dancing, they came close to each other again and again.

Suddenly, his cell phone vibrated in his pocket. Deftly, he took it out while dancing and looked at the display. Claudia.

For a moment, he wondered whether to press the green button or the red button. Why did she call now?

Back at the hotel, he accompanied Monica to her hotel room. At her door he stopped irresolutely.

»Monica, thank you very much for the super nice evening! I don't want to deceive you about how I feel about you, I'm sure you know that by now.«

Monica was silent. She looked at him seductively. He pulled her to him and kissed her. Monica released herself from his arm.

»Come,« she said, unlocking the door.

As soon as the door closed behind them, he embraced her tenderly.

»I'm sure of it. I want to share my life with you if you feel the same way. I feel like you've bewitched me.«

Instead of an answer, she simply threw her arms around his neck and kissed him.

Thomas knew he had arrived.

The Author

Vera Wagenvoort (pseudonym) is a graduate business economist and certified business trainer and coach. She is passionate about exploring the twists and turns of life, both personally and professionally. For many years, she has worked in the coaching field, focusing on career counselling, life balance, personal development, goal management, as well as love and relationships.

In our society, those who struggle with their problems are often labeled as weak or failures. Through her novel, the author offers readers the opportunity to find themselves and examine behavioral patterns. Drawing on her extensive experience in working with people and their issues, she provides insights and guidance.

»Women Won't Let Him Go« reflects many relationships in our society. It playfully addresses various problems while aiming primarily to entertain readers.

Dive into the captivating world of Vera Wagenvoort's new coaching novel about love and relationships! Originally conceived two decades ago, this gripping work has been catapulted into the present to shed light on timeless themes of love, relationship strategies, and communication in a modern and engaging way.

Experience profound conversations between the protagonists that not only break the boundaries of fiction but also offer real insights into the challenges and joys of relationships. Vera Wagenvoort, a pseudonym that represents not only captivating romance novels but also a familial background dating back to the 16th century.

In this revised edition, we encounter not only timeless questions of love but also modern aspects of life in the 21st century. No more printing emails, no more Walkmans or film cameras – the changes are reflected not only in the lives of the characters but also in the writing style.

Vera Wagenvoort invites you to embark on a journey of self-reflection and the discovery of true love. Immerse yourself in a world where coaching novels and love stories merge, offering not only entertaining reading hours but also valuable insights for your own love life. Look forward to a story that warms the heart and stimulates the mind.

Welcome to the world of Vera Wagenvoort!

* 9 7 8 3 0 0 0 7 6 3 0 5 2 *